Managed Care

Joe Barrett

D0488031

Black Rose Writing | Texas

Second printing

This is a work of fiction. Names, characters, businesses, places, events and incidents are either the products of the author's imagination or used in a fictitious manner. Any resemblance to actual persons, living or dead, or actual events is purely coincidental.

ISBN: 978-1-68433-140-6
PUBLISHED BY BLACK ROSE WRITING
www.blackrosewriting.com

Printed in the United States of America
Suggested Retail Price (SRP) $20.95

Managed Care is printed in Plantagenet Cherokee

For Michelle, Joe and Sophie

Managed Care

Frank

"Wake up, Mr. Johnson. You have a visitor!"

"What time is it?" I ask and roll over to look at the nurse.

"It's nine a.m."

"Who the hell gets visitors at nine a.m.?"

"Do you know how many people in here would love to get a visitor at any hour of the day?"

"Then parade my visitor around to those people," I say, turning back into the pillow. "And bring him or her back in no less than an hour."

"Whoring out your visitors is not one of the services that's included in your package, Mr. Johnson," the nurse says sweetly. Her name is Betty, I think. I can tell that the administration has told her to be nice to me. After I'd complained to the administration about all the snarky nurses in this place.

"Who is it?" I ask after realizing that there's no way I'm getting back to sleep. It's been more than thirty seconds of conscious thought. After thirty seconds, you lose the cloudy aura of sleep, the hole closes up, and you are effectively awake. I've had enough experience with this phenomenon over the past six months that I now refer to it as "the thirty-second rule." I roll over onto my side and lift myself from the bed. I stand in front of the nurse, wearing only adult diapers. Enjoy that view, nurse.

"You broke the thirty-second rule," I say, stretch and yawn. She knows what I'm talking about, "I'm going to lodge a complaint."

"Lodge away, Mr. Johnson. I don't think I'm going to get in trouble for breaking your thirty-second rule this late in the morning."

"This is supposed to be a managed care facility. I've paid the management to have you take care of me. Breaking the thirty-second rule makes me think that you don't have my best interests at heart."

Betty is a husky woman, maybe thirty-five years old. Dyke cut hair, really thick legs. She could probably take me, especially now, given all the muscle tone that I've lost here over the past six months.

"It wasn't me that asked your visitor to stop by in the middle of the morning," Betty says brightly.

"Since when is nine a.m. the middle of the morning?"

"I get up at five-thirty and I'm here at seven."

"Within this facility, I mean," I say in a nasty tone. I'm peeing strenuously into my diaper, hoping it's not so absorbent that she can't discern the gesture. "I don't mean in the outside world. Who is it, anyway?"

"I think it's your brother."

"Did he identify himself as my brother or is this just conjecture on your part?"

"He didn't identify himself as your brother. But he looks like you might look if you were forty pounds heavier, and clean, with a haircut, shave and, well, if you looked more normal."

"I resent that. You're very judgy this morning. Now I'm going to change my diaper, which is something that you are actually paid to do as part of my package. But I'll take care of it myself today, though you're more than welcome to stay..." I'm talking to the back of her head as she walks out the door.

I pull on clean diapers, a pair of sweatpants and a Motley Crue t-shirt. Slide my feet into paper slippers and walk down the hall to the living area. I scan the room. See my brother, Johnny, sitting on the linen couch, engaged in an awkward conversation with Mrs. Liptenstein. Probably about her missing cat. Mrs. Liptenstein is living somewhere in the Nineteen Forties, when she is still a pre-tween, unaware that we are more than sixteen years deep into the following century.

"Excuse me, are you looking for a white cat with a grey hood?" I ask Mrs. Liptenstein.

"That's Buttons!" she replies eagerly.

"Oh, hey. Wow. I'm not sure how to tell you this, so I'll just come right out and say it. I just saw the garbage men scooping a white cat with a grey hood off the street outside. I guess they ran over Buttons with their truck." Mrs. Liptenstein jerks herself up from the couch, stands for a fraction of a second, and then begins to fall forward. I catch her by the armpits before she has a chance to shatter her knees on the shag carpet. I pivot her boney ribs so that her arms can reach a walker and she grabs it instinctively before tottering towards the doorway.

I take her place on the couch next to Johnny, cradle the back of my head in my hands.

"You are a very sick individual," Johnny says.

"What?" I ask, as Mrs. Liptenstein totters back with her walker and asks if we've seen a white cat with a grey hood. I tell her the same thing about the garbage truck, the dead cat. She startles but doesn't lose grip on the walker, totters back towards the doorway.

"Why?" Johnny asks.

"It's a little game I've got going. I'm trying to see if I can actually stop her heart one of these times."

"How can you possibly get off on being cruel to old people?"

"It's not cruel. It's the most excitement she gets all day. I'm helping her stay young and vibrant."

"By lying to her about her cat?"

"Oh, that actually happened. Her cat, Buttons, got run over by a garbage truck and died. Probably, like, eighty years ago. Stick around, I guarantee she'll tell you all about it. Apparently, her father also died around the same time in World War Two. Normandy Beach, I think. But she's all hung up on the cat. It's amazing how the mind works, isn't it?"

"How long are you going to keep doing this?"

"Probably until I blow one of Mrs. Liptenstein's gaskets."

"No, Frank," he says, raising his palms and gesturing to the room, "I mean, how long are you going to keep doing all of this."

"Oh, right. This," I say, thoughtfully. "Well, I paid for a year, so I guess I'll do this for at least a year. If Hardy continues to hold out. At first it was just a matter of principle, me staying here. But now I'm actually getting used to the lifestyle. I don't think I'm ever going back to big boy pants."

"You've made your point, don't you think?"

"My point will be made when the home reimburses me for the unused balance of the year I paid for, or when I leave at the end of a year's time. Not before."

"You're abusing the memory of Grandad," Johnny says.

"Oh, come on. You can't really think this is disrespectful to Granddad. Granddad would love what I'm doing. I never met anyone who was tighter with a dollar and had a greater sense of righteous indignation. If anything, this is a tribute to Granddad."

"It's embarrassing for our family."

"Are you serious? You guys all live, like, twenty minutes away. It's not like I'm shacked up in a storefront window on your Main Street. How could this life choice possibly be embarrassing to our family?"

"You don't have to blog about it."

"Come on, man. It's two-thousand-seventeen. What thirty-three-year-old guy is going to live in a nursing home and not blog about it? Especially when I've got a point to make here."

"Mom wants you to stop."

"Mom doesn't play into this. She might have some say if it were her side of the family, which it isn't. What does Dad think?"

"Let's talk about something else."

"No," I say, "you brought is up. And we both know that Dad thinks this whole stunt is awesome. I just wonder why he doesn't come to visit more often."

"Maybe he doesn't visit more often because he's embarrassed that his thirty-three-year-old son is living in a managed care facility, wearing diapers and eating mush, with people that are, on average, two generations his senior," Johnny rants.

"Well, it sounds like someone's embarrassed about it."

"Do you know what kind of example you're setting for my kids?"

"First of all, what kid ever benefited by adopting an unwed, childless uncle as a role model? And secondly, I still make more money than you do, so it's not like I'm living here because I can't support myself. This is a conscious choice, my man. Made strictly on principle."

I don't want to sound immodest, but I'm a pretty brilliant computer programmer. Software development comes naturally to me. I make a ton of money as a freelancer. And I can do my job from anywhere that has a high bandwidth Internet connection. My room at the managed care facility is actually a perfect office for me. There aren't a lot of visitors so it's pretty quiet, though we do get more than our fair share of ambulance sirens.

Johnny is an insurance salesman. Yuck. So, I can see how the fact that his older brother lives in a managed care facility could possibly mess with his credibility, his perceived stability as an insurance provider, a pillar of the community and all. But I can't let his lame career get in the way of my principles.

"You're making a fool of yourself," Johnny says.

"Deal with it," I respond just as fat Ed Hardy approaches the couch.

"Mr. Hardy," Johnny says and gets up to shake his hand. I remain seated, look out the window at a couple of late-season blue jays nesting in a dying oak tree. I refuse to look Ed Hardy in the eye, at least until he comes to his senses. He and I are in an old-school standoff.

"Any progress, Johnny?" Hardy asks, burrowing his glare straight into the side of my skull.

"Nope," Johnny says.

"Tell Mr. Hardy," I say to Johnny, "that I will gladly vacate his premises when he repays me for the unused balance of facility fees."

"You paid for a year in advance," Hardy says angrily, "with a twenty-percent discount! A twenty-percent discount *because* you paid in advance! That's how an advance payment works! You don't get your money back just because your grandfather died before he was able to move in here!" Hardy shouts. He turns gently to my brother, "Again, I really am sorry about your grandfather, Johnny."

"He lived a full life," Johnny replies.

"Tell Mr. Hardy," I say, my eyes still fixed on the blue jays, "that we've been through this countless times with his lawyers and my lawyers. Tell him that the advance booking his facility accepted was for me, Franklin Johnson. The fact that I am the namesake of our recently departed grandfather, also named Franklin Johnson, has no bearing on Mr. Hardy's contractual obligation to provide me with managed care throughout the duration of my stay at his facility. If Mr. Hardy would like me to leave his facility, I would be happy to do so in exchange for the unused balance of fees already paid."

"I'll rot in hell before I pay you back a penny of that advance!" Hardy shouts and garners disturbed glances from the living space population, but they're so old that it doesn't really matter to any of us.

"You can tell Mr. Hardy that I'll be rotting in room four-twenty-two until he comes around to my point of view."

Hardy storms off. I'm amazed that our stalemate has held out for a little over six months. It's difficult to believe that anyone can be as stubborn as Hardy. It must be torture on his wife and kids.

"Breakfast?" Johnny sighs.

"Sure," I say. "Let me put on some real shoes."

I can leave the facility as long as I'm accompanied by a visitor on my registered list. Only if I'm accompanied by a visitor on my registered list. And I'll be damned if I'm going to break any of their rules and get kicked out on a technicality.

Elroy

So, picture this. Your name is Elroy. You're in seventh grade and walking down the hallway of middle school, right? And it's just after lunch so there are crowds of kids and a few teachers buzzing around. And you look down at the floor in front of your feet. And you see a pair of underwear lying in the middle of the hallway. And it's your underwear.

It's the same pair of underwear that you wore just yesterday. So, like, not clean underwear. Not filthy underwear, because you don't have some kind of hygiene problem, but definitely worn underwear. And it isn't a pair of cool boxer-briefs from some premium athletic brand, because that's not what you get at a foster home. It's what they used to call y-fronts. Tightie whities. The kind of underwear that was popular in the nineteen seventies. Because that's all you get at a foster home. So, what do you do?

What you'd do, I imagine, is exactly what I do. I give the underwear a quick look of disgust, just like the other kids are doing, and I walk right on by. No way am I going to claim that off-white pile of underpants on the floor. This is middle school, and we're talking about underwear here. The janitor can pick it up. Not me. I don't even glance at it twice. I can get more underwear. Or I can just go commando if I run out. Either way, it's better than people knowing that it's my underwear lying there in the middle of the hallway.

But then I see the same t-shirt I wore yesterday on the floor, too, maybe ten feet in front of the underwear. And my eyes follow the t-shirt to one sock, then another. Then a pair of gym shorts... All of this dirty laundry forming a loose trail to my open locker. My gym bag, which I forgot to take home yesterday, hangs empty on the top corner of the metal locker door.

This is no accident. I'm a victim here.

"Ohhhh... My boy, *Elroy*, gots the *frighty-frighties*, 'cause the girls can all see his *tightie-whitieeeees!*" Jacob Hirschfield, standing three lockers away, baseball cap cockeyed on his head, oversized plastic sunglasses, light blue *Members Only* jacket. A huge silver Volkswagen emblem hanging from a chain around his neck. If I had parents, I don't think they'd let me dress this way.

"Welllll... *Elroy* gots some mighty *scares,* 'cause everyone lookin' at his *underwears*," continues Saul Lipski, varsity-style jacket with white leather sleeves, ripped jeans. He's the biggest of the three.

"Seeee... El-roy, he looking for a place to run, cause... uh, he afraid of the ladieeeezzzzz!" Isaac Rothstein, in addition to being the runt of the group, can't rhyme. Porkpie hat, Buddy Holly glasses, tweed jacket, he's going for the hip-to-be square look. In middle school. I think maybe Saul's dad works for Isaac's father.

"Isaac, dog, you suck," says Jacob, "you're supposed to just act like you're spinning, man."

"I had it, Jay," he whines, "I had it and then I lost it, dog."

I turn around, trying to make myself small in the crowded hallway, pick my clothes up off the floor, starting with my underwear. When all of yesterday's laundry is loaded into my arms, I walk back towards Jacob, Isaac and Saul, who are still posed, rapper-style, around my locker.

I reach for my gym bag and big Saul steps in front of me and blocks my arm.

"Ju... Ju... Just cut it out, Du... Du... Dude," I manage to spit out. Oh, yeah. The stutter. Sigh. I really only stutter when I'm super nervous. Otherwise it's usually just a random word glitch here and there. Hardly noticeable in normal social situations. Or it would be hardly noticeable, if I were ever involved in normal social situations.

"Jeh, jeh, jeh... Jew Crew in da houze!" shouts Isaac, mimicking my stutter. His compatriots give him an approving look. They call themselves the *Jew Crew*, a wannabe rap group styled after *The Beastie Boys*. They're seriously committed to this whole retro white rapper thing. It's obviously lame, but who am I to have an opinion?

Saul steps back, allowing me to reach for my gym bag. He feints an overly dramatic punch at my face and I flinch huge. "Yeaaaah, Boooooy," Saul shouts into my ducked head, then high-fives Jacob and turns to walk away.

I so want to do something. Like hit Saul in the back of the head with a cinderblock. But I don't have a cinderblock and I know that I wouldn't hit him with it if I did have one because I'm not some kind of psycho. So I just shove the gym bag back into my locker, re-hook the cheap padlock into the metal handle. And I try not to cry, because how much worse would that make everything.

So, you're probably thinking that this would be the time that I am approached by my one friend at this middle school. A geeky boy or girl, thick glasses and maybe a Math Club hoodie, offering calm words of comfort. Slinging his or her arm around my quivering shoulders, telling me to forget about those jerks.

The problem is, I don't have one friend at this middle school. I've only been at this middle school for three days. All I have is enemies, specifically the Jew Crew. Who I offended on Monday, just two days ago. A banner first day at my new school.

Frank

Breakfast with Johnny is more of the same badgering that I got at the nursing home. I'd walk out on him, but it's so awesome to have some real food for a change. They don't even let me order pizza at the home.

"You look terrible, you know," Johnny says to me between forkfuls of Belgian waffle. No syrup on his lips or his chin. Johnny's always been very neat when it comes to eating.

"Yeah, I've kind of let myself go. The exercise classes at the home aren't what you'd call strenuous. More like, stand up from your chair, raise your hands to the ceiling, sit down in your chair, repeat. Once a week we go to the YMCA for water aerobics, and that's really the same thing, but in a pool. We're only allowed in the shallow end. The instructors line us up in rows and columns. You can actually feel the warm urine leaving these old people's bodies in the water."

"I'm trying to eat, here."

"But you get used to it, just like anything else," I signal the waitress for more coffee, "Speaking of which, excuse me for a moment, I've got to pee." Johnny slides the table towards him, making room for me to get up. Instead I just sit there, looking directly into his eyes, a sneaky smile on my face.

"Oh, God, that is so gross," he says, realizing after a few seconds that I won't be getting up at all.

"Don't be so narrow-minded. You would be amazed at the advancements that have been made in the field of adult diapers. I mean, really, diapers are one part of this whole fiasco that I'm taking with me when I leave. You wouldn't believe how absorbent they are. There are these layers of dry mesh between your skin and the pads. Half a second after you're done it's like you don't even know that you peed. I highly recommend…"

"Mom is really worried, Frank. Justifiably so, I think."

"Mom is always worried about something. She'll get over it. You guys could give me a little more support while I'm in this thing, you know. Get behind it, rather than try to shut it down."

"We all thought it was very generous of you to pay for Grandad's managed care facility. Why do you have to ruin it by pulling this stunt? Just let it go. You don't even need the money," Johnny says, his mouth full of waffle.

"Stunt? I'm not doing this for the money. I'm doing it for our family honor. To keep Granddad's integrity intact. Do you think he'd be OK with the idea that the nursing home wouldn't refund a year's worth of living expenses even though he died before he had a chance to move in? That would have driven him bananas. So, being his namesake in both a literal and figurative manner, I found a loophole. And I'm going to continue leveraging that loophole until Hardy refunds what's left of the money or renders all of the services for which I paid. Which is exactly what Granddad would have wanted. This whole stunt, as you call it, is a tribute to that unreasonable and stingy old man we all loved so much. It will help him rest easier in the grave."

"You know we cremated him."

"Rest easier in the urn, then, on top of mom and dad's mantle. Looking down on us from somewhere, still beaming with pride for his elder grandson. And still tragically disappointed in his younger grandson, just like the rest of us."

"Being an old person has made you nasty," Johnny says. He waves to our waitress for the check. She brings it, thanks us, walks away as Johnny slides the check over to my side of the table.

"Just once it would be nice if you bought me breakfast," I say and grab the check.

"I'll buy you breakfast when this charade ends and you stop acting like a child."

"I'd say acting like a child is the exact opposite of what I'm doing. Why don't *you* start acting like a man and get a real job? Everyone hates insurance salesmen. You are part of a population of suck. Why aren't you at work, anyway? Is it the weekend already?"

"It's Wednesday. I have an appointment out this way at eleven o'clock," he says, looking at his watch. Who wears a wristwatch anymore? Just look at your phone, dude. "Come on, I've got to get you back."

I leave thirty dollars on the table, tipping generously, as is my nature. Johnny drives me back to the home, signs me in at the front desk. The reception nurse gives Johnny an awkward smile. She gives me a blank look. Not exactly nasty, but certainly not a friendly welcome back. I make a face at her in response.

"Do you even have your apartment anymore?" Johnny asks, extending his hand in a goodbye.

"I sublet it, month-to-month," I say. I grab his hand and pull him into a hearty embrace, with which he is obviously not comfortable, "Come on. You don't hug me anymore, man."

"These people hate you. You're messing with the vibe of this whole joint. I'm trying to disassociate."

"Say hi to Jane and the kids for me. Bring them around sometime, I'll buy them some Jell-O."

"They miss their stupid uncle Frank," he says, finally breaking my embrace.

"I thought they called me 'silly' uncle Frank."

"They did, before you moved into a nursing home. Now it's 'stupid' uncle Frank. I think Jane changed your moniker first, but it caught on with the kids."

"Your wife has always hated me," I say coldly.

"You've always given her good reason."

"You're just mad because I dumped her, which is the only reason that she married you."

My relationship with my brother's wife is awkward, to say the least. Almost a decade ago she and I dated, casually, for about three months. And then she starts talking about marriage. As in, getting married to me. Which forced me to abruptly cease all communication with her. Full stop. Totally ghosted. In retrospect, I would probably have played it differently had I known that she was ultimately going to be part of the family. Live and learn, I guess.

"Nice, Frank," Johnny says, walking away, "You were always great at goodbyes."

I turn around, make another face at the disapproving nurse behind the reception desk, walk back towards my room. I probably could have handled that situation better with my brother. But, stupid uncle Frank? Jane is such a Stepford bitch.

Elroy

How I offended the Jew Crew was, I always try to approach any new school with a positive attitude. Even though I've been to three new schools in the past five years, and it's never done me much good. Still, I try to be outgoing on the first day. Show a little personality. Which is, like, the opposite of who I am. And on Monday I was trying extra hard, because I'm in the seventh grade and figure that a lot of my classmates might be new to this middle school, too. So even though I'm wearing foster home clothes, a five-dollar haircut, maybe I still have a chance to make a first impression. Maybe hook into a friend for a change.

In retrospect, not a good idea.

So I go to this convocation in the gym on Monday morning, where all of the seventh and eighth graders are gathered to listen to the principal and staff talk about how the school works, how we're expected to follow the rules, what extracurricular activities are offered, that kind of thing. And I'm sitting on the end of the bleachers next to this kid who looks kind of like a skinny chicken. Cowlick hair, thick-frame glasses, maybe eighty pounds if he were soaking wet. He's wearing one of those vests that go with a three-piece suit, knit in the front and shiny in the back, over a white button-down shirt. Total geek. And I'm thinking, hey, this could be my guy. New friend material for the foster kid.

I really want to get this weird little guy's attention, but as usual, I'm having trouble coming up with a conversation-starter. I jerk my chin up at him slightly, the way I've seen guys sometimes say hey to each other. He glances at me and then looks straight ahead, avoiding eye contact. He's nervous, too, I'm thinking. Maybe he doesn't want to mess up the chance to make a new friend either. I lean my head forward, catch his eye again.

"I'm not gay, dude," the little weird kid says under his breath, eyes straight ahead. What?

"What? I'm not gay, either," I say, a little too loudly. As if a gay kid would ever dress this badly, poor or not. Plus, I'm only in the seventh grade. I don't even know if I'm ready to like girls yet. Then these two big eighth graders walk up to the bleachers. They're dressed like *The Beastie Boys*, circa nineteen ninety. One of them looks past me at the little weird kid. It's like I'm not even there.

"Yo! Jew Crew in da houuuze!" he shouts at the little weird kid.

At that moment, something in my head is screaming, opportunity! Not just the chance to make a friend, but a chance to step up to anti-Semitism in this new middle school. Maybe I'll take a beating, but it's so worth it. I rise to my feet, then realize that I should have thought about what my statement against bullying and anti-Semitism was going to be before I stood up.

"Hey," I shout, "he's no… no… not Jewish!" That came out totally wrong. I blame the stutter and the crowd. Too self-conscious to think clearly.

The big *Beastie Boy* kid looks at me, blinks his eyes a couple of times, confused. "Yeah, he is."

"I… I… I mean, you don't get to bu… bu… bully someone just because they're Jewish."

"What? The hell? Are you talking about?" The big kid asks, shaking his head slightly. "I'm Jewish, too. What, you got some beef with the Chosen People?!"

As he shouts this, the principal has stopped speaking and the whole convocation is watching our scene unfold.

"Hey!" the principal yells into the microphone, looking at me. "There is no place for anti-Semitism in this school!"

I raise my palms and look wide-eyed at the principal, at the other kids in the gym. The big kid grabs my collar and pulls me off the bleachers. I land hard on the gym floor, scrambling, but still on my feet, mostly because he's got my collar in a tight grip. This is not the kind of first impression that I was trying to make at my new school.

And then I hear this wild yowl from behind me on the bleachers. I rotate my head, collar still twisted in the big kid's hand. And it's the weird little kid. He's stepping up for me. *He's* going to defend *me* from bullying. Not how I thought this would play out, but I'll take it.

Like it's all happening in slow motion, I watch over my shoulder as the weird little kid makes this running leap, one leg extended and the other jack-knifed, like you see in Bruce Lee movies. He launches himself off the second bleacher, right at the big kid and me.

And he kicks me square in the back.

It knocks the wind out of me, and then I'm twisting around on the gym floor like a spastic, trying to catch a breath.

"Jew Crew in da houuuze!" he shouts into my face, staring down at me.

Then he high-fives the two *Beastie Boy* kids and I'm thinking maybe I misread the situation entirely. So, there I am on the gym floor, these gangsta-rap eighth graders pointing and shouting the worst stuff ever at me. All of the other kids have given us a wide berth and are staring open-mouthed as the principal finally runs over and starts yelling at us. All of us. As if there was any way that I, the shabby poor kid huddled on the floor, could be at fault for this circus.

All three of us get held after the convocation. And we all get detention for a week. And I'm thinking about me and this self-styled Jew Crew, all sitting in some empty classroom for an hour after dismissal, the whole first week of school. Not good. Like a prison shower, not good. And then the guidance counselor, this sweater-vest wearing pony-tail guy with a soft voice, makes an alternative offer.

"Bill," the guidance counselor says to the principal, "we do need more people to volunteer for community service. Maybe these boys would prefer to join my Outreach Club in lieu of detention."

Yes! The principal eyes each of us in rapid succession.

"Whatever, Tom," the principal says with a sigh, "You boys can choose. Either the Outreach Club or detention." He looks at me first.

"I'll ju… ju… join the Outreach Club," I stammer. He looks down the line.

"Detention," says the kid who is Saul, glaring at me.

"Detention," says the kid who is Jacob, eyes on the gym floor, simmering.

"Detention, boooy!" raps the weird little kid, Isaac, spreading his arms wide and then crossing them in front of his chest in a pincer motion.

And that's how I made enemies with the Jew Crew and simultaneously became a part of the Rudolphsville Middle School Outreach Club. The guidance counselor tells me to meet him in front of the school after dismissal bell, and he starts to walk away. I jog to catch up with him, asking random questions about the Outreach Club, more to get away from the Jew Crew than to garner any real information. Which is fine, because the guidance counselor offers me, like, nothing about the program.

It turns out that I am the only active member of the Rudolphsville Middle School Outreach Club. Apparently there is one other member, inactive, named Sally Berman. Sally is missing the first week of school because she had to drive down to South Carolina for her aunt's funeral. All I know about Sally Berman is that, according to Dr. Severs, her mother is a *huge supporter* of the Catholic Church and is also a *huge supporter* of the Rudolphsville Middle School Outreach Club, as well as a *huge supporter* of Dr. Severs personally, branding the image of Sally's mother as a giant jockstrap indelibly in my mind.

So, based on my impression of her mother, I assume Sally's either a giant community jockstrap exactly like her mother, or she's one messed up kid, because of her mother. I'm hoping for the latter, although I find it helpful to always maintain very low expectations for whatever life might throw my way.

So, anyway, on Monday afternoon it's just me. I'm picking up garbage from the side of the highway with a pointy metal stick. At first, I'm thinking that the metal stick is cool, like hey, I don't have to bend down to grab any of this roadside litter! But the novelty wears off after a few minutes and all that's left is me, like a convict without the badass orange coveralls, stabbing cardboard and paper from the grassy median of State Route Four-Twenty-Four.

And it turns out that the Rudolphsville Middle School Outreach Club is only in its first year. Its first days, actually. In other words, it really started with me opting-out of detention. This benevolent social club is the brainchild of second-year veteran guidance counselor Dr. Tom Severs, who apparently believes that middle school kids would thoroughly embrace the opportunity to form an organized effort to support our community. Wrong. Dr. Severs further believes that this organized effort would create a virtuous cycle of love among small business owners and the altruistic kids, somehow elevating our blue-collar neighborhood into what could become a model community for America.

The jury is still out on that one, since the dedicated children are just me and absent Sally Berman, personality type TBD. My first impression of Dr. Severs is that his feet are very far from the ground.

According to Dr. Severs, the whole plan looked a lot more convincing in his PowerPoint presentation to the school board than it does in the first days of practical execution. But these things start slowly and build momentum, he says. And it's not like I have any choice in the matter, belonging to this newly-minted club of one, I mean. I'm stuck here, at least for the first week of school, while I'm avoiding detention.

On Tuesday afternoon, the Rudolphsville Middle School Outreach Club spends three hours pulling weeds from a garden in front of the town's Episcopal church. Just me, dirt and weeds. Dr. Severs is in his car, parked by the curb in front of the church, listening to the Grateful Dead, reeking of marijuana. I'm twelve, but I know what marijuana smells like. And I know the Grateful Dead. Before I was moved to my current home, I spent two years with a forty-something foster mom who listened to nothing but music from the eighties and nineties, watched nothing but late twentieth-century reruns on television. It's like I was stuck along with this sad lady in her happy teen years.

So, I've probably seen every episode of *Happy Days* and *Laverne and Shirley* ever made. And I've watched *Say Anything* and *Reality Bites* so many times that I could confidently exchange movie lines with the college kids that used to come over to our house to buy drugs and have sex with my foster mom. Until she got arrested, that is, and the system sent me here.

On Wednesday, the day of shame when my underwear is exposed in the school hallway at lunchtime, the Rudolphsville Middle School Outreach Club is scheduled to read to old people at a nursing home. The old people thing is a co-op effort with the town's Jewish Community Center, an organization that must have some pull with the parents because it produces about thirty kids, all geared up to read to a bunch of nonagenarians. The Jewish Community Center kids pull up to the nursing home in a bus. I pull up at the same time, in the passenger seat of Dr. Severs' nineteen ninety-two Honda Accord.

"Don't screw this up," Dr. Severs says to me as I open the car door. "It took a lot of greasing to get this affiliation with the JCC."

"JCC?"

"Jewish Community Center."

"Do they ca... ca... call themselves the JCC?"

"I don't know. Maybe. What's the difference?"

"Nothing, I guess. Just tr... tr... trying to avoid any weirdness in advance. Like if I call them the JCC and they don't know what I'm talking about," I say.

"Good thinking," he replies and jams a Grateful Dead cassette into the dashboard stereo. "Keep your mouth shut and follow their lead."

Just who exactly has a cassette player in their car these days? I might be poor, but I'm not a caveman. He should at least get one of those things that looks like a cassette, the kind you stick into your player and hook up to your iPhone so that it can play music through the car speakers. Then I notice Dr. Severs' Motorola flip phone on the seat beside him.

I get in line behind the last of the JCC kids, wait to be given the name and location of the elderly person to whom I will read out loud for the next two hours. I'm not terribly nervous about my stutter because I figure reading to old people is like talking to your plants. They don't really understand what you're saying, but just the attention itself can be life-giving.

When I get to the nurse at the front of the line, she hands me an index card on which is written the number four-twenty-two. She then hands me an old, paperback copy of *Huckleberry Finn*, gives me a forlorn look, and points me in the direction of my old person's room. The forlorn look gives me the impression that maybe I'm on my way to read to some catatonic guy. Or a crazy person. Or maybe the guy in four-twenty-two just smells really bad. Whatever it is, it can't be good.

So I walk down the hallway, which smells like pee. I turn left, walk down another hallway, find the room and knock on the door. No answer. Maybe the old person is dead? I try the knob and it's unlocked. I slowly creak open the door, peek my head in. Then I let the door swing wide.

My old person is not as old as I expected him to be. His hair isn't grey, though his bare t-shirt arms do look dangerously brittle. And I can't help but notice that he's playing *Grand Theft Auto V* on a giant monitor, grunting quietly into his microphoned headset, as if someone in the home might overhear his carjacking plans.

I look at the worn copy of *Huckleberry Finn* in my hands, loudly clear my throat. Twice. And then I cough, also very loud. Still no response. Finally, I toss my book in the air and it lands on the floor behind him with a thump. A risky move, given the heart attack probability in this place, but I figure a dropped book won't jar him any more than gunning down a young mother in a grocery store parking lot, which is what he's in the process of doing on the monitor.

When the book lands, he jerks his head to the left. His shoulders don't turn, just his black-haired skull, and he looks at me from the tiniest corner of his left eye.

"Explain," he says.

As in, explain why I'm standing in his room and just threw a book on the floor at his back. I incongruously lean backwards and check the number on his door, as if there might have been a mistake. I lean back into the room, look at him again. His shoulders are still square to the monitor, so I address just the corner of an eye in his turned head. It unnerves me.

"I'm sup… sup… sup… supposed to read to you," I say. At this, he pauses the game, spins his swivel chair fully towards me, drops his chin to his chest and looks at me with irises rolled towards his forehead. I'm thinking maybe he's mentally disturbed or something. Maybe that's why he's in here.

"Seriously," he says flatly, a combination of anger and sarcasm. I don't respond verbally. Instead, I turn my palms to the ceiling and spread my fingers, like to say I'm just a kid doing what I was told to do.

"You tell the toolbox who sent you that I'm not going to stand for this type of intrusion. Tell him to read my contract. This room is all mine unless I specifically request a nurse or I'm having some kind of dying episode, which clearly I am not."

"Okay," I say, without a stutter. I turn around, walk out the door of his room, turn right, turn right again at the end of the hallway. I turn left in the lobby and walk out the front door to Dr. Severs' car, idling at the curb.

"What are you doing?" Dr. Severs asks me, a panicked expression on his face.

"He told me to tell you that he wouldn't stand for this type of intrusion," I say without stuttering, "He told me to tell you to read his contract."

"Who told you to tell me that?"

"The guy I'm su… su… supposed to read to."

"He kicked you out? What did you do? Was it because of the stutter? Man, you're blowing my chance to get something started here," Dr. Severs whines, anxious that my inadequacies might derail his grand plan for rebirthing a sixties-style culture of love in our community.

"I didn't even say anything." I'm getting worked up "He just ki… ki… kicked me out!"

"Really?" Dr. Severs asks, calming down, raising his eyebrows into a sympathetic arch. "Old people, right? Look, he's probably just confused or something. Maybe he's offended at the idea that he needs a kid to read to him. Put yourself in his shoes. It's hard getting old.

Anyway, I want you to go back in there and let him know that you're just there to help him relax. To spend some time with him. Maybe give his eyes a break, assuming he can still read on his own. Be cool and defuse the situation. Let him know that you're only there to assist."

"Do I have to?"

"Well, yeah, you have to. I mean, do it for the group. We've got an opportunity here to be part of something regular with the JCC. We can't blow it by bailing out just because some old guy is offended by the fact that he needs a kid to read to him. Think of the bigger picture."

"You do realize that the group is just me, right?"

"You and Sally, when she gets home. And I'm sure we'll create momentum with the other kids if we just keep it moving. This is important stuff we're doing here. Change can happen. Don't let us down."

"He isn't old."

"What?"

"He isn't old, the guy I'm supposed to read to, I mean."

"Yeah, man, I getcha," Dr. Severs says, with hippie compassion, "No one's really old. Age is just a number."

"No, I mean, he hasn't had that many years," I say. "He's like, your age."

"I'm twenty-seven," Dr. Severs says, more offended than I think he should be. "I just finished grad school two years ago. Don't be comparing me to some old guy living in a nursing home. I've got my whole life ahead of me."

"No, I mean, for reals. Maybe he's a little ol… ol… older than you." Everything between twenty and forty looks about the same to me, because I'm in the seventh grade. "But he's not like an old man. I mean, he looks fe… fe… feeble and everything, but he doesn't look, like, aged."

"Yeah, Elroy, I dig you. And that's just the attitude we want for this type of work. You go in there and you tell him what you just told me.

And you let him know that you're here to help, not to be some kind of yardstick of old age. No judgments, right?"

"Fine," I say. "Whatever."

I turn around, walk back into the building, left at the end of the hall. The door of four-twenty-two is still ajar. I push it open. His shoulders are square to the monitor and he doesn't notice me in the doorway.

"Hey!" I shout into his back.

He takes his time swiveling towards me. He doesn't look as psycho as when I'd first gone into his room. He just looks exasperated.

"I don't th... th... think you're old," I say.

"That's because I'm not old, you retard," the man says.

"I know. I just acknowledged that. Look, we're ob... ob... obviously both in a weird situation here. How about you just let me read to you for a while and then I can go home?"

"Then read away," the man says lightly.

He adjusts his headset and swivels back to the computer monitor.

Frank

These days, aside from the rare visit, online gaming is pretty much my only source of social interaction with people born after nineteen forty. Still, most of the gaming crew is ten-to-fifteen years younger than me because everyone, aside from college students and recent graduates, seems to have day jobs. And mostly, I write code at night. So daytime is when I kick back.

Right now, me and user-name "Footjob" are playing *Grand Theft Auto V*, wreaking havoc at a strip mall somewhere in suburban Los Angeles. The stuff you do in video games these days is truly atrocious.

When I hear a loud thud on the floor behind me, I instinctively control my startle, quickly put on my game face. It's not unusual for the nursing staff to try and mess with me, especially when I'm immersed in gaming. With my body still facing the monitor, I turn only my head. I put an evil glint in my eye, leering sideways towards the intruder. The problem is, it's more pose than practical, and I can't really see who's standing in the doorway.

"Explain," I command in my creepiest voice. And then this stuttering kid voice says something about reading to me. Come on, man! What kind of game are you playing here, Hardy? I swivel the chair, face the urchin, give him my death stare. The kid is only eleven or twelve years old. It looks like someone dragged him through a Salvation Army shop in lieu of dressing him. On his feet are beat up Hush Puppies, the imitation suede shiny in spots, the thick gummy soles detaching at the toes. Sad. Like he was plucked from the chorus of a modern-day version of *Oliver Twist*. Is Hardy trying to shame me with street kids? How is that going to work?

"Seriously," I say, challenging him through my death stare. He makes a face and kind of shrugs, hands raised, as if he doesn't want to be here anymore than I want him here. I give him a message for

Hardy and mention my contract so he'll know I'm serious. Hardy doesn't want to pony up lawyer fees any more than I do, both of us having already spent way too much on those parasites when we argued the legality of my contract to move in. So now lawyers are more like a game of chicken between us, as opposed to a serious threat.

But I'm more than ready to bring back the bloodsuckers if Hardy doesn't flinch out of this metaphorical stare-down and leave me the hell alone. Footjob is yelling at me through the headphones, cursing me for letting our victims get away. But my death stare seems to work, because the kid says okay and then walks out of the room.

I try to get my head back in the game, but this little episode of reality has effectively distracted me. The thirty-second rule applies to immersive gaming as well as sleep. Point to you, Mr. Hardy, well played. Footjob calls me a loser and logs out of the game. I continue to stare at the screen, alone in my room.

I actually think about writing some code, even though it's the middle of the afternoon, but within a few minutes the kid is back. I can sense him in the doorway. He shouts "Hey" at the back of my head. I swivel around and look him in the eye. He tells me that he doesn't think I'm old. Not like he's exposing me for not being old, despite the fact that I live in a nursing home. More like, he's saying that I shouldn't feel bad about myself just because I'm old. Which I'm not, so none of it makes any sense.

"That's because I'm not old, you retard," I say, kind of regretting the last part because I don't know anything about this kid and maybe he does have some special needs. Filtering has always been a problem for me.

"I know. I just acknowledged that," the kid says without any hint of stutter. "Look, we're ob... ob... obviously both in a weird situation here," ah, the stutter returns, "how about you just let me read to you for a while and then I can go home?"

"Then read away," I say and pull the headset back over my ears and turn to face the computer monitor. I hear the kid sit down on my bed and open his book. He starts to read *Huckleberry Finn* out loud.

I'm not sure what to do. I don't want to be mean to this kid, but any gesture of kindness feels like it would only be playing into Hardy's game, whatever that may be. I pop open iTunes and put some music on the headset to drown out the kid's voice, making this whole scene a little less awkward. For me, at least.

I'm jamming to *How Do You Afford Your Rock and Roll Lifestyle* by *Cake* when I realize there are more people in my room than just the kid. They can't have been here for very long since the kid only started reading just one song ago. Standing in the doorway is Hardy, arms crossed. He's probably got an angry expression on his face, but I wouldn't know because I refuse to look him in the eye. Next to Hardy is some sweater-vested hippie. If there is one extreme prejudice that I harbor, it's that I can't stand hippies. I find them utterly revolting. No pun intended. The kid stops reading. Apparently he was so engaged in the book, he didn't notice that we had company either.

"Can I help you gentlemen?" I ask politely and glance at the kid for any kind of explanation regarding their presence. He just raises his eyebrows and shrugs. I don't think he can provide me with an explanation for his own presence, much less theirs.

"We're just checking on Elroy," the hippie says.

"Elroy?" I ask, not so much for identification because I know it must be the kid. But who, outside of George Jetson, names their kid Elroy?

"That's me," the kid, Elroy, answers.

"Nice, Johnson. A kid volunteers his time to read to you and you ignore him, listen to music on your headphones instead of treating him like a human being. I'm sorry, Elroy," Hardy says to the kid.

"Elroy," I say, addressing the kid, "Could you tell Mr. Hardy that he didn't have to send you to my room in the first place. He is well aware of the fact that I can read all by myself."

"Ahhhh," Elroy looks from me to Hardy, not sure what to do, "He sa... sa... said to tell you..." But Hardy waves him off before he can finish. And I'm glad, because it seems cruel to use a stuttering kid as an intermediary to communicate with someone who's standing in the same room as you. But I'm not going to break character and address

Hardy directly, because my refusal to look him in the eye really seems to be getting under his skin. Someday it might just be the thing that cracks him and finally gets me out of here, my money and dignity intact. Although I guess the dignity part would be a matter of perspective.

"It's part of the service you pay for, Johnson," Hardy says.

"Hey, Starflower," I say to the hippie, who responds with a mildly offended glare. "Tell Hardy here that it's not nice getting other people involved in a quarrel that I'd be perfectly happy to keep between ourselves."

"You've got everyone that lives at this facility involved in our quarrel, Johnson!" Hardy shouts.

"Moonbeam, please tell Mr. Hardy that I'd be more than willing to negotiate a departure. Assuming we can come to terms."

"What terms?" Hardy asks directly, not bothering to use the hippie as a go-between.

"If he's wondering," I address the hippie, "then you can tell Mr. Hardy that I'd be happy to leave in exchange for the remaining balance of credit against services rendered. And not a penny less."

"You can go to hell," Hardy says and storms off down the hallway. Leaving me, the hippie and Elroy staring at each other in my room. Awkward.

"Uh, I'm Doctor Severs, Mister…"

"Mister," I reply.

"Mister, uh, Mister?"

"Yeah," I say, "It sounds like the pop group, I know. But my last name is spelled with a 'u' at the end. So, it's actually pronounced mis-tuh, like in the old South. Mister Mis-tuh, you can call me. Or Mis-tuh Mis-tuh, if you happen to be from the South. Or just Mister Mister. I'm pretty flexible about it."

"Really?" Severs asks.

"No, not really, you moron. My name is Frank Johnson. Hardy called me Johnson at least twice in the last two minutes. Or did you think Johnson was some kind of derogatory euphemism? I mean, did you think he was calling me a dick? In front of the kid, here?"

"No, I... I wasn't really paying attention, I guess."

"Okay, let's move on. Why are you in my room?"

"Well, Elroy is my charge, see. And I just want to make sure everything is OK with the reading and stuff."

I'm wondering why Severs is being so polite, especially following Hardy's violent departure, when it occurs to me that he must think there's a reason that I'm living in a managed care facility at the unripe age of thirty-three. A reason having to do with a lack of mental stability or something. I don't see any harm in letting that thought play out.

"Everything is quite alright, Doctor Severs. Quite alright," I say, businesslike, "Elroy and I were just about to try on some of my old diapers. That's a thing, you know. So if you could give us, say, fifteen minutes, it would be great. Strip down, Elroy!" The boy doesn't move from the bed.

"Uh, I think I'd better stick around," Dr. Severs says.

"Even better," I say, "but no touching. Otherwise they'll give you a shock with the Taser gun. Big time ouchies." I walk over to the garbage pail in the corner of my room, pull out three soggy adult diapers. "First we wear them. Then we eat them. Yum, yum, yum!" I stick the elastic waistband of a diaper into my mouth.

"Elroy, go to the car!" Dr. Severs shouts.

"Wait!" I yell, the diaper falling from my mouth to the floor. "I need four ounces of his saliva – and a stool sample – for a project I'm working on! Elroy, stay!" The kid is still sitting on my bed, *Huckleberry Finn* open in his hands, a look of amusement on his face. He clearly digs the fact that I'm messing with Severs.

"Elroy. Car!" Severs yells. Severs probably knows that I'm screwing with him. But he doesn't know the extent that I'm damaged, or if I'm potentially dangerous, so he's disoriented. He's thinking about personal liability. Anything that might lead to his termination at whatever job entails shuttling kids around to old people homes. I can so read people.

"Elroy. Stay!" I say. He still hasn't moved from the bed. The three of us exchange glances for about ten seconds.

"I'm going to get a nurse!" Severs finally shouts. "Leave the door open." He pounds down the hallway, yelling, "Nurse!" As if anyone in a managed care facility is a fast responder.

By the time Severs, Hardy and a male nurse are standing in my doorway, Elroy and I are already on level three of Super Mario Brothers, two-player.

"Eh? What's up, Doc?" I say in my best Bugs Bunny, as I turn towards Severs and the nurse, my eyes conspicuously averted from Hardy's.

Sally

"She's with Jesus, Sally," Mom says.

It's kind of nice seeing Aunt Sadie in the casket. I know that sounds totally morbid, but really, she looks good. Peaceful, I mean. Well rested, for a change. Aunt Sadie never looked that happy when she was alive. She's just lying there, in the middle of all of the hymns and prayers and hushed voices around her, with this little Mona Lisa smile on her waxy face as if to say that Mom can do whatever she wants because none of it bothers her anymore. Honestly, I really think this is the happiest I've ever seen her.

And in my mind, I tell her so. And in my mind, she says thanks. And in my mind, I tell her that I don't want to sound selfish because it is her day and all, but she did kind of let me down because I'd always planned to run away from Mom, her sister, and come live with her. And now that plan is shot. And in my mind, Aunt Sadie gives me a trademark chuckle, a sarcastic "sorry" – like, sorry for living, which she is obviously not any longer. And in my mind, I tell her that I want to keep her in my mind like this, for a while at least. And in my mind Aunt Sadie says that would be alright.

And then my weepy, God-fearing mother hugs me from behind and ruins our moment.

"She is with Jesus forever, you know, Sally," Mom says.

I picture Aunt Sadie at a wooden card table in an old-fashioned parlor, playing Gin Rummy with Jesus. Aunt Sadie wearing the same dress she's wearing in the coffin, Jesus in his traditional garb. Both drinking sacramental wine, eating little round crackers. Aunt Sadie complaining about the taste of it all. In my mind, Aunt Sadie laughs at the scene. But it isn't the Aunt Sadie playing Gin Rummy with Jesus who laughs. It's the Aunt Sadie who was talking to me before Mom interrupted us, like she's standing beside me in my mind, looking at the parlor scene with me.

A part of me tells myself that I'm the one creating Aunt Sadie in my mind, that she isn't speaking or laughing by any volition other than my own and I can make her do or say anything I want because she is really only me. But I shove that part of me away. I don't test the thesis. Because, crazy or not, I want Aunt Sadie in my mind just the way that she is right now.

"You were her favorite niece," Mom says, through her tears.

"That's saying a lot," I reply, an only child without any cousins, a de facto favorite.

"You were kind of like her namesake."

"Sadie and Sally are different names, mom."

"Yes, I know. But Aunt Sadie had her problems, as you know, so we weren't exactly going to name you after her. Still, you're close to being her namesake." This woman is from hell. "I think she saw the Christ that she could be, in you. Maybe it was too much for her."

Seriously, is Mom implying that this is in any way my fault? What a psycho my mom is.

"She was my favorite aunt," I say. "Not just because she was my only aunt. She would have been my favorite, even if I had a dozen aunts. She was the closest thing I ever had to a real role model."

Mom's arms tense up and it's like I'm being hugged by a block of wood. I finally smile, the first one since Aunt Sadie killed herself.

Elroy

So they take me into this windowless office at the back of the retirement home and everyone wants to know if Mr. Johnson did anything inappropriate to me. Especially Mr. Hardy, who seems to have more than a few motives that are ulterior to my own well-being. When I tell them that Mr. Johnson didn't do anything inappropriate to me, that we just played Super Mario Brothers, they all act like I'm giving them the wrong answer. I mean, I was never an altar boy or anything, but shouldn't everyone be happy when I answer no, the older man did not do anything inappropriate to me when we were left alone in his room?

So they keep asking me the same question in different ways and I keep answering the same question in different ways, all of it amounting to the fact that we played video games for the five minutes that Dr. Severs left us alone in Mr. Johnson's room. No one is asking about the five or so minutes that I was alone in Mr. Johnson's room reading *Huckleberry Finn* on his bed before Dr. Severs and Mr. Hardy showed up the first time.

"It was fi... fi... fine. What do you want me to say?" I ask.

"It was fine doing what, exactly?" Dr. Severs asks.

"Playing video games. We don't have a Pl... Pl... PlayStation at the foster home where I live."

"See, that's how they trap you. Predators, I mean. They lure you in with candy or video games." Dr. Severs says.

"How could he have been trying to tr... tr... trap me when he didn't even ask me to come into his room in the first place? You're the one that sent me into his room, Dr. Severs. Even after I came back out to your ca... ca... car and told you that he didn't want me there, you made me go back."

Dr. Severs gives me a blank look.

"We're mixing up the issues here," says Mr. Hardy. "What about the diapers? And your saliva? And the stool sample? Johnson said all of that while Dr. Severs was still in the room."

"He was only me... me... messing with Dr. Severs. He also told Dr. Severs that his name was Mister Mister, like the po... po... pop music group from the nineties. The *Broken Wings* band. Dr. Severs actually believed him for a second."

Dr. Severs shakes his head as if he never believed that.

"But how do you know that he was just messing with Dr. Severs when he said the other stuff?" Mr. Hardy asks.

"Because he to... to... told me he was only messing with Dr. Severs. He told me that hippies are a disgrace, that they deserve to be messed with. Sorry, Dr. Severs, I'm only saying what he said."

"It's not your fault, Elroy," Dr. Severs responds, weakly.

"Look, I'll answer anything you want, but no... no... nothing bad happened. And I have to get home, eventually." That last part is a lie. I don't have to get home. I don't even know if my foster parents are aware that I live with them.

"You realize you're giving me nothing," Mr. Hardy says to Dr. Severs.

"If nothing happened, then nothing happened. He's right. Mr. Johnson didn't even want Elroy to come to his room in the first place. He said so, outright," Dr. Severs says.

Mr. Hardy gets this look, like he's the Grinch scheming a way to ruin Christmas in Whoville.

"What's on the Rudolphsville Middle School Outreach Club docket for tomorrow?" Mr. Hardy finally asks.

"Tomorrow? Tomorrow, Elroy, I mean the RMSOC, is going to work at the Soup Kitchen on Hickory Street." Dr. Severs replies.

"How about Friday?"

"We don't have anything set up for Friday yet. I typically schedule stuff a day or so in advance," Dr. Severs says, haltingly, like he's uncomfortable talking about the loose schedule of the RMSOC.

"Is there any way that I could convince you to have the RMSOC come back on Friday to read to our residents?" Mr. Hardy asks.

"After what just happened?"

"Nothing dangerous or inappropriate happened. You said it yourself. And I think it would be nice if we could entertain Mr. Johnson with a reader on Friday afternoon."

"I mean, I guess… we'd get credit for the hours of community service, right?" Dr. Severs asks.

"I don't see why we couldn't double, or even triple, the community service credit hours. Johnson being a kind of difficult case and all."

"Done," replies Dr. Severs, smiling huge.

"And what does next week look like for you guys?" Mr. Hardy asks.

And that's how the RMSOC, meaning me, got scheduled to read at the Hardy Managed Care Facility, specifically to Mr. Johnson, for the entire month of September. Dr. Severs even agrees to me working on weekends, earlier in the morning than I would have thought necessary. But I'm fine with it. It gets me out of the house, at least. Though I'm not sure how Mr. Johnson is going to feel about it. Bad, I suspect.

Frank

"But that's not fair to the other inmates!"

"Residents," Martha Hardy corrects me.

"You know what I mean, Martha. This is just another one of Ed's schemes to try and nudge me out of here."

"I'm just the secretary here, Frank. I shouldn't even be having this conversation with you," Martha says, looking every bit like Betty White, my favorite Golden Girl. But this isn't a time for me to get sentimental.

"I'm not going to baby-sit some twelve-year-old, every day, for the next month. I've got work to do," I say, pacing towards the doorway of her small office.

"I thought you worked mostly at night?"

"Yeah, I do. But I nap and generally rest up during the day. This is a clear violation of my rights as an inmate."

"Resident," Martha corrects me again.

"Whatever. He's your husband, Martha. Can't you talk to him? You know what he's doing to me is wrong. Not refunding the money, I mean."

"You of all people should know by now that when Ed gets his teeth into something, there's no way anyone except himself is going to get him to let go."

"Yeah, but how can he force volunteer work onto me when no one else in the home is getting the same treatment? There's got to be some kind of rule about that."

"There probably is, somewhere. But we're a private company. Meaning we make the rules as long as they're aligned with what the government tells us is OK for a nonprofit organization. Unless you want to get your lawyers involved in researching what seems to be an obscure and random precedent in the world of managed care law somewhere, I'd suggest you just deal with it. I mean, you've got, what, six months left? You'd probably be gone before the lawyers could even dig something up."

"Find me a loophole, Martha," I whisper after leaning over her desktop, my lips a fraction of an inch from hers, so close that I can smell the everything bagel that she had for breakfast. "I'll make it worth your while."

"Don't tease me, Frank," she breathes hot, stale air softly into my face.

"I'm not teasing you, Martha. How's another half-hour of afternoon lust sound?" I murmur.

"I'll look around, see what I can find for you. But I want my payment in advance," she whispers back, pulling her fat pink mouth into a warm smile, lipstick smudged above her upper lip.

"Well, I think that I can engineer a few more bangs," I say as she rises from her chair at the desk.

So, it's not what you're thinking, perverts. It is sexual, though. I'm not going to lie to you. It's one of the most intense sexual experiences with which I have ever involved myself. Which maybe says more about me than Martha.

Here's what went down. About a week after I moved into the home I began complaining to the administration office about how the snarky nurses were treating me. I knew I wasn't going to get anywhere with Ed Hardy, given the painful legal battle preceding my arrival at the home. So I went a step down, to administration. The administration office consisting solely of Martha Hardy. Martha being the person that actually keeps the retirement home chugging along on a day-to-day basis while her fat husband Ed glad-hands with all of the inmates. Ed isn't really fat, he's actually pretty normal for an older guy. I just like insulting him.

So, it's our first meeting, and I'm ranting to Martha about her cheapskate, idiot husband. And I'm really digging her response, which is like, indifference. Even though she's married to Ed Hardy, she doesn't take his side. She doesn't take my side either, but after dealing with the irrational belligerence of her husband for two weeks prior to the start of my residence, her neutrality felt like a victory to me.

The only thing that really bothered me during our first meeting was the fact that Martha was multi-tasking, toggling between two screens to enter invoices into the QuickBooks program that she uses to manage the facility's finances. It felt like she wasn't really listening to my problems. So, after scoping out what she was doing, I scooted her roller chair away from computer, sat down and wrote some code to automatically dump the invoice data into the accounting system via Intuit's public API. It's probably an exaggeration to say that the whole thing took me four minutes. "Bang!" I said, when I finished. Like that Creole chef Emeril on TV. I love solving problems with code.

"That's an hour of my day," Martha said to me, wistfully stunned, "every day."

"Great, so maybe now we can focus on my problem with your snarky nurses and jackass husband."

"You don't understand. You just gave me sixty minutes of my life back. Every day," she said softly, like close to tears, "You can't tell Ed!"

"Why would I tell Ed? He's a tool."

"I haven't watched *All My Children* in almost a decade."

"You're freaking me out a little bit, lady," I say, with just enough humor to avoid offending her.

"No, I'm sorry. You don't understand. How *could* you understand? It's just that I used to love watching the soap operas. When the kids were at school, I mean. *All My Children, As the World Turns, General Hospital.* Look at it from my perspective, Mr. Johnson..."

"Please, call me Frank."

"OK. And you can call me Martha."

"I was already calling you Martha."

"Well, you can continue to do so. What I was saying, Frank, is that I'm married to Ed. And I love Ed, very dearly. But Ed isn't big in the passion department, if you know what I mean."

"My preference is to defer to you on that subject."

"I mean, Ed's a very loving man. He's been a great husband and father to our children. But the daytime soap operas, all of that romance and lust during my otherwise empty afternoons, that's what really got me through the day. And then the kids went away to school and we bought this retirement home. And Ed can't do any of the bookkeeping, so it was all up to me. And it took all of my time. I lost everything that my daytime soap operas used to bring into my life. No more romance and lust. Until now, because you just gave it back to me. An extra sixty minutes every day. Assuming I can find a way to sneak a little television into the office and hide it from Ed."

"What are you talking about, a little television?"

"So I can watch the soap operas."

"Yeah, but what do you need a little television for?"

"So I can watch the soap operas," Martha says again, more slowly, like she's talking to one of the old people at the home.

I'm still sitting in front of Martha's computer terminal, so I start hacking away. I set up a connection to my media server. Bang! I log into my snatch programs and assign the names of the shows to grab from the Internet. Bang!

"Martha, you don't need a little television. I just set up your computer so that you can watch your soap operas from this large screen monitor, right at your own desk."

"What? No! Really?" Martha responds, jaw slack and hanging open, "You can do that?"

"I just did that. Bang!"

"And you're saying that I can watch soap operas that are playing on any of the networks?" she pants.

"No. That's not what I'm saying. I hooked you up to my media server and put a snatch program on the shows that you mentioned. So you'll be able to watch any of your soap operas, whenever you want. Bang!"

"Ummmuh," she moans, a sound you don't typically hear from a sixty-five-year-old lady in an office environment, "Wait a second, now. You're saying that I'm not ever going to miss any episodes."

"You're still not understanding me," I say. I project my two index fingers towards her. "As of right now, on this computer, whenever you want, you will be able to watch any episode of any soap opera that ever aired on any network at any time in history. You just search the titles and episodes, here, click on the one you want to watch, here, and hit play."

"Whooowhahha…" And I am pretty sure that I'm watching Martha Hardy have an orgasm. It's short, but poignant. When she recovers, she asks dreamily, "Let me get this straight. You just said that I can watch any episode of any of my favorite soap operas, ever made, from my computer, right?"

"It's already done, yes. Welcome to the Internet," I answer and she moans again, short panting breaths. "And now, Martha, here is the cherry on top of your sundae. If you walk me through your routine daily tasks, similar to how I watched you transcribing invoices a few minutes ago, I'm pretty sure I can automate away another two or three hours of manual work from your day-to-day activities."

"Meaning?" she says, breath heavy with anticipation, a dirty kid on an erotic Christmas morning.

"Meaning, instead of an extra hour to watch your soap operas," I say benevolently, "you should end up with at least two or three hours of extra time to watch any episode of any soap opera you ever loved, sequentially or non-sequentially, every single day. And Ed never needs to know about it. Bang!" I find it hard to describe the sound of Martha's multiple orgasms immediately following my explanation. Suffice it to say, there was a part of me that shared this experience with her, loving every second of her ecstasy, which lasted approximately two-and-a-half very intense minutes. Completely hands-free, by the way. Like she was having sex with God. And, at the same time, there was another part of me that remained preoccupied with the potential awkwardness of our going-forward relationship. Like there was going to be some sort of post-coital weirdness that no one had ever written a book about.

But, to my pleasant surprise, Martha behaved wonderfully following our impassioned meeting the first week of my stay. It was amazing, really. Like I crossed some rigid boundary in her psyche, and, once on the other side, she welcomed me with complete candor regarding her sexuality. No awkwardness or embarrassment. Nothing coy about her. And all pertaining to the daytime soap operas, you understand. Nothing physical every happened between us. I'm only thirty-three and she's a sixty-five-year-old married woman with grandchildren, for God's sake. Although, I've got to say that it was really hot being in the room when Martha had all those orgasms, regardless of her age.

But I was only there that one time. Not to say these extreme orgasms don't happen just as often when I'm not present, soap opera plot twists being what they are to the enthusiast. And, just keeping it honest, I find myself thinking about these Martha episodes a lot more often than I'd like to admit, given her age, our friendship and the fact that I hate her husband at a gut level.

So anyway, when I ask Martha for help, I always know that she will give me her best. And I was not about to be interrupted for a couple of afternoon hours, five-to-seven days each week for the next six months, by some stuttering kid trying to read classic literature to me. At least not if I could help it.

Elroy

My new foster parents, the Joneses, aren't bad people or anything. They're just old. Like really super old. Like, let's dry the cat in the microwave, old. Like, pennies floating in the Jell-O mold old. Underwear worn over the pants old. These are not hypothetical examples.

I guess the Joneses have kept foster children for a lot of decades, ever since their son drowned when he was a little kid. In a pond, I imagine, because I doubt they had pools back then. And as far as I can figure it, somehow, they've been in the system for so long that maybe nobody ever checks up on them to, like, make sure they're still in command of their faculties. Maybe when one foster kid gets old enough to leave the Jones' home, the system just ships them another one. No questions asked. But I think that I'm going to be their last one, given as how Mrs. Jones is serving me a frozen waffle for breakfast this morning. Still frozen, I mean, she skipped the toaster part. But I'm not going to try and eat the waffle anyway, because she pours dishwashing soap all over it, instead of maple syrup.

"Morning, Mr. Jones," I say as the old man walks into the kitchen. He's wearing a yellow cardigan sweater, open front, large imitation chestnut buttons. He's not wearing anything else. It's not the first time he's come into the kitchen bottomless. And I've only been living here for about two weeks.

"Hey there, Sporto." He doesn't know my name. "I thought we agreed that you were going to call me Dad."

"Okay, Dad."

"Aren't you going to eat your breakfast? Whatcha you got there, a waffle? Leggo my Eggo? The quicker-picker-upper?"

"Yup."

"I wish I could still eat a waffle for breakfast," he says nostalgically, and I wonder how long this waffle has been in their freezer, "but solid food just doesn't agree with me anymore."

"I'm sorry to hear that, Dad."

"Gives me the gas something awful," he says and sits down at the head of the table.

"That's really a shame."

"Want to see?" he asks, eagerly. I'm not sure exactly where he's going with this.

"No, that's okay."

He gets up anyway, stands with his penis lying flaccid right there on the table. He cups his chin in his hand.

"Now what is it I was going to show you?" He seems lost in thought.

"It's fine. You can show me some other time. I've got to get going to school, anyway," I say.

"No. Now, wait a second. It's right on the tip of my tongue. Ah, I got it!" he shouts and walks out of the room. Mrs. Jones is at the ironing board, oblivious to the scene taking place. Oblivious, also, to the fact that the iron isn't plugged in and there aren't any clothes on the board. She's just running a cold iron over the memory of a shirt from some time long ago. Thank Christ they didn't give these people an infant.

Mr. Jones, I mean Dad, lumbers back into the kitchen, still naked from the waist down. He's hiding something behind his back and I'm praying to God that it's not feces.

"Ta Da!" he shouts, slamming onto the table in front of me one of those cheap wooden paddles, a little pink rubber ball on an elastic cord affixed to its face. "What do you think of that, Sporto?!"

"Wow," I say, meaning it. Like, wow, about all of this. "I th... th... think I left my book bag up in my room. I'm gonna go get it." I step over my book bag, which is leaning against my chair, and walk toward the stairs.

"Tell Jimmy if he doesn't hurry up I won't be able to drive him to school," Mr. Jones yells. I think I'm going to stick to calling him Mr.

Jones, rather than Dad. Something tells me that this isn't going to be a long-term situation. Jimmy is their dead son, who I'd estimate would be about sixty years old if he'd survived to this day. Part of me wants to see if I can encourage Mr. Jones to actually get behind the wheel and drive Jimmy to school, just to see what would happen. But I'll save that for more desperate times.

A few minutes later I walk back into the kitchen, grab my book bag, tell them I'm off to school. Mrs. Jones hands me a cucumber from the ice box. Tussles my hair.

"Have a good day at school, Son," Mr. Jones says from behind a newspaper. He's sitting at the head of the kitchen table. The newspaper is upside down, but mostly covers his genitals. I walk out of the house.

My new foster home is only two blocks from the school, so that's convenient. I look both ways, making sure that I'm not going to cross paths with the Jew Crew, and make it to the school door just as the first bell rings. Many years of intensive bullying has developed in me a fantastic sense of timing.

I keep a low profile throughout the school day and avoid run-ins of any kind. I spend the majority of my mental energy trying to stay away from my new enemies at school, rather than trying to actually learn anything. But I figure that unless I prioritize my self-preservation instinct, I won't be around to use whatever I might have otherwise learned, anyway.

According to an arrangement that we made yesterday, I meet Dr. Severs at his Honda in the parking lot immediately following the dismissal bell. I'm surprised that he's so prompt. Then I open the car door and am almost knocked backwards by the thick smell of Jamaican. I guess he had the last period free.

"You're early, little dude," Dr. Severs says with a cough, a smile. I climb in, close my eyes and lean back onto the front seat. Pretty sure this is what a contact high feels like. We drive, like, two blocks to the soup kitchen on Hickory Road and I'm wondering why we didn't just walk, especially given the fact that Dr. Severs is high as a kite. I want to mention that it's a pretty poor judgment call for him to be driving around right now, in an official capacity, with a minor in the car, but decide to let it pass and enjoy the contact high instead.

There's no parking available in front of the soup kitchen so we circle the block twice and end up driving back to the school lot, parking about eight spaces over from the spot we left a few minutes earlier. Dr. Severs turns off the car and exhales loudly, as if he's just accomplished something. We walk the two blocks and stand in front of the soup kitchen.

"Is this the right place?" I ask.

"Sure. Why?"

"It doesn't look like there's anyone here."

"Of course there's someone here," Dr. Severs says in an annoyed tone. He bangs on the door.

"The lights are off inside," I say as he rattles the locked door, "Do you have a key?"

Dr. Severs looks at his key ring, squinting at each of his four different keys.

"You can probably rule out the Honda key," I say and he continues to look at his keys, "Have you worked here before?"

"No," Dr. Severs says, "this is my first time."

"Then it's probably a pretty safe bet that there isn't a key to this place on that ring, right?" He looks at me and smiles. How stoned is this guy?

"I'm hungry. Are you hungry? How about we go get something to eat and when we get back, there might be some people here?" Dr. Severs asks eagerly.

"I'm always hungry," I say, and it's true. My diet has been so erratic living with the Joneses that I was looking forward to tapping some of whatever brew we were going to be serving at the soup kitchen. Also, I notice that the little bit of contact high that I got from the car ride seems to have helped control my stutter. Good to know.

"Let's roll, then," Dr. Severs says and starts to walk back towards the car.

"We could just go to that diner on the corner," I say and point to a neon sign that's about half as far away as our car.

"Done," he says, and we walk across the street.

"Triple decker turkey club sandwich," Dr. Severs says to the waitress after we're seated, not bothering to look at the menu. The waitress looks at me.

"I'll have the pancakes."

"Short stack?"

"No, the regular stack."

"Bacon or sausage?" I look at Dr. Severs, who just smiles at me.

"Both, actually," I answer and the waitress nods.

"Something to drink?"

"Do you have milkshakes?" I ask.

"We do."

"Then a chocolate milkshake, please."

"Oh, yeah. Definitely. Two of those!" Dr. Severs shouts. The waitress gives us a strange look.

"I'm his guidance counselor," Dr. Severs says, apparently to dismiss any idea that he's on a date with a twelve-year-old boy. The waitress gives him a tight grin, nods, walks towards the kitchen. Dr. Severs does kind of look like a pedophile, with the long hair and beard, the little John Lennon glasses, the sweater vest. I'm thinking this probably isn't the first time he's had to clarify his position as a kid's guidance counselor.

"So…" Dr. Severs says.

"So." I respond. And we do not say another word to each other for the next five minutes. I'm glad Dr. Severs still seems pretty stoned because it makes the silence less awkward. When the food arrives, we tuck in like a couple of animals.

"Brain freeze! Ugh!" Dr. Severs grimaces, slamming the table with his open palm, but not fully removing his lips from the straw in his milkshake. I give him a full mouth smile. Within minutes the food is gone.

"Anything else?" the waitress asks, tearing the check from a pad in her apron.

"Ah, two checks, please," Dr. Severs says, smiling at her. The waitress cocks her head, screws up her face. My mouth hangs open.

"I don't ha… ha… have any money, Dr. Severs."

"What?!" he shouts, any trace of being stoned now gone as a result of the food, as well as the revelation about my empty pockets.

"I th… th… thought you were paying."

"What made you think I was going to pay for your food?"

"Because you asked if I wanted to go to a di… di… diner."

"I never said anything about paying for your food!"

"I'm in seventh gr… gr… grade and you're an adult."

"So?" he whines. The waitress, frozen at our table throughout this brief dialog, looks appalled. Dr. Severs grabs the check from her hand. "Eighteen dollars?"

"The check is for twenty-nine dollars and eighty cents," the waitress says curtly.

"Yeah, but his stuff cost eighteen dollars? You've got to be kidding me! Why didn't you just order the whole menu?" He glares at me, spitting the words. "How much have you got?"

I look at him like he's got to be kidding. Reach into my pockets and pull out a crumpled dollar bill. A quarter, a dime, three pennies. I drop it all on the table. He grabs the dollar, leaves the change on the table. Pulls two tens, a five, and five singles from his Velcro canvas wallet, throws them on top of the change.

"You owe me seventeen dollars," he says to me and slides out of the booth.

"So, I'm assuming the fifty-eight cents is my tip?" asks the waitress, disgusted.

"Hey, I'm getting screwed here, too!" he shouts, still glaring at me, "Ask the freeloader for more tip." And he walks to the door.

"I… I… I'm sorry," I say to the waitress, mortified.

"Don't you worry, honey," she says, taking a single from the pile, sliding it and the change towards my side of the table, "You take your money back."

"It's okay." I slide the money back towards her.

"No, I insist," the waitress says, smiling. And then she turns from the table, "Cheap-ass hippie stoner, come in here again and he'll be eating a whole lot more than what he orders from the menu."

As she walks away, she makes a sound like she's pulling phlegm from her smoky lungs. I put the money in my pocket, slide out of the booth. I catch up with Dr. Severs at the soup kitchen.

"This is just great," he says, looking at the still-locked doors.

"Are you sure we were supposed to help at the soup kitchen today?"

"Don't you talk to me," he says without looking my way, "Damnit! What a day I'm having!"

"So, I'm going to go home, okay?"

"What, you don't need me to drive you?"

"I live right over there. It's closer than the car."

"You're reading at the managed care facility tomorrow. Meet me in the parking lot right after dismissal. And don't be late or I'm leaving without you!" he shouts at the back of my head, still making no sense at all.

Frank

The kid doesn't show up on Thursday, so I'm thinking maybe this whole scheme Martha told me about might not actually happen. But come three-thirty on Friday he's knocking on my door, *Huckleberry Finn* in hand. I get up from my computer and let him in.

"We need to have a discussion about this," I say to the kid. Elroy. How do you forget a name like that?

"I... I... I'm sorry, Mr. Johnson..."

"Frank," I say, "Call me Frank."

"El... El... Elroy," he replies, nodding.

"I know. I remember. So Elroy, first off, is there anything we can do about that stutter? I mean, not to be insensitive, but that stutter is super annoying, you know?"

"It go... go... goes away when I'm not nervous."

"Okay, so try not to be nervous. What do you have to be nervous about, anyway? You're talking to a thirty-three-year-old man who lives in a nursing home," I say and Elroy smiles. "And, do you have to read to me? I mean, do they check up on you? Like, give you a test or anything when you're done?"

"No."

"Good. So that's good. I mean, worst case we can just sit in here and play age-appropriate video games until they see that you're not really bothering me and Hardy gives the whole thing up."

"Okay," Elroy says.

It seems like he's trying to use one-syllable words, avoid full sentences, to minimize the stutter. Considerate. But the last thing I need is to start thinking too much about this kid's well-being. I remind myself that Elroy is an instrument of abuse, regardless of his own intentions, and I've got to find a way to turn this situation to my advantage. But he seems trustworthy enough, so I decide to treat him as an ally, give him some background information.

I tell him about my grandfather dying and this whole performance art piece that I've created to try and get my money back. About my feud with Hardy and the lawyers and the principle at stake. He's looking at me as if I'm crazy, sure. But he's also pursing his lips in thought, nodding conspiratorially.

"So, look, Elroy. I don't have anything against you, personally. You seem like a nice kid and all. But we're going to have to work together to make the best of this situation, right?" I ask and he nods. "And it starts with our posturing when other people are around. When anyone else is in the room, or if we're walking around the hallways or living areas, it's got to look like we hate each other. Like we really can't stand each other. Can you do that for me?"

"Okay," he replies, "But, we… we… well, why?"

"I'm not exactly sure how it will work to our advantage yet. But the first rule of warfare is to always try to make the other side think the opposite of what's really going on, anywhere and anytime you can. Remember that. It might help you someday. You don't drive, do you?"

"I'm twelve."

"Okay, right. So how do you get here?"

"Dr. Severs drives me."

"That hippie who came to my room the other day?"

"Yeah."

"He can't be happy about dropping you off and picking you up every day. How far away do you live?"

"I don't know, ma… ma… maybe about two or three miles. I'm right by the middle school in town."

"I don't know where that is. Do you think they'd let you ride your bike out here, instead of having that hippie drop you off?"

"I don't have a bike."

"You're twelve and you don't have a bike? What the hell?"

"I don't know. I live in a fo… fo… foster home and the people there didn't buy me a bike. I don't think they have a lot of money. And they're ol… ol… old so they don't really think about stuff like that."

"How can you be twelve years old and not have a bike? Anyway, it might not even matter. I just want to see if there's any way to ditch the hippie. You know, remove him from this whole equation, at least part of the time," I say.

"Why?" Elroy asks.

"I don't know why," I reply. "I'm talking at a raw material level here, just trying to see what we have to work with. The answers will come. Don't rush me."

"Okay."

"So what's this Severs like?"

"He's a dick." No stutter on that one.

"Obviously. But what's he like?"

"He's a cheapskate. I ow...ow... owe him seventeen dollars."

"Okay. Weird, but fine," I pull out my wallet and hand him a twenty. Probably best to erase any debts if both these guys are going to be deep in my stuff for the near term. His eyes widen and he takes the money, puts it in the front pocket of his lousy jeans, thanks me. "That's for Severs. Pay him back what you owe him so the slate's clean. What else?"

"It seems like he sm... sm... smokes a lot of pot."

"Makes sense," I say. "Why wouldn't he? We'll keep that one in our back pocket in case we need it later. What else?"

"He's really into the RMSOC. It's like his ba... ba... baby. He ta... ta... talks about it like it's going to make his career or something. Like it's go... go... going to be some kind of national movement."

"The what?"

"The RMSOC. The Rudolphsville Middle School Outreach Club."

"And what does this RMO-whatever do, exactly?"

"RMSOC. As of now, we're supposed to re... re... read to you, for the whole month."

"As I understand it, that's just what you specifically are supposed to do."

"Yeah."

"What do the other members do?"

"There are no other me... me... members."

"We've really got to work on that stutter," I say. "So you're telling me that this pothead hippie counselor has organized a do-gooder club for the community consisting only of yourself?"

"Yeah. And one other gi... gi... girl, who's away because her aunt di... di... died."

"Why, in the name of God, would you ever join a lame-ass club like that?"

"If I didn't join they wo... wo... would have given me detention. I kind of got in a fight the fi... fi... first day of school."

"Oh. That makes sense. Did you win?"

"No."

"Too bad. Next time, right?" I say and Elroy smiles at me. "Okay. So we're going to take a walk now, go see a friend of mine. And remember, when other people are around, we act like we can't stand each other, right?"

"Right."

We walk down the hall, my hand on Elroy's shoulder, like a teacher marching him to the principal's office. Colonel Adams, an agile old war veteran who has no idea what's happening in the world around him, puts his hand on my shoulder and falls in behind us like he's joining a conga line. I shrug his hand off before any other ambulatory inmates take cue, keep walking down the hall. I can't see Elroy's expression, but he must be doing a good job of looking pissed off because the nurses smile sadly at him when he passes. To me, no expression at all. God, I hate this place. Ed Hardy is chatting with a nurse at the reception desk when we pass.

"Taking a break from the reading, boys?" he calls smugly.

"You can tell Mr. Hardy that this garbage will not stand," I say to Elroy, loud enough for Hardy to hear. Elroy doesn't bother to relay the message. I consider making a public announcement to the inmates about how it's unfair for the home to provide me with a daily reader when everyone else does not have access to the same privilege, but figure it's way too complicated a message to stir them up. Instead I make an overly dramatic pointing gesture at the kitchen door and shout "Sweet Jesus! Is that a rat?!"

Over the past six months I've found that short, vivid blasts of melodrama are most effective in riling up this particular peanut gallery. It really doesn't matter what you're saying, either. "Oh, sweet Christ! Is that a penny?!" when accompanied by stage actor gestures would have garnered pretty much the same response as what I'd just said. The rat thing was strictly for Hardy's benefit.

The room stirs as if all of the old people were buzzed with mild electrical shocks. Hardy gives me the stink eye, jogs to the center of the room, his hands making a patting-down gesture at the air in front of him.

"Mr. Johnson is just making a joke, everyone. Not funny, Mr. Johnson! He's just trying to give you all a scare! I guarantee that there are no rats in the facility!"

We can still hear him shouting down the hall as we walk into the administration office.

"So, this is your new friend," Martha says, looking up from the computer monitor, pressing pause on the keyboard.

"We ha… ha… hate each other," Elroy replies. Good boy.

"It's okay, E. Martha is one of the good guys. She's on our side," I say and then turn to Martha, "So what do you have for us?"

"Us?" Martha asks brightly, "So you two are a team, now. That was fast."

"We're making the best of a bad situation," I say. "Look, Martha, I gave you an extra half-hour of lust yesterday, what have you got for me?" Elroy looks at me, like, what? I give a dismissive headshake to imply it's not what he's thinking.

"Well, I haven't *got* anything specific," she says, "but I was thinking about this last night. So tell me, what do you want more than anything right now?"

"To get my refund from your husband and blow this popsicle stand."

"Yes, well I can't help with that," she says, "What's next on your list?"

"To be left alone." Elroy deflates when I say the words, "No offence, dude."

"It's okay," Elroy responds, like he's used to people not wanting him around, making me feel even worse.

"I don't think so," says Martha, "I mean, if you have to keep living here, Frank, I think what you really want is to get out more often."

She's right.

"Martha, my love, you are one-hundred percent accurate," I say. "If I'm going to be here, then I'd rather not be here. As much as possible. Where are you going with this?"

"Well, I think we might be able to use your forced-friendship with Elroy to engineer some flexibility in terms of your coming and going. As long as Elroy is on board to help, that is."

Elroy purses his lips, nods.

"Thanks, E. Go on, Martha."

"So, you obviously are aware of the fact that, aside from facility sponsored outings, you can only leave the premises with someone on your registered list, right? Well, what if we could get Elroy on your registered list?"

"That would never fly with Ed, Martha. He'd see right through it."

"I'm twelve-years-old," says Elroy.

"And I'm sixty-five, boys. I'm not stupid. I wouldn't have brought it up if I didn't think there was a way that we could finagle it."

"Sorry, Martha. You talk. Shut up, Elroy," I say and give the kid a wink.

"Elroy, instead of just reading aloud, do you think you can arrange excursions through this organization of yours?"

"Dr. Severs sets everything up. I ju… ju… just do what he tells me to do," Elroy responds.

"I understand," Martha says, "But do you think he'd be open to suggestions? Especially if you're recommending super boring stuff. Things that Frank would hate to do?"

"Maybe."

"This doesn't sound like it's shaping up all that great, Martha," I chime in.

"Is this your plan or mine?" Martha asks pointedly and I shut my mouth. "Look, our facility has the right to coerce obstinate but physically adept residents to participate in certain excursions that management considers beneficial to their well-being," she says in quasi-legalese, "It's in your contract."

"And?" I ask.

"And, if we can establish a precedent to convince Ed that excursions with Elroy's organization represent an effective vehicle to torture you, Frank, then I'm sure he'll buy in. Ed wants you out of the home almost as much as you want out yourself. And that would get you off the grounds, which is a critical first step. From there, who knows? After a few painful excursions, you might be able to open things up a lot more."

"Okay. I mean, it's worth a shot. And you think you can plant the seed with Ed?"

"Sure. When you guys leave I'll tell him that you were down here complaining about Elroy invading your privacy, and I told you that you were lucky we weren't making you go on outings with... What's the name of your group, Elroy?"

"The Rudolphsville Middle School Outreach Club, or RMSOC, for sh... sh... short. It's a joke."

"It really is. He's the only member of the club," I say.

"Th... Th... There's a girl, too. Sa... Sa... Sally Berman. She's away this week. It's run by this id... id... idiot, Dr. Severs. He's a dick."

"That probably works in your favor," Martha says to me. "So let me bait Ed and we'll see if he'll make the first move. In the meantime, why don't you guys go back to Frank's room and come up with some good ideas for bad first dates?"

"Wouldn't Ed and Severs be the ones coming up with the excursions? I ask. "I mean, it's not like they're going to rely on Elroy's recommendations, at least at the start."

"Ed isn't going to come up with anything. And didn't this Severs guy just commit Elroy to read to you for the entire month? You think he isn't looking for someone else to come up with suggestions for his club? As far as everyone knows, you guys don't like each other, right? So if Elroy is slick about it, I'm sure he can work some ideas into the mix right from the start. Especially if these ideas look really painful for you, Frank."

"How about ch… ch… church?"

"No way," I say. I've had enough church to last a lifetime.

"Perfect," says Martha.

"Uh-uh, bad idea."

"Why, you're Catholic, aren't you, Frank?"

"Catholic by upbringing. Not practicing. Me and the Catholic Church have a tenuous relationship."

"What's their problem with you?" Martha asks.

"They don't have a problem with me. I have a problem with them."

"Great, that will work fine, then. Ed's a big time Catholic. He'll love it. And the fact that you're strongly opposed to going to church makes it a perfect place to get started."

"How about a Buddhist temple, instead? Or maybe wherever Taoists go?"

"Won't work. First of all, you might actually enjoy it. And secondly, Frank thinks those people are heathens."

"What? Why?"

"Because he's ignorant. And he's Catholic. So Catholicism is right and everyone else is wrong."

"That's ridiculous."

"I don't make the rules. You want to set a precedent for escape, you start with the Catholic Church. That's your best bet."

"Thanks, Elroy," I say with a heavy dose of sarcasm. "Are you Catholic?"

"I'm no… no… not anything," Elroy says.

"Better for you," I say. I look at Martha. "Fine. If this is what it takes to get me out of here, I'm on board."

So we thank Martha, put on our game faces and stomp grumpily back to my room. From the corner of my eye, I see Ed staring at the pair of us with a mean smile. What a tool.

Elroy

"So, how'd it go?" Dr. Severs asks as I climb into his Honda. The car is musty, but it doesn't reek of pot like yesterday. I wonder what he's been doing for the past three hours.

"Bad," I say. "Awkward."

"Did you read to him?"

"Yeah," I reply.

I reach into my pocket and pull out the twenty that Frank gave me earlier. I should probably just keep it. God knows I need the money. But I give it to him anyway. Not because I feel like I owe Dr. Severs, but because I don't want to feel like I'm stealing from Frank.

"Hey, thanks!" Severs says, grabbing the twenty and stuffing it in his wallet. "Look, I don't have any singles right now, but I'll owe you the two dollars, okay?"

"It was th... th... three dollars. I only owed you seventeen."

"I'm pretty sure your food was eighteen bucks, Elroy," he says with finality, like he's ending the discussion. I've been bullied enough to recognize the tone. He knows that he's trying to gyp me out of a dollar, which I suppose is worth more to him than any sense of personal integrity. But I continue on principle. Maybe Frank is rubbing off on me.

"I ga... ga... gave you a dollar and change at the restaurant."

"Fine, whatever. I owe you three dollars. Happy?" From the way that he says it, I know I'll never see that three dollars. He pulls the car away from the curb and gets back into character as the head of the RMSOC, "So, was Mr. Johnson nicer to you this time?"

"He wasn't anything to me. He just seemed mad that I was invading his privacy."

"He'll come around," Dr. Severs says. "Just remember it's a good thing you're doing."

"Reading out loud to a thirty-three-year-old man, who's living in a nursing home in order to prove a point? That's a good thing? Really?" There's something strange about this conversation. I mean, stranger than just the subject matter.

"It's a good thing for the RMSOC. Mr. Hardy is giving us triple credit for the community service hours that you spend with Mr. Johnson. You're doing a lot to legitimize the club. What are you reading to him?"

"Still *Huckleberry Finn*. Can I bring my own book from the library tomorrow? He doesn't even listen when I read, anyway." There it is again.

"Let's just stick to reading the books that they give you, at least for the first week, okay? We don't want to create any waves, here. Did you read the whole time?"

"Yeah, why?" I'm a little worried that maybe Dr. Severs has read *Huckleberry Finn* and is going to start asking me questions, catch me in a lie. This whole discussion is a lie.

"Because when I went into the room yesterday, you guys were playing video games."

"Mr. Johnson doesn't want me coming to his room every day. So he said we couldn't play video games, even though we did that first day. And he said that I had to start calling him Mr. Johnson, instead of Frank. He said that if I was going to invade his privacy, then I'd have to suffer through it, just like him. And he said that I have to take off my shoes and my shirt before coming into his room, too - like he's shirts and I'm skins, like we're playing basketball against each other."

I throw in that last part on the fly, figuring it might help later, when they're deciding whether it's best that Frank and I stay closed up in his room all day. But I'm a lot more interested in what's happening to me during this lying session than I am about tactics to encourage my excursions with Frank.

"He makes you take off your shirt?"

"Yeah. It's fine, I don't think it's sexual or anything. At least not yet."

"It's not fine. You tell that weirdo that I said all RMSOC activities must be performed fully dressed."

"What about if we, I mean the RMSOC, are doing landscaping or gardening when it's hot outside?" I ask.

"That would be alright, I guess. So tell him that all RMSOC indoor activities should be performed fully dressed."

"What about if we went to a pool or something? Mr. Johnson said that he sometimes goes to a pool with the old people. What if I have to read to him then?"

"Elroy, I'm trying to help you out here. Work with me, would you?"

"Sorry. The RMSOC is really important to me," I say.

And I am amazed at the fact – and it's a fact – that I haven't stuttered once since I started lying to Dr. Severs. So, okay. Maybe I only stutter when I tell the truth? When I'm lying, do I talk like a normal person? I have to test this, flat-out lie with no agenda.

"Dr. Severs, can I ask you something? As a guidance counselor, I mean?"

"Sure, kiddo," Dr. Severs replies.

I've suddenly made him feel important. Good to know.

"Does wearing women's underwear make you gay?"

"What?"

"Like, say a twelve-year-old kid was wearing woman's underpants. Does that mean he's gay? Like homosexual?"

"Before I answer in any official capacity," Dr. Severs says, "can I ask why?"

"You mean like why would it be gay for a boy to wear panties?"

"No. I mean, why are you, specifically, asking me that?"

"Okay, fair question. So my foster parents, they're not big on doing laundry. And I've only got, like, four pairs of underwear. Actually, three. Because I threw one pair in the garbage."

"Why, did you crap yourself?" Dr. Severs asks, snort and giggle.

"Yeah, actually. On Wednesday a kid at school punched me in the back of the head so hard that I blacked out. And when I woke up, I realized that I crapped myself. Does that answer your question?" What a dick.

"Whoa, little dude. Jesus, really? I'm sorry, wow, I didn't know. Are you sure you don't have, like, a concussion?"

"I'm not sure of anything. I just woke up in the hallway after lunch with a huge egg on the back of my head and I'd messed up my underwear. So I went to the boy's room and threw up. And then I cleaned myself and threw my underwear in the garbage. I'm not saying that any of this is your fault, you being the guidance counselor and all. I just want to know if wearing women's underpants can make a kid gay."

I intentionally elaborate in order to draw out my sentences. No stutter. Wow.

"Should I take you to the hospital or something?"

"No, I think I'm through the worst of it. I haven't blacked out at all today. I really just want to know what you think about the whole women's underwear thing. As a counselor, I mean. Because on Thursday morning I didn't have any clean underwear, so I borrowed a pair of my foster mom's panties because they were the only underpants that were clean at the house."

"Really? Is she hot?" Dr. Severs asks.

What the hell?

"She's li... li... like a hundred years old." Okay. Stutter's back. Random peek into the perverted mind of Dr. Severs must have thrown me. Get back into character. "But yeah, she's kind of hot. For an old lady, I mean. Why does that matter?"

"Forget it. I didn't mean to ask that. So you wore old lady panties for a day, that doesn't mean you're gay, Elroy."

"Yeah, okay. But, well, I could have worn my own underwear today."

Dr. Severs pauses, then lifts his head and nods.

"Ah, I see. So today you *chose* to wear your foster mom's panties. Not, like, out of necessity. Well, I'm not technically a psychologist, Elroy. But that does sound pretty gay to me. You might want to keep an eye on that kind of behavior."

"That's what I thought. Thanks."

Amazing. So I only stutter when I'm telling the truth. Obviously, this stutter thing is a psychological problem, not a physical one. I'd always wondered about that.

"Good talk. So, tomorrow's Saturday. Pick you up at nine?" Dr. Severs asks

"That's fi… fi… fine," I say. "Hey, Dr. Severs? You know how they do confession at St. Cecelia's church on Saturdays at ten? I was thinking that maybe we could take Mr. Johnson there."

"Are you Catholic?"

"No."

"Then how come you know there's confession at St. Cecelia's tomorrow at ten?"

"It's just something I know."

"But why do you want to go to confession, if you're not Catholic? Do you want to talk to the priest about the gay stuff?"

"I'm not saying that I want to go to confession. I'm saying maybe we should take Mr. Johnson to confession."

"Is Mr. Johnson Catholic?"

"I think so, yeah."

"Does he want to go to confession?"

"Probably not, but don't you think it would be good for him? He's a pretty angry guy. I mean, he's mad about me reading to him. And he likes to mess with Mr. Hardy and the old people. And he said all that stuff about the diapers and experiments to you on Wednesday. I mean, maybe going to confession will help him be less angry all the time."

Dr. Severs is completely oblivious to the fact that I haven't been stuttering. What an insensitive jerk. But I can see the wheels turning in his head. He's still pissed off at Frank for calling him names and messing with him.

"What if he doesn't want to go?" Dr. Severs asks.

"I don't know. Maybe I just read to him, then. Or maybe Mr. Hardy can make him go. It doesn't really matter to me. How about you talk to Mr. Hardy about it when you drop me off tomorrow morning?"

Dr. Severs nods and I climb out of the car. I'm still totally intrigued by the fact that I don't stutter when I lie. Wonder why I never noticed it before? I guess I've never been much of a liar. That's going to change.

But there's a part of me that wants to explore this newfound self-awareness further – like, see if I can leverage the fact that it is so clearly a psychological problem in order to stop my stuttering altogether. Though that type of self-exploratory knot-untying seems like it would be a lot of hard work. So maybe I'll just focus trying to lie more in my day-to-day life.

Sally

~ You know, Aunt Sadie, I'd read on the Internet that you can kill yourself with a necktie. And it's painless. You just knot the tie part to your bedpost and put the loop part around your neck, and then you just let yourself lean into it. Not fast, like you're trying to break your neck or anything, because that's not how it works. And you breathe normal, because you're not trying to suffocate yourself either. Apparently, the loop part just squeezes your neck and stops the blood from getting to your brain, so you eventually pass out and die. But all you feel is like you're going to sleep. It's really popular with kids who are part of, like, suicide epidemics. And you don't have to cut yourself or see any blood or anything. Why didn't you do something like that?

~ *I don't know, Lambchop. I've never had a problem with blood. Or with cutting myself, for that matter. You know how much I cut myself when I was growing up. They had to put me in a mental hospital. I mean, think about it. It could have been a whole lot messier than wrists and a warm bathtub if I'd really put some thought into it. But I didn't do a lot of research before the fact. Actually, it was kind of spur of the moment.*

~ You didn't know you were going to kill yourself?

~ *I mean, I knew I was going to kill myself. It was really just a question of when. But I didn't know it was going to be on that specific night, you know? I'm actually surprised that I finally went through with it. It wasn't the first time I tried.*

~ I'm going to do some research. I like the idea of the necktie thing, but I don't think it would make enough of an impact. The visual of Mom finding me all peaceful and blue-faced, kneeling by my bed, like in prayer, I don't think it would jolt her enough. She'd probably call Father Mcloughlin and have him come over, so she could show him how angelic I look.

~ *You could still do the necktie thing; you just need to add some props. Like, cover yourself in cow's blood and finger paint satanic symbols all over your walls. Or get your mom's laptop and go to some really twisted clown-porn website and leave it streaming in front of you. Or do both. Use your imagination.*

~ Maybe. Did it ever bother you, knowing how much you were going to hurt me when you killed yourself?

~ *Lambchop, this had nothing to do with how much I love you. You're up in New Jersey and I was down in South Carolina and every day was sadder and sadder. And your Mom wouldn't leave me alone, you know? Even when she left me alone, she wouldn't leave me alone. I love you so much, but you were just a little bright spot in a very dark life.*

I wonder if I'm putting words into her mouth, like words I want to hear. Then, I think, of course I am.

~ I could have run away. My life is miserable, too. Ever since Dad. Before Dad even. She's the same with me as she was with Dad and you. She doesn't treat me like a person, more like a Sunday school project. She destroys everything near her with all the Catholic stuff. I could have gotten on a bus and come down and lived with you. We could have been miserable together. That would have been something, at least.

~ *Yeah, I don't think my lifestyle was conducive to raising a twelve-year-old.*

~ It would have been better than me being on the street.

~ *Marginally, at best.*

~ Are you in, like, heaven now?

~ *Sweetie, I'm in your mind. That's all.*

"Sally?" Mom asks from the front seat, "Why are you moving your lips back there?"

"I'm praying, Mom," I sigh. I'd climbed into the backseat to try and take a nap. I wonder how long she's been watching me in the rearview mirror.

"Good girl," Mom replies. "Say a prayer for your Aunt Sadie. Pray that she's with Jesus and that He can finally help to heal her, if not in life then in death."

The melodrama makes me want to throw up.

"Who do you think I'm praying for, Mom? I mean, we're literally driving home from Aunt Sadie's funeral."

"Don't use that tone with me. We're *all* having a hard time right now." *All* is just the two of us. "We'll be home in time for Sunday mass tomorrow, and it's probably a good idea for you to have a talk with Father Mcloughlin afterwards. Sort out your feelings."

"I thought that's what parents were for," I say. She ignores me.

"And then you have to walk Sister Francine Glucko around the church grounds for a while. I have to give a talk to the CCD kids. You know, the Confraternity of Christian Doctrine school that you used to go to on Sundays?"

Mom says this to shame me because I don't go to CCD anymore.

"Sure, whatever." I try to get Aunt Sadie back, but the moment is gone. So I just look out the window and imagine myself living in all of the towns that we pass along the highway. Living in any town but my town. Living with anyone but my mother.

Frank

"Fr... Fr... Frank," the kid is shaking my shoulder, whispering for me to wake up. What time is it anyway?

"Don't ever touch me when I'm sleeping, E," I croak, cranky from a long coding session last night. "I can't be held responsible for what might happen. What time is it?"

"It's ni... ni... nine-thirty. Confession starts at ten."

"So it's a go, then?" I say and swing my legs over the side of the bed, stand up. Knowing that Elroy would be arriving early, I'm wearing boxers over my diaper.

"I do... do... don't know yet. Dr. Severs is ta... ta... talking to Mr. Hardy now."

"So we wait."

"Right," Elroy says, pausing thoughtfully, "Hey, Frank."

"Yeah?"

"Can I talk to you about something?" The kid seems nervous, uncomfortable.

"Sure. What's up?"

"I wanted to talk to you yesterday but didn't know how to bring it up. I mean, I'm not really sure how to say this, maybe I should just come right out with it." Weird, it seems like the kid really has something to say. What could he possibly have to say to me that would make him uncomfortable? Even if he's, like, dying or something, it's not like it would be such a big deal to me. I just met him on Wednesday. On the bright side, I think, his stutter seems to have cleared up.

"It's about the real reason I'm here, Frank," Elroy continues, hesitating but deliberate. "I didn't get into a fight at school. That was a lie. I found out you were living at this nursing home. I joined the RMSOC because I knew that we would be reading here. I made sure that I would be assigned to you, Frank. Because I wanted to meet you. I've always wanted to meet you. Because, well, because you're my biological father."

I don't know what kind of expression is on my face. Inside my head it's like that scene in *Raiders of the Lost Ark*, where the Germans open the Ark of the Covenant and all around it's a blazing chaos of demons. But there's an Indiana Jones part of me in there, too, and he's trying to look away and work out the math because something doesn't seem right. Thirteen years ago? I'd have been twenty years old. Two thousand four. Junior year at college. Ah ha! The yellow fever! And just like in the movie, all of the demons get sucked back into the Ark and my mind goes quiet.

I spent, like, a year-and-a-half between sophomore and junior year of college only hooking up with Asian women. I was obsessed. And then, the fascination just stopped, cold. Weird. I wonder if that happens to a lot of guys. But there's nothing Asian about Elroy. So there's no way that I could be his biological father, I think, almost positive. Still, it's going to be an awkward conversation. Good thing I was wearing diapers, though.

"No," I say and try to keep my voice from cracking, "Sorry. kid, you're misinformed. The numbers don't work. I'm not your biological father."

"I kn... kn... know," Elroy says, smiling, "I made that up. But di... di... did you notice anything?"

"Dude, so not cool," I say, collapsing onto the bed. What is the matter with this kid?

"Didn't you no... no... notice? I do... do... don't stutter when I lie," he says. "Neat, right? I fi... fi... figured it out yesterday."

"Congratulations," I say in stroke victim voice, "Maybe you could have come up with a demonstration that didn't involve a minor heart attack on my part?"

"So... so... sorry," he says. "I'm wearing women's underpants. See? That was a lie and I didn't st... st... stutter!"

"That's great, Elroy. Just make sure you don't tell the truth, like ever, and it will make you a lot less annoying."

"That's actually what I was th... th... thinking, too," Elroy says.

I'm about to correct him the way a responsible adult might, tell him that constructing a life of fabrication is kind of a low-road approach to fixing his stutter. But at that moment Hardy and Severs appear in my open doorway.

"Are we interrupting something?" Severs asks.

"I imagine you're always interrupting something, Dreamcatcher," I say.

"It's your lucky day, Johnson," Hardy says, "We've got a little outing planned for you."

I flash Severs what I think is a hopeful expression, still refusing to look directly at Hardy. But Hardy continues to talk at the side of my head.

"When was the last time you went to Church, boy?"

I argue indirectly with Hardy about my contract, my rights as an inmate. Hardy is adamant about the rights of the managed care facility as per that same contract. We're volleying comments through Severs, who looks like a judge at a Wimbledon. Within minutes, Severs is signing me out on behalf of the RMSOC at the front desk. I glare at the reception nurse, who's a temp worker and clearly doesn't understand where my hostility is coming from. We climb into a piece of garbage Honda and drive to town.

The air outside is magnificent. It really is. It's just magnificent. Different than when I was outside with Johnny on Wednesday. I don't really know why. The hippie who's driving still makes me want to vomit. But when I stick my head out the window, there's something good there. Like a freedom in the sun and the breeze. Into my head pops the image of a chick cracking out of its egg. I might be having a nervous breakdown or something because I haven't felt this good for no real reason in a long while.

"Forgive me, Father."

The priest pauses on the other side of the screen.

"For you have sinned...?"

"No, I just burped really big. It wasn't intentional. I don't want you to think I'm rude."

"It's alright, my son. I didn't notice."

"You'd notice if you were on my side of the closet. Beef stew last night. You want to know what hell smells like, stick your nose to the grate."

"We're getting a little closer to my thinking you're rude now, son. Would you like to confess your sins?"

"Do I have to?"

"It's typically what people do when they come to confession."

"I know, but I was thinking we could talk a bit first, you know? Get to know each other." I am so starved for lucid adult conversation.

"If that would make you more comfortable," the priest replies. Just a hint of Irish, like he's probably been in America for the past twenty or thirty years.

"You have an accent."

"I do."

"I've always liked an Irish accent. It's goofy, but there's a warmth to it. Not like the heathen Scots. It should be illegal, what they've done to the English language. Australians and New Zealanders too. It's torture listening to those accents. It's like they're actually trying to be annoying, talking like that. But a brogue is tolerable, sometimes even pleasant, you know?"

"I'm glad you approve. Are you homeless, my son?"

I guess I am kind of rambling.

"Homeless? No, I have a home. Funny story, it's actually a managed care facility…"

"Ah, I see," the priest says knowingly.

"It's not what you think, Father, but I get that reaction a lot."

"What can I do for you, my son?"

"Well, Father, certain circumstances in my life have brought me back to the Church, right? And I've got to admit, I was pretty bummed about it at first. But the ride over here was so great, you know? I mean, the car was garbage and smelled like a dorm room ashtray, and the guy that drove me here is a disgusting hippie – lord knows the world would be better without another one of those, right? But the outside air, I mean, it was so sunny outside, and warm and fresh. And the kid's okay, too. Aside from the stutter, I mean. So right there on that car ride, I decided that I wasn't going to poison this experience with a bunch of contention or negativity. There's been so much of that in my life these days. I decided, instead, I'm going to give it a fair chance. Embrace the opportunity, I mean."

"I'm glad to hear it, my son."

I can tell by the tone that he still thinks I'm some variety of special needs, but I'm coming into something here. I'm having a moment. Maybe a religious experience.

"Oh, it gets better, Father. So much better."

"How so?"

"Okay, so here's how I see it. And I don't want to offend you or anything. I want to keep this discussion positive, you know? But I think we can both agree that the Catholic Church is in pretty bad shape, right?"

"Ah, no. We don't agree on that point."

"Okay, okay. I get it. You're on the inside. You probably have to say that. It's alright. Just remember, we're on the same team here. And I'm just saying that the Church has spun pretty far out of orbit, in terms of, like, its original purpose and intentions. You know, like what the historical Jesus would have wanted? Before the politics and control, I mean. Come on, you know the history."

"I'm not following you, my son." The priest is getting grumpy now.

"Okay, sorry. Let me take a step back. This is all just coming to me so quickly. Let's take a second. What's your name, anyway?"

"Father Mcloughlin."

"So your parents named you Father Mcloughlin?"

"My parents named me Rory Mcloughlin."

"Rory! That's perfect! Rory the Irish priest. You are a gem, you know that? You know what we're going to do, Rory?"

"I think I'd prefer Father Mcloughlin."

"Why would I call you Father Mcloughlin when you have such a perfect name like Rory? This father-son business is all part of the problem. Rory. You can call me Frank. Can you feel me, Rory? We're so much more connected right now just because we're using each other's first names. It's like a sign. Think of how far we can take this thing!"

"I'm still not following you, my son."

"Frank," I say.

"I'm still not following you, Frank." He's humoring me. It's time I get to the point.

"We're missing something, Rory. It's what I've been missing for the past six months at the home, maybe for a long time before that. But it's the same thing. It's the same thing that the Church is missing. It's why people like me would rather suffocate with a plastic bag taped over our heads than go to church. And you know what it is, Rory? It's intimacy, Rory. Intimacy is what we're missing! But we can fix that. We can fix it, Rory! Starting right here with this church!"

"Ah, there are other people waiting to receive the sacrament, my son."

"Rory," I say, seriously, "you were going to call me Frank."

"Frank," Rory says, exasperated.

"Not a problem, Rory. I've got a lot of thoughts pin-balling around my brain right now, and I'm sure you do, too. So let's take a breath, let it settle. But in the meantime, before we meet again, I want you to think about how we're going to bring some real intimacy to this church. Think about how we're going to tear through the red tape of hierarchy and politics and repetition and propaganda – and give the church back to the people. Intimacy, Rory. Not all of this God and worship nonsense. Real people getting to know each other on a deeper level. Real people – talking to each other, helping each other, drinking and eating with each other, maybe even having sex – who knows, right? But you and me, Rory, we're going to bring this thing back to the human level. No pretense, just pure intimacy."

"My son… Frank, I mean."

"Shhhhhh. Don't ruin the moment, Rory," I say.

I step out of the confessional closet. I feel so good. The church air smells like incense and I breathe deep. Then I bang twice on Rory's closet door with my open palm and shout, "You and me, Rory! We're gonna bring it back! We're gonna go old school – no... ancient school – on this bitch!"

I smile and wink at an old lady kneeling in the pew outside of the confessional, walk to the center aisle, spread my arms and slowly spin, taking it all in. Purpose. It's like a drug. I can't stop smiling.

I walk to the back of the church. Severs and Elroy are standing there, both slack-jawed, watching me.

"Boys," I say.

"Right now, you're reminding me a lot of how Hollywood movies try to portray a modern-day Satan," Severs whispers at my smiling face. He's not smiling. Elroy is.

"If only I could burn you to a crisp, Starflower," I reply benevolently, "that would punctuate this moment perfectly."

I slam open the big wooden door, spread my arms wide in the sunshine and walk toward the parking lot.

Elroy

Picking up Frank from the nursing home on Saturday morning goes off without a hitch. Frank complains and yells and argues. He gives me dirty looks, like I'm one of the bad guys. Thankfully he's using Dr. Severs as an intermediary for his phony rant with Mr. Hardy, so I can just stand there and look stupid.

When we get in the car, Frank doesn't say anything. He just lets his head hang out the passenger side window like a golden retriever that's been shot with tranquilizer dart. And I'm wondering if he's mad at me for the way I showed him my stutter thing, that lie about him being my father. I hope I haven't messed things up.

When we get to the church, Frank goes on ahead of Dr. Severs and me. I follow him in through the sets of wooden doors, then stand at the back of the church as he walks up to the line of people kneeling in the pews, waiting to make confession. Dr. Severs joins me a few minutes later.

"Did I miss anything?" he asks, his breath heavily masked with black licorice.

"No," I say, "he di... di... didn't go in yet."

"Right," Dr. Severs says, nodding. He obviously toked up in his car a minute ago.

"I was found in this church," I lie to Dr. Severs.

"You were what?" Dr. Severs whispers.

"When I was a baby, I mean. They found me in this church. This is where my parents left me."

"In this church?"

"Yeah."

"Wow. Is it, like, traumatic to be here?"

"No, I don't remember it. Maybe just the smell. I think I remember the smell." No stutter. I could do this all day.

"Do you want to, like, wait outside or something?" Dr. Severs asks with uncharacteristic sympathy.

"No, I… I kind of like it in here. It somehow feels like home. Not my foster home, I mean. Like my real home. Like this is where I'm supposed to be."

"Maybe you want to be a priest," Dr. Severs whispers, giggles, "I mean, you've already got the whole gay thing happening." What a douche bag, I think. If I said this out loud I'm pretty sure I would stutter.

"I don't think I'm gay. I mean, yeah, I'm wearing my foster mom's underpants again. But do you really think that has anything to do with being a homosexual?" I ask. This is all a lie, sure, but even stoned, I'd expect the guidance counselor in him to provide some kind of insight.

"I'm no expert, Elroy. But yeah, I'm pretty sure it does."

"I like the robes that priests wear, I guess."

"That's because they're a lot like women's clothes, probably," Dr. Severs says, seriously.

"And I guess being a priest would give me a pretty good access point, if I wanted to experiment with being gay, I mean. Like, after I hit puberty, obviously. Priests are always around a lot of altar boys."

"Wouldn't be bad for my business, that's for sure. Anything to steer more kids towards the guidance counselor's office," Dr. Severs says in a distracted voice as we watch Frank step into the confessional.

Am I really standing in the back of a church, having a lighthearted discussion about the potential upside of physical relationships between priests and altar boys, with a licensed counselor? Maybe I should try smoking pot, take the world a little less seriously. But for now, I decide to guide this conversation onto some new tracks. Maybe something a little more *Oliver Twist*, less cross-dressing and pedophilia.

"Anyway, when I was little I used to get letters from the priest who found me."

"Really?" Dr. Severs asks.

No, not really.

"Yeah. My first foster parents used to read them to me. I was small so they didn't make any sense. He kept saying that he was sorry. Sorry that he couldn't keep me. At the church, I guess. Obviously, you can't raise kids at a church, so I don't know why he kept apologizing."

I'm trying to see if I can get a nibble on this plot twist.

"Yeah," Dr. Severs says, "that's weird."

Nothing. The guy is a dim bulb.

"And the priest would send me little presents on my birthday. Nothing expensive, just like army men or rubber balls. One year he sent me a baseball glove."

"That was nice of him."

"One time the priest visited me at my foster home. He acted strange in front of my foster parents and me. Kind of weepy and embarrassed."

"Priests can be strange, I guess."

"Once, when my foster parents left the room, he hugged me really tight. He kept looking at my eyes – not like, looking into my eyes – more like studying them."

Dr. Severs crooks his neck, looks at my eyes.

"Your eyes are green," Dr. Severs says flatly. "That's kind of rare. My eyes are brown, see?"

Come on, man. Am I going to have to spell it out for you?

"You know what's weird, Dr. Severs? The priest's eyes were green, too. I just remembered that."

"Maybe that's why he was so attached to you. Like, people with green eyes should stick together or something. The green eye club," Dr. Severs giggles.

Seriously?

"And you know what else I remember? He got all weirded out when I called him Father. Like he was going to have a panic attack or something. Can you think of any reason why the priest who found me orphaned at church would freak out when I called him Father? Any reason at all?"

If he doesn't bite this time, I'm giving up.

"Whoa. Dude." Dr. Severs puts his fingertips to his forehead, pop spreads them away from his face, gesturing a blown mind, "Hear me out on this. Did you ever think that this priest might actually be your father? Like your biological father?"

No way! You think?

"No!"

"Yes! Think about it."

"It couldn't be. Nobody knows who my father is."

I have now laid the groundwork that will allow me to fib seamlessly throughout any interaction with Dr. Severs. As long as he's around, I'll never stutter again.

"Dude, it has to be him. Beyond any doubt. I'm sure of it."

I know he's stoned, but I still question how responsible it is for someone in a position of authority to try and convince me that a priest secretly fathered me and then gave me up to foster care. I mean, what if I hadn't made the whole thing up? He'd be seriously messing with my emotions right now. But I guess this is the same guy who thinks cross-dressing means you're gay and gay means you'd be a good priest and church pedophilia is good for the business of guidance counselors. I don't know how much of this to blame on the weed and how much is just because he's a freaking idiot. It's kind of sad, really.

"I guess. Maybe. It never occurred to me."

"How could you miss it? Jesus, there were signs everywhere."

Does he really need to try and make me feel stupid for not figuring this out on my own? Like, how would that be helpful if I hadn't, in fact, made all of it up?

"I don't know. I never thought about it. Do you...do you actually think that priest could be my real father?"

"Definitely. I'm one hundred percent sure of it. Do you know this priest's name?"

"I don't know if I remember."

At that moment, we see Frank step out of the confessional. He starts to walk away, then stops, turns and bangs on the priest's door.

"You and me, Rory! We're gonna bring it back! We're gonna go old school – no, ancient school – on this bitch!" Frank shouts at the priest's door. Then he goes over to the center aisle and spins around with his arms outstretched, smiling like a maniac. And I'm thinking, maybe I want to try this confession thing.

"Boys," Frank says, nods. Dr. Severs tells Frank that he reminds him of Satan from the movies. Frank tells Dr. Severs that he'd like to set him on fire.

This church thing is awesome. We've got to come back.

"What do you think that was all about?" Dr. Severs asks me after Frank has banged through the doors at the back of the church.

"I don't know. Maybe he feels better after confessing his sins."

"Maybe," Dr. Severs says and we look up at a priest walking towards us from the confessional.

"Were you boys with that man who came into the confessional a minute ago?" the priest asks. I think he left an old lady in the closet so that he could come and talk to us.

"Well, I wouldn't say we're with him. But yeah, I guess. We took him here from the managed care facility up the road. So, I guess, he's with us. Why?"

"Is he...alright? Mentally stable, I mean?"

"Definitely not," Dr. Severs says. "He's a nut job."

I grab Dr. Severs sleeve, yank.

"Is that why he lives in a managed care facility? Because he's disturbed?"

"No. Why he lives in a managed care facility is a long story, but it's not because he's been committed or anything. Why?"

I yank on Dr. Severs sleeve again. He shrugs me off.

"But he's not dangerous or anything?" the priest asks.

"Only to himself, in my professional opinion. I'm a licensed guidance counselor."

"Great, that's fine." The priest looks at me. I'm looking at Dr. Severs, still tugging on his sleeve. "Well, okay then. Thank you," the priest says, walks back to the confessional.

"What do you want? Quit tugging my sleeve," Dr. Severs says to me.

But I'm excited. I have a feeling that we'll be coming back here and I don't want to miss this opportunity.

"Dr. Severs. That man," I say, "that priest. It's the one who visited me in the foster home. I'm sure of it."

"That's the priest? The guy who's your father? No way! Are you sure?"

"As sure as I've ever been about anything in my life," I reply, stutterless.

"Whoa," Dr. Severs makes that "you're blowing my mind" gesture with his fingers and forehead again.

Frank

It's been a long time since I've felt this good. I know it's just a manic high. That I'm going to have to rein it in, like quick, and get back into character. The little episode in front of the altar, the bright-eyed exchange with Severs at the back of the church, those were mistakes. Big time mistakes. The last thing I want is for Severs, much less Hardy, to get the impression that I was happy when I came out of confession. It could spoil everything.

I've got to turn it around, make Severs think that I don't want to come back here, like, ever. But, damn, I feel so good. How long has it been since I've felt like I had a clear purpose? Ever?

I see Elroy and Severs walk out of the church, maybe a football field distance from the parking lot. They'll be here in less than a minute. That's my normal transition time from dream world to reality. The thirty-second rule, applied to spiritual awakening. I try to tuck Elmo into some dark corner of my psyche, go back to being Oscar the Grouch.

"That was interesting," Severs says and looks me up and down, as if something about my physical appearance might have changed because of my performance in church. He points to a Starbucks on the corner. "I need a latte. You guys want anything?"

"Sure, dark roast, grande, black." I say.

"A wa… wa… water would be good," Elroy says.

Severs just stands there in front of us.

"That's it," I say. Severs pushes his hand outward, turns his palm up, points it at Elroy. Is he really asking for money? From a twelve-year-old? What a douche bag.

"Don't worry about it," Elroy says, and then he perks up. "Oh, wa… wa… wait. You can take it out of the three dollars you owe me."

"Yeah, guy, sorry," Severs says to Elroy. "I only have a fiver. My latte costs, like, four-fifty."

What a dick. He turns to me, same palm held upward.

"You want anything other than water, Elroy?" I ask and pull a twenty from my wallet.

"No, that's okay."

"Seriously, dude," I say. "Did you have breakfast?"

"Not really, no."

"Do you eat meat?" I ask him.

"I eat meat," Severs says, apropos of no question from me.

"I eat anything," Elroy replies.

"Starflower, get him a couple of those egg and sausage English muffins. You want orange juice? They have it at this Starbucks. Fresh squeezed."

"I've never had fresh sq… sq… squeezed," Elroy says.

"You don't know what you're missing. Lovechild, get him a large orange juice, too. The fresh squeezed kind."

"Oh, man, I love fresh squeezed orange juice," Severs says.

"Yeah, it's delicious. Get me one, too." I hand him the twenty.

"I don't think a twenty is going to cover it," Severs says hesitantly.

"Sure it will. One grande coffee, two large orange juices, two egg and sausage sandwiches. Eighteen or nineteen bucks. Tip the extra dollar."

"What about mine?" Severs asks.

"Moonbeam, in no universe will I ever buy anything for someone that owes money to a twelve-year-old kid. Bring me the receipt. And don't make me go back and ask the barista how much you left as a tip."

"What about something for the effort?"

"You were going to Starbucks anyway. You asked if we wanted anything. I don't remember you ever putting yourself out for hire as a Starbucks runner."

Severs is staring at me like I'm being totally unfair. I pull another twenty out of my wallet and stick it into Elroy's front pocket, look at Severs. "That's just because I like him."

"Whatever, I don't care," Severs turns, sulks towards Starbucks. And I realize that I'm completely out of character. I'm supposed to hate Elroy. Man, it's getting really hard to keep everything straight, especially after my epiphany at church.

"Dude, give me back the twenty," I say to Elroy, loud enough for Severs to hear. "And you're going to owe me for the orange juice and sandwiches." I give Elroy a wink, gesture with my eyebrows for him to play along.

"I already owe you twenty dollars!" Elroy shouts at me. "How am I supposed to pay all of that back? You should pay! Or you shouldn't try so hard to impress Dr. Severs! Either way, it's not my fault. I don't want any of it!"

The kid's a natural. And Severs has obviously heard his performance because he picks up his pace, jogs out of earshot before Elroy can retract the order.

"No stutter at all on that last outburst. Pretty impressive," I say and eye the window of Starbucks before I stick the twenty back into Elroy's front pocket, "Let's improv some when he gets back with the stuff, make sure he doesn't figure out that we actually like each other."

Elroy's eyes literally brim when I mention that I like him. Christ, what a low bar. Has anyone ever been nice to this kid before?

"Yeah, sure. No pr... pr... problem. Thanks for the fo... fo... food. And for the money, too. I really need it." He's looking at the ground, avoiding my eyes.

"What do you need the money for?"

"To buy more fo... fo... food, I guess. Like later or tomorrow."

"Don't they feed you at the foster home?"

"Yeah, but it's kind of a weird situation."

"Are you okay? I mean, are they, like, meth heads or something?"

"No, no. They're nice. They just pr... pr... probably shouldn't have a foster kid. They're really old. Re... Re... Really old. I mean, co... co... compared to them, the inmates at your nu... nu... nursing home look like bright young kids."

"So, can't you tell someone? Get a transfer or something?"

"The devil you know," Elroy says, more mature than he should be at twelve. "I've li... li... lived with a lot worse."

It's a hard knock life, I guess. And I thought I had it bad at the nursing home.

"We'll talk more about that later," I say. "How did it go with Severs at the church?"

"Gr... gr... great. I told him some excellent lies. Didn't st... st... stutter once when I was with him, and I talked the whole time."

"Awesome. Good for you. Catch me up later, okay?"

"Yeah. What about you? It wasn't wh... wh... what I expected, when you came out of confession."

"I know. I got a really good idea, got excited and pretty much nuked our whole cover story. How bad is it? I mean, in terms of damage control? I know my slip-up in the parking lot didn't help either."

Elroy blushes. His face actually turns red when I mention my slip-up in the parking lot, where I mistakenly let on that I really do like him, with the food and money and actually saying it and stuff. I look over at Starbucks again, ostensibly to check on Severs, but more to deflect the awkwardness of Elroy's reaction. He shakes his head and gains some composure.

"It might not be as bad as you th... th... think. Dr. Severs was pretty stoned in the church."

"When did he get stoned?"

"He la... la... lagged behind in the car. He was totally stupid when he came into the church. And I made up a whole bunch of st... st... stuff that blew his mind. Between the weed and my lies, he was pretty di... di... distracted when you came out of the confessional and spun around in the aisle."

"Ah. Well, that helps. I think I know how to play it. Now get into character. He's coming back."

Elroy is staring at the ground while I curse at him about nothing when Severs walks back, bag and tray in hand. He hands Elroy the bag, me the tray. I shove the tray in front of Elroy and he refuses to pick up his orange juice.

"Trouble in paradise?" Severs quips.

Elroy drops the bag at my feet.

"Just a misunderstanding, Dreamcatcher. No business of yours. How about that receipt?"

"How about you tell me what happened at confession? You looked pretty chipper when you came out of there," Severs says, handing me the receipt.

"Did you tip the dollar seventy-five?" I ask, looking at the total.

"Yeah, I did."

"Really?"

"Yeah," Severs whines.

"Then you won't mind if I check." Statement, not a question. I start walking towards Starbucks.

"Oh, for Christ sake, it took her, like, five minutes with those sausage sandwiches. She didn't deserve a tip! I deserve a tip more than she does."

I walk back to him, my palm outstretched, into which he deposits my change. I've seen it before and I don't think this type of greed has anything to do with money, the actual amount, I mean. It's more like it's a perverted obsession, wanting to always get away with more than whatever is fair. I've shared a pizza with guys like Severs, the type of person that wolfs down his first two slices in order to vie for the fifth, regardless of whether he's still hungry. A complete disregard for his own integrity. People like this should be put down, like rabid dogs. How this one became a guidance counselor is beyond me.

"You're a class act, Moonbeam."

"Whatever. Why were you so happy after confession? Did the priest let you give him a foot massage or something?" Severs laughs at his own joke, then looks at Elroy and tightens up. "Sorry, dude."

Elroy scowls, looks at the ground.

"What, Rainbowbright? They didn't have sarcasm on the commune where you grew up? You'd have to be stoned out of your gourd to miss the irony of my behavior in there." I pause, staring at him, until he looks away guiltily. "I'll remember to wear a sandwich board next time I'm sarcastic around you."

"I didn't think you were being serious," Severs backpedals.

"You asked me why I was happy, like, two or three times."

"Maybe I was being sarcastic, too," Severs grins wide, like checkmate.

"Oh! *Double* sarcasm. Sarcasm in response to my sarcasm. Very subtle," I say. "You're obviously a comic genius."

"Did you tell him about your dad?" Severs asks Elroy. I look at the kid, raise my eyebrows.

"Uh, Dr. Severs? That was more like a private student-to-guidance counselor conversation we were having in the church. I don't think I want to share it with everyone."

"Of course, Elroy. Definitely. That's none of your business, Mr. Johnson."

I like the fact that he's still addressing me formally.

"Posolutely, Starburst. It was rude of me to ask."

"Sa… Sarc… Sarcasm," Elroy says, smiling for real.

Elroy

No one says anything on the car ride from confession back to the nursing home. I really want to eat one of the sausage and egg sandwiches while they're still hot, drink the orange juice while it's still cold. But I leave the bag on the floor of the car. The tray is sitting on the backseat beside me, because Dr. Severs' car was apparently built before the invention of rear cup holders. Frank's got his head out the passenger side window again, soaking up as much sun and air as possible outside the grounds of the nursing home.

I think Dr. Severs is still rattled by the fact that Frank alluded to him being stoned back in the church parking lot. I'm kind of surprised that it even shook him up. I mean, it's not like he goes to any great lengths to hide the fact that he smokes pot, at least from me. But I guess he thinks that I'm too young to know what he's doing, what he smells like. Or maybe he just thinks I don't matter enough for him to care one way or the other.

"Grab the food and juice, Elroy," Frank says in a nasty tone. "You might get hungry with all of the reading that's on the docket for today."

Thank God. I had absolutely nothing to do for the rest of the day. That's not a sarcastic thought, by the way. I'm totally serious. It's, like, really good news that Frank isn't just going to leave me in the car and go back to the nursing home.

"Wait a second. You want Elroy to read to you? I was going to take him home," Dr. Severs says.

"I don't think so. You two made me go to confession, which is something that I didn't want to do. Now I'm going to make Elroy read to me, which is something that I'm sure he doesn't want to do. And you're just going to have to wait in the car or come back and pick him up. Happy Saturday, guys."

"For how long?" Dr. Severs whines, oblivious to how this impacts me.

"Church kind of put me in a Mark Twain mood," Frank says. "I'm thinking we've got a few hours of reading ahead of us this afternoon."

"Can't do it," Dr. Severs says, "I've got a date."

"*You've* got a date?" Frank says, deadpan.

"What? I go on a lot of dates. Lots of dates. Girls dig what I put out there."

"Uh, huh. Well, I guess you're going to have to call Mom and cancel because Elroy's going to be reading to me for the next few hours."

"It's not my Mom and I'm not going to cancel."

"Well, it's only a couple of miles into town. I figure a taxi can't cost more than five or six dollars."

"I'm not paying for a taxi, either. If you want to torture Elroy by making him spend all Saturday afternoon reading to you, then you pay for a taxi."

"Let me get this straight. You're okay with me abusing Elroy and you getting off scot-free, as long as I pick up the associated costs of five dollars? You're all heart, Sunburst. Okay, fine. I'll pay for the taxi," Frank says, then glares at me. "But it's going on your tab, Elroy."

"Dr. Severs?" I say and give the rearview mirror my best look of shock and pleading.

"Sorry, Elroy. We did commit to the whole day. Do it for the RMSOC, huh? You know, take one for the team. Oh, and I'll pick you up at eleven-thirty tomorrow at the school."

"Why?" I ask. Not just that he's picking me up tomorrow, but why not at my house, which is only two blocks away from the school?

"We're going to Sunday noon mass."

"What? We just went to church!" Frank shouts.

"Yup, and we're going back tomorrow. I arranged it with Mr. Hardy this morning."

"You're pushing it, Dreamcatcher," Frank says. "Come on, Elroy. Hey! Don't forget the breakfast sandwiches and orange juice."

"If Elroy's not going to eat those, I'll take them," Dr. Severs says hopefully.

"That's okay, Lovejuice. There's a garbage can right there," Frank says. He walks toward the door of the nursing home.

"I can't believe how selfish that guy is. I mean, if all he's going to do is throw that food out, what a waste," Dr. Severs says as I climb out from the backseat. By the time I've caught up with Frank, Dr. Severs has driven away.

"Here, let me take those." Frank grabs the bag of breakfast sandwiches and the tray of plastic orange juice cups and hides them behind the garbage can in front of the nursing home.

"You're just coming into the lobby to sign me back in. After that, turn around and go back out the front door. Grab the Starbucks and sneak around back of the home. You'll see a hill in the back yard, and behind the hill there's a bench. Wait for me there. I should only be about fifteen, twenty minutes. Starbucks always makes the breakfast sandwiches too hot so they should be perfect by the time you eat them. And drink the orange juice slow, don't gulp it. It's fresh squeezed, so you want to appreciate the taste."

"Wa… wa… wait a second. You're going to sneak out? If Mr. Hardy catches you, aren't you going to get kicked out of the home? I mean, if you can just sn… sn… sneak out, then why are we doing all of this stuff in the first place?"

"Easy, E. Yes, I am going to sneak out. And by doing so, I am at risk of being kicked out of the home. But these are unique circumstances, Elroy. Circumstances that warrant a calculated risk. I'll explain when I see you. Now go run around back and enjoy your breakfast on this fantastic Saturday morning."

Frank grabs my shoulders and gives me a shake. Then he puts on his game face, grumpy and mean, and marches me into the nursing home. After I sign him in, give the front desk nurse a sad smile, I go out the front door and sneak around back to wait for Frank.

There's only one bench on the back side of the hill behind the nursing home, so I know I'm in the right place. But I still feel kind of lost because I don't know if I'm allowed to be back here and I don't know anything about Frank's plan. For a minute I wonder if I should hold off on the feast of breakfast sandwiches and orange juice, in case Frank's plan involves a picnic on this bench. But then I remember that he specifically told me to enjoy the breakfast while I waited for him, so I decide to go ahead and eat.

You're probably not going to get this, but I'm going to describe it anyway. Because, if you're not an orphan who has spent the past twelve years in homes that actually need foster kid income in order to pay their bills, and if you haven't spent your life eating the food that's available in those homes, then none of this is going to make any sense at all. But indulge me.

I have never sipped anything so glorious as fresh squeezed orange juice. My first sip is a cinematic experience. Meaning that the world around me actually seems to turn cartoon. Like in one of those nineteen-sixties Disney movies. The trees and rocks and grass all smile at me and love me. There are animals. Sweet, like in Bambi, bunnies and squirrels and skunks all smiling and loving me. The sun smiles at me and loves me. I am filled with all the love in the universe. That's what fresh squeezed orange juice tastes like to me. And I sip it slowly, like Frank said, swirling it around my tongue and letting it slide down my throat almost without swallowing, so that I can taste every bit of it.

When I'm halfway through the plastic cup of orange juice, I put it on the bench beside me. I glance at the orange juice lovingly and I unwrap the first breakfast sandwich. Once again, Frank was right. It is still warm inside the foil. I take a bite from the corner of the sandwich, big enough to make sure that I don't just clip the end, miss the egg, cheese and sausage. Make sure that I get the full symphony of tastes in my mouth.

Now, I've eaten breakfast stuff at diners and fast food restaurants before. And it's good, don't get me wrong. But I want to be honest, here. Prior to today, the best meal that I'd ever had in my life happened about a year ago when I saw a worker at McDonalds toss a trash bag full of breakfast sandwiches into the dumpster behind the restaurant. And this garbage bag was mostly filled with just these McSandwiches, maybe only a little bit of regular trash, so it wasn't dirty or anything. And the McSandwiches were still in their wrappers, still warm, just like what McDonalds would have served to paying customers fifteen minutes earlier, before breakfast ended.

But they were better than what McDonalds serves to its paying customers. Because they'd sat just long enough for the steam and the grease from the egg, cheese and meat to soak the English muffin so that it just kind of melted perfectly in my mouth. The muffin, egg and cheese were the consistency of thick icing on a cake, so that all I needed to chew was the meat inside. It was a life changing experience. I ate those McSandwiches until I threw up.

And then I ate some more.

I bring up my McDonalds dumpster experience not only because, until today, it was the best meal of my life. But also because these Starbucks breakfast sandwiches are similar, only so much more so. In the same ballpark, but luxury box seats instead of the nosebleed section.

First of all, the bread is square. That's classy. And it's not really an English muffin. It's more like a small Italian loaf. And the bread part, under the crust, is just as steam-soaked as my McSandwiches were. But the crust part, even though it's thin, it stays chewy. Unlike my earlier McSandwiches, which were like a delicious porridge surrounding breakfast meats, these thirty-minute old Starbucks sandwiches still have the consistency of a sandwich. The crust, the steam-wet bread, the meat, the cheese, the egg – all of them keep their different textures, like a real sandwich should. Like you're eating one thing and many things at the same time.

And where do you find sausage with this kind of spice? Or cheese, or egg, with these kinds of flavors? I feel like a king or a count, somewhere in Europe, where fairytales are real and this is what people eat. Like I said, you're probably not going to be able to relate to this, unless you're me.

I'm sobbing on the bench when Frank shows up. Not because I'm sad that the orange juice and breakfast sandwiches are gone, but because I'm so happy. Really and truly happy.

"Dude. What the hell? Did somebody steal your food?" Frank asks, a mix of kindness and ridicule, if there can be such a thing.

"It was so good," I say, wiping the tears from my eyes, "It was so good."

"Uh, okay. You know we can, like, get Starbucks anytime we go out, right? It's not really that big of a deal."

I stand up and shake myself back into reality. He isn't going to understand and I feel kind of stupid, crying about how good the breakfast sandwiches and orange juice were, so I decide it's time to move on.

"What now?" I ask.

"Now we wait," Frank says. "It shouldn't be more than ten minutes or so."

A few awkward minutes later, a car at the bottom of the hill honks three times. I follow Frank down to meet it. That thing about not getting into a stranger's car? It doesn't really apply to orphans like me. I mean, who's going to care if I don't ever come back? Plus, I'm with Frank. He's kind of like an adult.

Sally

So, about my mom. No. First, about my dad. My mom is still alive. I can get to her later.

I still remember Dad, even though I was only four when it happened. I remember him the way you can still remember a really good dream even a lot of years after you had that dream. I remember things like his scratchy face against my cheek, and the fact that he smelled like cologne even though I can't remember what the cologne smelled like. I remember being hugged and wanting to be hugged.

I didn't find his body when it happened. Nothing indelibly traumatic like that. I just remember that the police came and they made me stand outside the house for, like, ever. Then I remember a lot of time in church, and a lot of church people visiting our house after it happened. But no one really told me that Dad wasn't coming back. When I asked where Dad was, they just hugged me and told me to pray. I suppose, how do you explain a father's suicide to a four-year-old? I guess, instead, they thought it was healthier for me to just gradually figure it out on my own. Or at least less awkward for them.

Why Dad married mom was, well, me. The math is easy to do. Why he killed himself was, well, because he was married to Mom. So, you might say that my being born was the real reason that he took his own life. That's called deductive reasoning. No me, then no married to Mom, then still Dad.

But I don't blame myself. I only blame Mom.

Here's the thing about Mom. Religion is fine, I think, if it's personal. If it's about you and God, whatever god you want. But Mom's religion isn't personal. It affects everyone around her. My mom's religion is like the stink of a skunk. It's not going to outright kill you or anything, but it hangs there in the air making things unpleasant. Lingering even when she's not still there. And if you're around her

Catholic stink long enough, it can make life unbearable. I'm thinking that's what happened with Dad. And at the very least it contributed to Aunt Sadie.

Here's how it is. Every single time you have anything to do with Mom, she gets her Catholic all over you. Some of it is straight guilt, with her playing the part of the martyr. Like, God forbid you ever need her to do something for you, which is kind of hard to avoid when you're twelve and she's your only parent. Though it was a lot worse when I was younger, before I was allowed to bike to places on my own. Back then it was like...

"Mom, can you pick me up from choir tomorrow?" (I'd ask this, like, every Wednesday in the fourth grade.)

"Tomorrow? What time tomorrow? Tomorrow I have to do a teen abstinence workshop with the high school kids, which always takes longer than we plan for. And I've got to coordinate the busses for the Right to Life march just after that. And I've got physical therapy for my foot at three pm and you know how that exhausts me. What time do you need me to pick you up?"

"Four thirty."

"Oh, I'm supposed to help Sister Martha set up the chairs for the Youth Group between four and five, and I've already committed to that. So I guess I can try to move some stuff around. Maybe if I go straight to the auditorium and start setting up the chairs instead of icing my foot after physical therapy like I usually do, maybe I can make it work. That's going to be rough on my foot, but I'll find a way to make it work."

"I guess I could..."

"No, I'll find a way to make it work. If Jesus could haul a couple hundred pounds of wood up the hill at Calvary to die for our sins, then I can change my schedule and manage the pain in my foot so that I can pick you up. Even though I probably won't be able to sleep tomorrow night because you know I can never sleep unless I ice my foot after physical therapy, but it's only one night and I can offer it up to God, anyway."

"Well, as long as you're sure it isn't any trouble..."

"I'll be fine. Really. I get my happiness by doing things to make you happy. That's what selflessness is about. Finding happiness in your sacrifice for others, even if it means pain for yourself. Someday you'll know what I mean."

She doesn't even have a job. We live off the money that Dad left us. The torturous grind of her daily life is totally on a volunteer basis. Other than the stuff she has to do for me, because I'm her daughter, I mean, everything else is just stuff she decides to do. No one is making her do any of it, except maybe Jesus, and that's only in her head anyway. And it's not even that much, really. It's not like she's a single mother holding down two jobs to pay for my schooling. I go to public school.

But anyway, every time she has to extend herself, even just a little, it's the same long-winded martyrdom routine. Can you see how that would make you want to kill yourself? I mean, if you were stuck with it? If you were family with her or married to her? If you couldn't just walk away and never look back?

Oh, and then there are the times when she wants something from you. But it always comes across as if she's over-extended herself to create a special situation in which you are allowed to participate. And it would be unthinkable for you not to want to participate, especially after all of the trouble that she's gone to. So, it's like...

"Oh, Sally, there's someone you just have to meet. She reminds me so much of you, well, of what I see in you, of what you could be. You're going to love her."

"Who?"

"Sister Francine Glucko. She's visiting our parish from Siberia, where she's spent the past seventy years sucking infection from sores of Siberian leper children (or something like that). *Honestly, you look into her eyes and... and it's what it must be like to look into the eyes of Jesus Christ. I made an appointment for you to see her at three-thirty tomorrow."*

"Does she speak English?"

"Oh, no, Honey. She doesn't speak at all. But she's sharp as a tack. There's a lot going on in her mind. You can tell just by looking into

her eyes. It's a life-changing spiritual experience, just looking into her eyes."

"What am I supposed to do with her? If she doesn't speak, I mean?"

"You just walk her around the church parking lot for an hour or two. She's in a wheelchair. You're going to thank me. You're going to remember this for the rest of your life. It's like a one-on-one with Mother Theresa, only better because not everyone knows how holy Sister Glucko is. You're going to gain so much from her spirituality."

"Mom, I've got study group at Karen's tomorrow after school."

"Well, you have to change it. This is a once in a lifetime opportunity that I've created for you."

"How long is she going to be here?"

"I think this is her last stop. She could die any day. And I would never forgive myself if you missed the opportunity to really experience, first hand, the Christ that's in her."

"Fine. Can you pick me up, after?"

"Oh. Huh. That might be difficult. Tomorrow I'm working at the soup kitchen until noon, and then I'm helping out at the burn victim unit until two-thirty, and you know I've got physical therapy for my foot at three..."

This is no hypothetical example. Since before we left for Aunt Sadie's funeral, I've walked this holy-potato-with-a-pulse around the church parking lot, like, four times. Meaning four different days of walking her, sixty-to-ninety minutes per session, depending on when the nurse from the convent shows up to retrieve her.

This is my hell.

But like I said, Mom never asks for your help. Instead she creates an opportunity for you to experience something for your own benefit, to which she has, incidentally, already committed your time. Every one of her requests is like an ugly Christmas sweater from an awful relative. It's bad enough when you receive it, but even worse because you'll have to wear it later when they're around.

At least, now that I'm twelve, she lets me ride my bike to school and church and whatever, so I don't need her to drop me off and pick me up so much. But that just diminishes the frequency of me asking stuff of her. It doesn't change the dynamic. She didn't have to drive Dad or Aunt Sadie around, and the two them still offed themselves rather than deal with her any longer.

I guess it's up to me to make sure Mom scores the hat trick.

But that's why I really want to think about how to do it right, you know? Because even though two of the three people closest to Mom killed themselves, she seems to be oblivious to the pattern here. So I want to make sure it's crystal clear. That it's obviously, totally and completely because of Mom, when I take my own life. Not because she ever hurt me so deeply or set too high a bar for me to reach. Not because she's mean or spiteful or jealous or cruel. Not because of any heavy-weight reason at all. Just because she is… So. Fucking. Annoying.

Frank

Everything seems like it's back on the right track when Severs drops me off, leaves Elroy for the afternoon. I hide the Starbucks breakfast behind a garbage can, tell Elroy to sign me in and pick it up on his way out, then to go wait for me behind the facility.

Elroy signs me in and leaves without a word. No questions asked, the little trooper. Once I'm back inside, I go straight to Martha's office, hoping she's there on a Sunday. I knock and then open the door to her office. She's sitting behind the desk, watching her soap operas, masturbating.

"Oh! Wait just a second...! Oh, it's you. Thank God, I thought it was Ed," Martha says. She lifts her hands from between her legs and clicks pause on the monitor. Utterly shameless, this lady is. At least with me. And I am thoroughly impressed with her candor. "I thought you had confession today?"

"Just got back," I say. "How are the soaps?"

"There are no words."

"You want me to give you a minute?"

"No, that's okay. I can rewind it when you leave."

I like the fact that she still talks in analog. It adds a quaintness to our otherwise progressive relationship.

"Good, because I'm short on time. Is Ed here today?"

"No, he's fishing. But I thought he might have cancelled his trip when you barged in. Other people usually wait after knocking. You know, to see if it's okay to come in."

"You could just lock the door when you're having a moment."

"Ed would think that's suspicious. If the door were locked, I mean."

"Right. Anyway, it's great that he's not here. I need you to do me a favor. A couple, actually."

"As evidenced when you walked in, I remain substantially in your debt. What do you need?"

I ask Martha to tell the nurses to leave me alone for the day, both the first shift and the second shift. To tell them that Ed pushed me a little too far with the church thing. That I'm going to bed and it would be in everyone's best interests not to disturb me. She tells me that's not a problem. Then I tell her that I need to call my brother. From her phone, not mine, because he usually doesn't pick up when I call from my cell phone.

"Do you want me to give you some privacy?" Martha asks, pushing her phone to the front of the desk.

"You and I don't have any secrets, Martha," I say sweetly. I take the phone and dial Johnny's home number.

"Johnson," Johnny says when he picks up.

"Is this John Johnson? John, son of John? I bet you wish you were first born and named after Grandad."

"Frank," Johnny sighs. "What's up?"

"It's time, Johnny. I'm waving the white flag. It's over."

"Thank Christ."

"Yeah, checkmate Hardy. I know when I'm beat. But I've got to do it my way. And I need your help."

"Anything you need. I'm just glad you've come to your senses."

"I need you to pick me up, like now."

"No can do. Wendy has a soccer game in five minutes. I'm just walking out of the house."

"So drop her off and come pick me up."

"Jane doesn't like leaving the kids alone at their games."

"Oh, grow a set, would you? What, you guys think that some wild pedophile is going to rush the field and grab Wendy, out of like twenty kids, with a couple dozen parents capturing video of the game on their iPhones? Come on, Wendy is safer than the Pope on that soccer field. Just drop her off and come pick me up. Jane doesn't need to know anything about it."

"What if Jane comes by the game when she's done with her mani-pedi? It's happened before."

"What if I decide to keep living in the nursing home for another six months because you won't help me?"

"Fine. I'll be there in twenty-five minutes."

"Great. But I need you to drive around the block and pick me up behind the facility. I'll explain when I see you. I'll be on the hill, back side of the nursing home. Honk three times."

"Why do I have to pick you up behind the nursing home?"

"I told you, I'll explain when you get here. Why do you have to ask so many questions?"

"Because you're obviously an insane person and it's not beyond you to try and get me mixed up in your schemes. Do you want some examples from our childhood?"

"Oh, stop. This is legit. I'm sitting next to Martha Hardy right now. Here, I'll put you on speaker." I press the speaker button on the office phone.

"Hi, Johnny," Martha says sweetly.

"Hi, Mrs. Hardy. Sorry to bother you, but you know."

"Not a problem, Johnny."

"Okay, Frank. I'll see you behind the nursing home in twenty-five minutes."

"You still have my car, right?" I ask.

"No, I sold it to the Baker kid next door," Johnny jokes feebly. It's a shame when all of the wit in the family is inherited by only one of the children. That said, Johnny has much better hair than I do, so I guess it all comes out in the wash. "Of course I still have your car, why?"

"Great. Just double-checking. See you in twenty-five minutes."

"Are you really leaving, Frank?" Martha asks, in all seriousness, when I hang up the phone.

"Of course not," I say dismissively. "I'm here until Ed pays me back my money or until my twelve months is up. But our plan is working. So I just need to sneak out this one afternoon to make some arrangements."

"Don't get caught," she says.

"Make sure the nurses don't come into my room. If you can do that for me, then we're golden."

Back in my room, I lock the door, rig up a Ferris Bueller type of sleeping arrangement and turn off the lights. It's obviously not as complex as Ferris Bueller's. I don't rig any sound or jerry-rig any moving parts in the sleeping pile of clothes arranged under my covers, but it should get the job done in case a nurse peeks her head in. Especially with the lights off and shades down. And since I'm in my thirties and less of a death-in-bed risk than most of the inmates, I expect they'll all follow Martha's orders and leave me alone anyway.

Once the scene is set, I flip back the shade, hoist my first-floor window, and scoot out onto the lawn.

I find Elroy on the bench behind the home. It looks like he's been crying. This is why I don't want to get married and have kids. None of it makes any sense.

"Dude. What the hell? Did somebody steal your food?" I ask.

"It was so good," Elroy says, wiping the tears from his eyes. "It was so good."

Tears of ecstasy for a Starbucks breakfast sandwich, fresh squeezed orange juice. It is unfathomable how much good people with money could do for the world, if that money were only pointed in the right direction.

"Uh, okay. You know we can, like, get Starbucks anytime we go out, right? It's not really that big of a deal," I say, awkwardly.

I'm not looking to empathize right now. It's so tragic I don't think I could take it, and anyway I've got my own stuff to do. Fortunately, he starts to shake it off.

"What now?" Elroy asks.

"Now we wait," I say. "It shouldn't be more than ten minutes or so."

And the silence is mildly awkward as I allow Elroy to regain his composure while I scroll through stuff on my phone. A few minutes later, Johnny pulls up to the curb at the bottom of the hill, honks three times. I gesture with my head for Elroy to follow, walk down toward the car.

"Who's this, then?" Johnny asks as Elroy climbs into his backseat. The kid doesn't say anything, waits for my lead.

"Great to see you, too, bro. I've been good, thanks."

"Who's this?" Johnny asks again, shrugging his chin toward the back seat.

"That's Elroy. He's an orphan," I say and glance back at him. "He's a friend of mine."

"Since when did Mr. Hardy start taking in orphans?"

"He didn't. Elroy is just someone that I picked up along the way. He's not the Artful Dodger to my Fagan, if that's what you're worried about. Just be nice."

This seems to satisfy Johnny.

"Hey, Elroy. Good to meet you."

"Ni... ni... nice to meet you, too."

"He stutters," Johnny says to me.

"Only when he's telling the truth," I reply and poke Johnny's belly behind the steering wheel, "while you're fat all the time. Tell me, which is more offensive?"

"Your mouth is far more offensive than his stutter or my weight. And what do you mean anyway? I hardly weigh more than I did in college."

"You were this fat in college?"

Johnny isn't fat. I've come to realize that everyone gets self-conscious when you say they're fat. Except for people like Elroy, who is so skinny he could be a stand-in on a Sally Struthers commercial about adopting kids from Africa.

"Where am I taking you?" Johnny asks.

"Your house. My car."

"I have to pick up Wendy first."

"That's fine. You mind if Elroy and I use the car ride to catch up a bit? A lot went on this morning."

"Whatever," Johnny says.

Elroy

So we're in the car with Frank's brother, Johnny Johnson, and at first I think they're just messing with me but it turns out that it's his real name. Frank and Johnny have this relationship like brothers on a sit-com where they bust each other's chops, but you can tell that they really love each other underneath it all.

Especially after those breakfast sandwiches and the fresh squeezed orange juice, I'm starting to get sentimental. Maybe just a little bit resentful that I've never gotten to experience anything like this in my own life. But Frank breaks the momentum of these thoughts when he launches his adult body over the front seat of Johnny's BMW to join me in the back.

"Dude, these are leather seats!" Johnny shouts at Frank, who ignores him.

"Okay, bud. Let's sync up on this morning," Frank says to me.

"What happened this morning?" Johnny says from the front seat.

"I went to confession," Frank replies.

"*You* went to confession."

"Yeah. I've decided I'm going to spend some more time at church."

"*You're* going to spend *more time* at Church. You haven't been to church in, like, fifteen years."

"Yeah, that's because I didn't know how to fix it. And I'm trying to catch up with Elroy, here. So how about you just keep your eyes on the road and your mouth shut?"

"I don't remember agreeing to be your chauffer when you asked me to pick you up."

"And I don't remember agreeing that every conversation in your car was going to include you. Just give me fifteen minutes here, Johnny. This is important."

I really wish I had a brother that I could talk to like this.

"So, E," Frank says, looking me in the eye. "Tell me everything. What did you lie to Dr. Fairydust about? Leave nothing out."

"Who's Dr. Fairydust? Are you guys dropping acid? He's a minor, Frank."

"Johnny, I'm asking you one more time. Don't test me. Go on, Elroy."

So, I explain to Frank that I told Dr. Severs I was found in the church when I was a baby, the same church we were at this morning. Frank bobs his head and nods, as if this is a reasonable lie. And then I explain to Frank that I told Dr. Severs that the priest who found me kind of pestered me, showed up at my foster homes and stuff, until Dr. Severs finally offered up the idea that this priest might be my biological father.

Actually, I tell Frank, I had Dr. Severs convinced that this priest was my biological father. And Frank chuckles, nods for me to go on. So then I explain to Frank that the priest who did confession with him came over to Dr. Severs and me, after Frank left the church. To ask about him, about Frank, that is. And Frank gets this satisfied look on his face, like I've confirmed something for him.

And then I explain to Frank that I told Dr. Severs that this priest who asked about him, asked about Frank, was also the same priest that visited me in my foster home back when. So, I explain, now Dr. Severs thinks this priest who did confession with Frank is actually my biological father. And I didn't stutter once throughout the whole conversation with Dr. Severs, I tell Frank. Even though I'm stuttering a lot while I'm explaining all of this to Frank.

"Dude, seriously?" Frank says to me when I'm finished. "You threw Rory under the bus?"

"Who the hell is Rory?" Johnny asks from the driver's seat. "And also, because I feel like I'm in a David Lynch adaptation of a Charles Dickens novel, how much of what that kid just said is true?"

"Rory is the priest that I talked to when I went to confession. And he's also my partner in crime. He's going to help me turn the Catholic Church inside-out. And he's also Elroy's fictitious biological father, as far as Elroy's hippie guidance counselor is concerned. That last connection is coincidental. We didn't try to set it up that way or anything.

"The priest that did your co... co... confession is named Father Rory?" I ask.

"No, it's Father Mc something-or-other, but his first name is Rory. He's Irish. We connected. We're on a mission to bring the Catholic Church back to the people. That's my story, that's why I was so pumped this morning, I mean. I've got a new project."

I feel a stab of jealousy towards Father Rory McSomething, hope this new project doesn't distract Frank from the project that he's working on with me.

"I di... di... didn't know he was your friend," I say to Frank. "I wouldn't have said that st... st... stuff to Dr. Severs if I knew."

"Not your fault, Elroy. I never met him before this morning. I don't even know what he looks like. But when I was talking to him, behind that screen, we both had, like, an epiphany."

"What, so you're going to become all Catholic now?" Johnny asks Frank.

"No. Catholic is going to become all me," Frank replies. "Me and Rory, I mean."

And I'm thinking, where do I fit into all of this, now that Frank's crushing on this Rory character.

"Okay, brother of mine," Johnny says slowly, like he's talking to a dimwit, "I'm not trying to rain on your parade, here, but do I need to bring up the many childhood examples of you assuming too much allegiance? Especially with people that you don't know very well?"

"Easy, boy," Frank says to Johnny.

"Dude, do I have to remind you that you were, literally, the kid who jumped off the bridge after mothers asked their own children if their friends jumped off a bridge, would they do it, too?"

"And I was fine. What, I had a cast for eight weeks, it was nothing. If the rest of them jumped like they said they would, we would have been legend. We called ourselves 'The Lemmings,'" Frank asides to me. "It was ironic, a statement club. I had t-shirts printed up and everything. And then they chickened out at the last minute." Frank turns his eyes back to Johnny's in the rearview mirror, "And anyway, that's a random example."

"Yeah, you're right," Johnny says to Frank. "And let's conveniently forget about the time that you were the only kid to streak down the middle school hallway at lunchtime, back when you were in eighth grade."

"Come on, you're going to bring that up? They all promised. Even you promised. You guys were weak. You totally let me down. But I wasn't going to let myself down."

"You're making my point," Johnny continues, "and, might I add, it's pretty messed up being a sixth grader when all the girls in your middle school have seen your brother's penis. Back me up here, Elroy."

"You did that?" I ask Frank, suddenly feeling not so bad about my underwear in the hallway last Wednesday. Suddenly feeling like this guy isn't just my friend, he's maybe my hero, too.

"He's exaggerating. Probably less than, like, a third of the middle school was even in the hallway and saw my junk," Frank says to me.

"Your date-rape witch hunt with the high school football team. Your social justice crusade against the fraternities at college. Your solo version of Occupy Wall Street, three years before it became a thing. Shall I go on?" Johnny asks Frank.

"I still maintain that I was the one that actually started Occupy Wall Street," Frank replies. "It was just a slow burn on a long fuse."

"Listen, dude," Johnny says, "what's remarkable isn't the ridiculous number of bad choices you make, it's the way you run with them. Like, every time we think you've hit rock bottom, you somehow find a drill."

"No stone left unbroken," Frank says.

"Whatever. Let's just agree that you have a tendency to believe that people are a lot more behind you than they actually are. Remember, you graduated when I was a sophomore in high school. I spent ten years watching you make these William Wallace speeches and then charge full-steam, alone, straight into brick walls. And get pulverized. And then do it again. It wasn't easy, Frank. It wasn't easy for you and it wasn't easy for me to watch happen. So, I don't know who this Rory is, or how you two are planning to (air quote) 'fix' (end air quote) the

Catholic Church. But, as your only brother, I advise you to take a long look at your history and use a modicum of sense and caution as you move forward with this—clearly insane—scheme of yours."

"Johnny, you are such a buzz kill," Frank replies. "It's no wonder that I'm the one with a lot of money and you're the insurance salesman, struggling to make your mortgage, caring about what everyone in the community thinks of you."

"Fair point, Frank," Johnny says, "but I live in a house, with a wife and two kids. And you are thirty-three years old, single, currently residing in a nursing home with a bunch of clueless nonagenarians. And you wear diapers."

"You're we... we... wearing diapers?" I ask Frank.

"Yeah, I am. Adult diapers. It's a life choice, one that I stand behind. Everyone should give it a try, at least before they ignorantly criticize me for it."

But Johnny Johnson doesn't engage Frank because he's pulling his BMW into the parking lot of a soccer field just in time for us to see the teams shake hands, tell each other good game. He jumps out of the car and runs to the sideline, the only parent cheering for his daughter during this lame post-game ritual. It's idiotic. Both the Johnny cheering part and the draggy high-fives that never mean anything to anyone anyway.

But there's a part of me that wishes I were Johnny's daughter, that wonders what it's like to have a parent that actually gives a damn. To have a parent at all.

Sally

We get home from Aunt Sadie's funeral on Saturday afternoon. I start to unpack the car while Mom tells me about how she doesn't want to tell me how bad the drive was for her foot because she doesn't want to make me feel bad. I tell her I would have been happy to take the wheel if I'd known it was an option.

She tells me that she isn't going to tell me how insensitive I've been to her during the past week. That she isn't going to mention the fact that I didn't once ask her how she was doing, even though her only sister had just died. Because if she did mention any of this I would probably feel really bad about it.

I thank her for being so considerate.

She tells me that she's not going to talk about my attitude problem, because I already know about it, and I'm just going to have to work on it myself because nothing that she does seems to help, no matter how hard she prays. She tells me that I don't have to ask her if she's still going to keep praying for me to grow up and stop being so snippy because she's going to keep praying for me, whether I know it, whether I like it, or not.

I tell her that all of this not telling me stuff is kind of exhausting.

She tells me that I'm her daughter so she has to love me, but she doesn't have to like me.

I tell her, right back at you.

She drops her duffle bag on the front lawn and stomps into the house. I carry my stuff in, leave her duffle bag where it sits. It can stay there overnight for all I care. I hope it rains.

Frank

"Look what I picked up," Johnny says and opens the back door of his car.

"Stupid uncle Frank!" Wendy shouts.

"Stupid kid Wendy!" I reply and get out of the car and lift her up in a hug.

She's gotten really heavy. Or maybe I've gotten really weak over the past few months at the home. Either way, she feels more like a big sack of flour than a spry five-year-old girl.

"I'm not stupid," Wendy says, her cheek pressed against mine.

"Neither am I," I reply, putting her down.

"Mommy says you are."

"Well, your mom is a bitch."

"Frank!" Johnny shouts.

"What's a bits?" Wendy asks, cute.

"It's not a nice word," Johnny tells her.

"There are worse," I say.

"Who are you," Wendy asks, addressing Elroy, before getting in the back seat with him.

"That's Elroy," I intercede. "He's my new friend."

Elroy waves to her, keeps his mouth shut, probably to avoid having Wendy ask about his stutter. Poor kid.

"Is he a cousin?" she asks me.

"That works," I say.

"I never had a cousin before."

"Me ne... ne... neither," Elroy replies.

"Why do you talk funny?" she asks.

"Wendy!" Johnny says. "Sorry, Elroy."

"It's okay," Elroy says, turning to Wendy. "It's ju... ju... just something I do."

"Are you broken?" Wendy asks with the kind of innocence that only a child can get away with.

"Yeah," Elroy says.

"Great, stupid uncle Frank," Wendy says. "You get me my first cousin and it's broken."

"She's her mother's daughter," I say to Johnny.

"Wendy, stop. Be nice to Elroy." Johnny says to the backseat.

"Sorry, cousin Elroy. Do you have an iPhone?"

"Uh-uh," Elroy says.

"What kind of phone do you have?"

"I do... do... don't have a phone."

"Why not?"

"Because no one ever bo... bo... bought me one."

"Daddy, phone!" she shouts, and Johnny reaches back with his iPhone.

It just amazes me what a bitch Johnny has become.

"Another short leash, I see. Do they ever give you back your balls, even for a little while? You know, so you can remember what they look like?" I ask him.

"I'm doing you a favor, here. How 'bout you lighten up."

"Here," Wendy says to Elroy and holds the phone face-up between them. "It's air hockey, two pucks."

And Wendy proceeds to beat Elroy in six straight games of air hockey, two pucks, on the ride to Johnny's house. It wouldn't be so bad, but for the trash talk. She really lays into Elroy, especially for a five-year-old. She is definitely her mother's daughter.

"I'm home!" Jane yells as she walks into the kitchen. "Oh, Jesus Christ!"

"Nice to see you, too, Jane."

"So, what, you're out now?"

"Temporary leave."

"Who's this."

"This," I say grandly, "is your nephew, Elroy."

Jane looks at him, shakes her head slowly, doesn't bother to ask.

"Stupi unca Fwank!" Timmy says from behind his mother.

"Real nice, Jane," I say and walk over to Timmy and pick him up. "I can't wait until these kids are teenagers. Say 'hi' to your cousin Elroy, Timmy."

Timmy hides his head in my neck, shy in front of strangers.

"I'm sorry, Elroy," Jane says.

"For wh… wh… what?"

"For whatever is happening to you. Do you want something to drink?"

"Not going to comment on the stutter, Jane? Do you want Elroy to step out of the room so that you're more comfortable talking about him?"

"I see you've matured a lot in that old folks' home."

"Like a fine wine."

"Johnny says you're wearing diapers now."

"Yup."

"Maybe someday stupid uncle Frank will be able to wear big boy pants like you, huh Timmy?" Jane says to the boy in my arms.

"I free," Timmy says and finally looks at Elroy.

"You're fr… fr… free?" Elroy asks.

"He's three," Jane says to Elroy, turns to me, "Is this going to be a long visit, then?"

"Sadly, no. I just wanted to stop by. Say hello. Picture you naked. And then we've got to bolt," I look her up and down, still holding her son, "Okay. Ready, Elroy?"

"Ugh. You're such a creep."

"And you're a bloodsucking harpy."

"Pig."

"Cun…"

"Hey! Hey, hey!" Johnny interrupts me, walking into the kitchen with Wendy in tow. "Get a room, you two." He takes Timmy from my arms, kisses Jane on the lips.

"Stupid uncle Frank called you a bits, Mommy," Wendy says.

"Did he, now? And what did Daddy say about that?" Jane asks, looks at Johnny.

"Nothing," Wendy replies.

"Really."

"That's not true. I told her that it wasn't a nice word. It's not the type of word that a little lady would use," Johnny says, looking at Wendy.

"And yet it's still a part of Frank's vocabulary," Jane says.

"I only acted like a little lady when that's what you asked for, kinky McGee," I say.

"Honestly, could you guys please…" Johnny whines.

"Fine. Car keys?" He throws them to me. "Always a pleasure, Johnny." I give the kids a kiss, look at Jane. "Bits." She smiles, mouths two words at me. I give her a thumbs-up.

"Bye," Elroy says to everyone at once and we walk out the door.

My car is around back, on the lawn off the edge of the driveway. It's still got a half-tank of gas and starts up fine after six months of rest. Johnny should have covered it up, but I don't want to go back in and complain. Elroy climbs into the front seat.

"Nice ca…ca… car," he says, petting the dashboard. I push a button and the ragtop automatically unfolds. What a day. How much have I missed this car, this whole world around me?

"Can you drive a stick?" I ask, and Elroy rolls his eyes. "You've got to be able to drive a car with manual transmission, E. When you're old enough to drive, I mean. No woman will ever respect a man that can't drive a stick."

Elroy

I know it's stupid, but it made me feel really good when Frank told that little girl, Wendy, that I could be her cousin. And I'm telling myself that I'd better watch it. How good I've been feeling, I mean. Like I shouldn't get too attached to Frank, too used to this feeling. Because I just met him on Wednesday and it's only Saturday and he's obviously insane so there's no telling when all of this could be pulled out from under my feet. But it's just so good to feel like I'm a part of something, instead of how I usually feel, which is like I'm hanging around where I don't belong.

Even at Johnny's house, which was obviously awkward with the way that Frank and Johnny's wife talk to each other, I still felt more welcome than I do, say, at school or at my foster home. I didn't feel like, given the choice, I'd rather run away. I felt like I was happy enough, right where I was. Like I wouldn't really want to be anywhere else. Which is hardly ever the way I feel.

And now I'm speeding back to town in a Chevy Camaro ZL1 convertible, triple black with oversized quad pipes. Like I'm the coolest kid in the entire world. Frank's driving like an escaped convict on the outside edge of a police manhunt. Getting the feel of the car again, he tells me. And part of me is hoping we crash spectacularly, so hard that there's nothing left but dust and smoke, because I'd be fine if this excellent moment were the last of my life. Because there's not much chance it's ever going to get any better than this.

Frank is shout-talking at me over the wind. I don't look over at him because every time I look over at him he looks back at me, right in the eye. And we're hair-pinning turns and doing single lane passes and even maybe catching air sometimes, and I think he should be keeping his eyes on the road. So, I just stare straight ahead, point at my ears, shake my head, and thoroughly enjoy the adrenaline rush of what I consider to be my first near-death experience.

We're back in no time and I'm expecting Frank to just drop me at my house, but he pulls over onto the side of Main Street and stops the car.

"Dude, what I was trying to tell you in the car is that I'm sorry if that whole thing at my brother's house was weird for you. There's some history there. Jane and I used to date, like a decade ago. And she hates me because she wanted too much from me in a pretty short amount of time, so I cut her off completely. Hard stop. Which probably didn't make her feel too good about herself. And I hate her because I think she's ruining my brother and she cuts out my legs with my niece and nephew. So, I apologize for dragging you into it, okay?"

"Frank. Honestly. This has ma… ma… maybe been the best day of my whole life."

Frank looks at me, trying to figure out whether I'm being sarcastic, and when he realizes that I am totally serious, I can see something in his eyes. Then I think he throws up in his mouth. Which is something that everyone does sometimes. The trick is to make sure you get it back down, instead of letting it spew through your lips. But he swallows it, like the hero he is. And then he looks back at the road.

"The day's not over yet, bud," he says. And we pull away from the curb.

Frank

Okay, so I'm being honest, here. This kid, Elroy. He, like, totally crushes my heart.

And, really, that doesn't happen often. Almost all the time, crushing my heart would be like trying to make wine by stomping on a raisin. I'm a pretty hard-edged loner, if you haven't picked up on that yet. But when I try to give him a bro-apology for the awkwardness at Johnny's house, and he comes back at me with how this might have been the best day of his life? And he's not being ironic or anything? I almost sob right in front of him. I swear, it's like I'm eight years old and they just shot Ol' Yeller. Which is maybe the last time I'd let out an impetuous sob, I think.

It's like with the breakfast sandwiches. A perfect example, it illustrates exactly what I'm talking about. It's like, relativity, you know? Used to be, I didn't believe in relativity, just like I don't believe in squirrels. Things just exist. What things are has nothing to do with how they compare to other things. Relativity is just a human invention that helps us think we can understand the world and the universe. Like time and space. We humans made it up. Fit the universe into a vacuum that our human minds can understand. Or at least that's what I've thought for a long time.

But really, for me, Elroy actually proves the theory of relativity. Because I don't fold over in ecstasy when I drink fresh-squeezed orange juice or eat a Starbucks breakfast sandwich. I don't consider the crap of today to be one of the best days of my life, even with my epiphany and all. But Elroy does. So, the depth of greatness is all relative to a person's experience, I guess.

"The day's not over yet, bud." I say as I pull the Camaro away from the curb.

"Where no... no... now?" Elroy asks.

"Well, kid, I was going to bring you back to your foster home. But then I recognized a flaw in my logic. See, when we ditched Severs after church, I figured that was the first step in ditching him for good, right? I'm mean, he'll be around tomorrow, sure. But as of today, we've set a precedent where it's alright for you to come to the nursing home without him. Solo, I mean. And so, on the back of that thought, I called my brother so I could get my car and leave it parked at the facility. What I figured was, for our outings, I could just pick you up at your foster home instead of you coming out here to get me."

"Yeah, but what about me signing you out? And then signing you back in, when we get back?" Elroy asks.

"Exactly. That's where I totally blanked. It happens. So now, we've got to set it up so that I can coordinate with you directly, and you can get out to the home to sign me out and in."

"So how do we do that?"

"We're gonna get you a phone and we're gonna get you a bike. We're going to outfit you for on-demand travel." I'm about to say "just like a real chauffeur," but then I look at his over-brimming eyes.

Elroy

I'm getting a bike. And a phone.

Sally

You know how in movies, when women get pissed off, they sometimes chop off all their hair? Yeah, well I just did that. How you like me now, Mom?

Frank

So, I'm totally negotiating against myself here. And I've negotiated enough programming contracts, and I know myself well enough, to understand that what I am doing is totally counter-productive to my original goals. Here's how it goes down at the bike shop.

"Alright, we're not gonna go overboard here, Elroy. We just want something functional. No bells and whistles. Just something that can get you to and from the managed care facility. With enough safety to avoid a lawsuit."

"Look! This one's perfect. And it's the cheapest one they have," Elroy shouts.

"Okay. We don't have to go with the cheapest one they have," I say. "The cheapest one is usually a sucker bet. Let's just work backwards from what we need, and what we need is value, not just cheap."

"Okay, well, they have more used bikes behind the shop."

"We're not getting a used bike. If we get a used bike today, we might as well set up an appointment for next week because we'll have to come back and get another bike. Because the one we would have bought today fell apart." I wave over a sales associate and he steps up. "Hey, man. We're looking for a commuter bicycle. One to get this kid maybe two miles back and forth to where he's going. Maybe six or seven days a week."

"I'm Bill," the sales associate says, extending his hand, which I ignore.

"I don't do first names with sales people, dude. Just find me the best quality for what we need, at the best price, because there are other bike stores." When I play, I play hardball.

"I think I've got exactly what you're looking for," Bill says and leads us over to a rack of bikes hanging from the ceiling. He describes and I reject. Many times.

Elroy just stands there, watching, saying how we don't need this or that. The kid clearly does not know how to buy a bike. We get to the end of the rack.

"Okay, so compared with Cannondale Elite's race geometry, this Cannondale Synapse 8W Claris 2015 Road Bike has a taller head tube, and a gently sloping top tube, a slightly headed angle and a longer wheel base. What does that mean? It means a combination that provides a more upright riding position and a lively, yet stable feel. So it will inspire confidence and at the same time will allow him to relax while avoiding the sluggish feel and awkward handling of most 'comfort' road bikes," Bill recites. They must make him memorize this stuff.

"We'll take it," I say.

"What?! It's ni... ni... nineteen hundred dollars," Elroy whines. "Let's go back and lo... lo... look at the used bikes, just for a minute."

"Elroy, we're not buying a bike for tomorrow or next week. I don't want to come back here and shell out another few hundred dollars when some used piece of crap or cheap China tin can clunks out. You'll never go wrong investing in quality. Remember that."

"Well said, sir," Bill remarks.

"Frank, I can st... st... steal a bike. I can st... st... steal a bike from here, right out back. And they'd never catch me. And even if they do, wh... wh... what would happen. I'm a foster kid. They're not gonna put me in ja... ja... jail."

"Hey, now!" Bill says to Elroy.

"Sc... sc... screw off, dude! Frank, you're not going to buy me a nineteen-hundred-dollar bike. I ca... ca... can't take care of something like that!"

"We'll take it," I say to Bill.

"Great," Bill says. "So I assume you're going to need a helmet?"

"No," Elroy says, "we don't need a helmet."

"Kid," Bill says to Elroy, but looks at me, "New Jersey State Law says that everyone under seventeen-years-old needs to wear a helmet when they ride a bike."

"So, get him a good helmet," I say. "Not, like, a hair-top or anything fancy, just a good, safe helmet."

"I recommend our best seller. Top-of-the-line safety at an affordable price. Color?"

"Black," I say. "He's not a girl."

"And a lock?" Bill asks.

"Yeah," Elroy says, like we've hit on something important to him, something he's finally ready to spend my money on, "A bi… bi… big lock. If we invest in anything, it should be se… se… security."

"We have a SpyBike GPS tracker for one-hundred-fifty-three dollars, not including the pay-as-you-go SIM card. It's like a LoJack for bikes. You can track it anywhere."

"We'll take it," Elroy says.

"Uh, dude? One-hundred-fifty-three dollars for bike security?" I ask.

"Get me a ch… ch… cheap bike and a ch… ch… cheap lock, that's fine. But you're ki… ki… killing me, here. If you want to spend nineteen-hundred dollars on this thing, then we've got to invest in se… sec… security. I guarantee, a bike like this, it's going to get st… st… stolen, probably before Monday."

"Sounds like he knows what he's talking about," I say to Bill and hand him my credit card. So, I drop over twenty-three hundred bucks at the bike shop. The whole time, Elroy arguing with me to spend less, me arguing with Elroy in a way that ends up costing me more. A very backward negotiation. It's not much better at the Apple Store across the street.

"Are we married now?" I ask Elroy as we walk the store. "Because this is how married couples talk to each other. Are we a married couple?"

"No," Elroy says.

"Have you ever bought a piece of daily-use technology before? Like, in your life?"

"No," Elroy says.

"So how about you let me do the thinking, here? Huh?"

"Fine," Elroy says.

"You want last year's model. For what? To save some hundred-and-twenty dollars? The iPhone Seven is worth twice as much as the Six. What? You want to just throw my money away?"

"No, Frank. The Seven is great."

"Damn straight, it's great," I say to Elroy and turn to the tattoo-covered Apple Store hipster chick. "We'll take it. Give me a case, black, and whatever normal accessories, too. And I want to add it as another line on my Verizon account, can you do that from here?"

"We can do it from the Verizon site, as long as you've got your account information."

"Great. Let's do it then."

Just like the bike store. I've successfully negotiated with Elroy, against myself, on behalf of Elroy. And he's not playing me. He's really uncomfortable with the amount of money I'm spending. Like the perfect wife. But, whatever. He's got transportation and communication. And I've got six months of relative flexibility, not to mention a newfound purpose to reform the Catholic Church, so who's complaining? Aside from Elroy, I mean, who can't believe how much money we just spent.

"Okay, dude," I say, outside the Apple store. "Good day, right?"

"Wow," Elroy says, shaking his head, "You know I know that this stuff is yours, right? Like, you own it and I'm just using it, right?"

"Look, man, if you're more comfortable thinking about it that way, then fine. Whatever floats your boat."

I take his phone, tap in my number, hit the call button, answer my phone, hang up. I go to recent calls, add contact "FRANK" from my number, stick it into his Favorites. Then I do the same with his number on my phone.

"Okay," I say. "You're all set. You can figure out the thumbprint access and the apps and stuff on your own. It's all pretty intuitive."

"I'll figure it out," Elroy says.

"Cool. Well, Elroy, this is where we part. You can get home on the bike from here?"

"Yeah, it's only a few blocks."

"Great. So, remember, when we see Severs tomorrow, none of this stuff happened, right? You spent the afternoon reading to me. Maybe we spent a little quality time, hating each other in silence. And then I stuck you in a taxi. We cool?" Elroy nods. "Great. I'll see you tomorrow when you guys pick me up, then?"

"Yeah," Elroy says, and then his eyes get all wet and brimming. "Hey, Frank…" and suddenly my eyes are stinging, too, and there is no way I'm going to emotionally unravel right now. Not here on the street in front of the Apple Store. No way.

So I interrupt him by putting my hand up, palm out, fingers splayed, directly in front of his face. The classic STOP gesture. It looks like I'm giving him "the Heisman." And I imagine what I'm doing looks pretty rude to the other people on the street. But whatever. Things were about to get mushy, like, out of nowhere. I walk to my car, get in and drive away.

Elroy

So, I walk the bike seven blocks to my foster home. Because, naturally, I don't know how to ride a bike. Even though I'm twelve.

But it makes sense, right? I mean, who would have taught me? What would I have practiced on? There isn't some foster kid supply house where they've got samples of all the stuff a normal kid has, where we can learn about this normal kid stuff, like how to use it. Of course there isn't. So why does everyone just naturally assume that I should know how to ride a bike?

Oh my god. I have a bike. And a phone. I wish I had someone to call. Other than Frank, I mean. I don't want to start bugging him and I don't really have anything specific to ask him because he only just left and he totally doesn't seem like the type who likes to chat on the phone. So, I just walk home with the bike, checking corners and alleys, as if there might be robbers waiting to ambush me. The bike is, like, feather-light when I carry it up the front stairs of my foster home.

"Who's that?" Mrs. Jones squawks from the living room when I pull my bike in the front door.

"It's just me, Mrs. Jones."

"Me, who?"

"Me, Elroy."

"Elroy?"

"The foster kid. I'm living here?"

"Oh, fine, son. Fine," she says. "Elroy. You're home from school early today."

It's five pm and it's Saturday.

"Yeah, they let us out early, for Valentine's Day."

"Oh, my! Valentine's Day! My mind must be slipping. It seems to come earlier every year. I'll go bake a cake for you and Mr. Jones."

She hobbles into the kitchen. I'd stop her, from baking the cake, I mean, because it's totally not Valentine's Day. But I'm pretty sure that by the time she gets to the kitchen, she'll forget what she went in there for in the first place.

I haul my bike up the stairs, try to find a place for it in my room where it's out of the way. But the room is so small. It's like all bed. With a little desk at the foot of the bed under the window. And these, like, stacks of newspapers. So, I'm going to have to climb around this bike to get to my drawers and closet, to walk in and out of the room. But I so totally don't care because this bike is probably worth more than everything else in the house combined.

I lean my bike against the closet door. I take the plastic tie-string Apple bag to the desk. I unpack the contents, appreciating all of the innovative Apple packaging as I do so. I plug it into the charger. I don't have a computer and there's no Wi-Fi in the house, so I can't get to the iTunes account that we set up for me in the Apple store.

I go to the app store from the phone, download a free version of Air Hockey. I launch the app, select one-player, and spend the next four hours mastering the game. Next time I see Wendy Johnson, that little five-year-old is dead meat.

Sally

"There's a frozen pizza in the ice box. You can make it your... Oh, good Lord! What did you do to your head?"

"I'm in mourning, Mom. Get over it."

"My God, Sweet Jesus, Holy Virgin Mother."

"And-a-partridge in a pear-tree," I sing. "Like it?"

"Sally. Why?"

"I felt like it."

"Oh, Sally, how could you? You look like one of those punk rock people or some kind of devil worshiper. You don't live in an orphanage. Why do you have to make yourself look like you live in an orphanage? Your hair was so beautiful."

"It's still beautiful. Upstairs on the bathroom floor. Feel free, it's all yours."

"Well, I'm not going to talk about how this is going to make everyone at church think that I'm a bad mother, make them think that I can't raise my own daughter. And I'm not going to tell you how people are going to be worried about getting counseling and guidance and prayer help from a woman who can't even raise her own daughter properly. And I'm sure you know, so I don't have to say it, that I slave every day helping people at the church and you are making it even harder for me to do my work. And I know you don't care about me, but what about the people I help? Did you think of them? Did it ever occur to you that there are people who wouldn't be able to get out of bed in the morning unless they knew that I was there to counsel them, to pray with them? I'm their rock. And I'm fine giving my life to my calling. But did you ever ask yourself what mutilating your head would make these people think? How it would affect their trust in me, their impression of me? You've not only damaged yourself, but you've also damaged my reputation and the people that I help. And it's hard enough already, Lord knows. Why do you have to make it even harder? Do you think I do what I do just to make myself feel good?"

"Yes, actually, that's exactly why I think you do what you do."

"You would think that, wouldn't you?"

"Yes. And I do."

"Well, I'm not going to argue with you. Go ahead and make the world an ugly place, if that's what you want. Go ahead and hurt my reputation, give me another load to bear. Go ahead and work out your teenage aggression. If you need a place to put it, put it on me."

"I'm twelve."

"It won't make any difference, you know. I can bear it. That's what I'm here for. You might make me cry, but I can take it."

"That's great, thanks. Did you say something about a frozen pizza?"

"Someday you'll understand me. You'll see everything that I do for you. And it scares me to think how bad it will make you feel."

"I already understand you. And, yeah, bad is how I feel. Though probably not in the same way you want me to feel bad."

"Why would I ever want you to feel bad, Sally?"

"I don't know, to help you feel better about yourself?"

"Nonsense. Does it make you feel good, being so hateful to me?"

"No."

"Then why do you do it?"

"Just killing time, Mom," I say, walk into the kitchen to heat myself the frozen pizza.

"I've made an appointment for you to talk to Father Mcloughlin, tomorrow after mass," Mom calls out from the other room a couple minutes later. "You'll have to bike to church and back because I've got to be there early for a prayer group for the elderly, and I have to do some committee stuff after mass."

"That's fine!" I shout back from the kitchen.

Elroy

"Hey!" I say.

"Hey. I just want to check to see if the new phone is working," Frank says. It's nine pm.

"It's gr... gr... great!"

"Are you too young to know who Tony the Tiger is?" Frank asks.

"From, like, fr... fr...Frosted Flakes?" I ask, hesitate, then understand the lame joke, "Oh, yeah. Fu... fu... funny."

"Listen, kid. I just wanted to give you a heads-up. When you guys pick me up tomorrow, I'm going to be, like, mentally preparing myself for something. So I'm going to be, like, quiet and distant, okay? But we can talk after mass, alright? I just didn't want you to think that I was acting weird because of anything you did."

"Sure. I pr... pr... probably would have thought that."

And I would have. If Frank was acting distant and I didn't know why, especially after he bought me the bike and the phone, then I would have been a wreck the whole time at church. But what's really cool is the fact that he thought of this, too. To the point where he actually called me on my new iPhone. I'm trying to think if anyone has ever cared that much about me. I don't think so.

"Thanks, Frank. I me... me... mean it. For everything."

"Big day tomorrow, kid. Sleep well," he says, hangs up.

I close up Air Hockey, leave my new iPhone plugged in, get into bed. I'm smiling when I go to sleep. I think that's maybe another first.

Sally

I wince when I look at what's left of my hair in the mirror. Maybe I took this thing a little too far.

~ *I used to feel like that when I cut myself. I'd get, like, lost in the process of carving myself up, because once you start, it doesn't really hurt. And then when I came out of it, the process, I mean, it always freaked me out. And when I looked in the mirror later, I would be all like, eww-ouch! I'd physically cringe. It was like I didn't recognize myself. I mean, I recognized myself in the mirror, but I couldn't recognize what it was in myself that made me want to do something like that. You know?*

~ You're kind of stealing my thunder here, Aunt Sadie. I mean, all I did was cut my hair. I didn't even shave it. I could probably even go to a stylist and they could fix it and it could still be pretty cute. It's not like I took a straight razor to my own skin. And don't get me wrong. I'm not saying that it wasn't cool, how you used to cut yourself. I think it was super cool. I just don't think I could ever do it, you know. I'm not as brave as you. Or maybe I'm not as desperate as you. Or maybe a combination of both.

~ *It's not a contest, you weirdo.*

~ Aunt Sadie, sorry to say, but you calling me a weirdo doesn't carry too much weight.

~ *You still make me laugh.*

~ You still make me cry. Especially at night, when I go to bed. The rest of the day I can usually just pretend to myself that you're still down in South Carolina, that I'm going to see you again sometime.

~ *That's a serious glass-is-half-full attitude you got there, missy. We never used to talk like this when I was still alive. Even when we talked on the phone and you used to think it was the closest you've ever been with someone, it wasn't like this.*

~ Maybe. But at least you were alive. There was still the potential that I'd feel this way with someone, like, in real life. This is really nice. It is. But you're a voice in my head. And I don't ever want you to leave or anything, but it's different than having something this close with, like, a living person. No offense.

~ *Do you know what it would take to offend me?*

~ Fair point. So, what? You just show up like this, whenever you feel like it. So, do you have any advice you can give me? A message from beyond or something? Because I'm way open to anything right now. While I'm still alive. I'm wide open to pretty much anything, I mean, before I do it. Before I get around to killing myself. So, do you have anything for me?

~ *My advice? Just stay way, wide open. Not just to anything, but about anything. I'm not saying you shouldn't kill yourself – I mean, coming from me? But maybe, while you're still, like, in the world, maybe you let everything be a lot more fluid – what you're going to do, what kind of relationships you want to have, what's bad about your mother or what was good about your father, or me. Maybe, you try not to have a ridged opinion about anything. Maybe, you just let happen, happen. For a little while, at least. Oh, and I advise you to get your hair fixed. You don't look good like that.*

I pick up the scissors that I'd used earlier. Smooth out some of the lawnmower spots, round off some of the edges. When I'm done, I still look awful. But not so much struck-by-lightening, cancer patient awful. More like, really-bad-fashion-decision awful. Implying not that this bad hair happened to me, but instead that I happened to it.

Frank

Game day!

And a beautiful Sunday morning it is. I scroll up the shades, pull the window wide open, breathe in the dewy, fresh-cut grass. Go to my bathroom, throw up. Surprised that there's so much solid food in my stomach, having been given the opportunity to digest all night.

But, hey! It's time to jump in. You know what you have to do, Frankie boy, so just turn off the mind and let your unconscious guide you.

I shower, powder my nethers, pull on a fresh diaper. Three deep-knee bends. A push-up. Jumping in place, shaking it out. I swan-dive into a burpee, my left shoulder and chest plate taking almost all of the impact, and stopping, I believe, my heart on the point of impact. Everything so much grey-metal pain, like the worst headache ever is actually the whole universe around me. Like a kick in the groin from God. But it fades and I breathe and the beating heart comes back. Probably a purple bruise from chin to chest, but no long-term damage, and all will be covered when I'm dressed.

I'm feeling manic. I know the feeling. I've had this feeling before. Unfortunately, Johnny's litany of my failed causes runs through my head because before each, I'd felt just like this. I'm sure there were other times, too. More successful times I've felt like this. I just can't think of any.

If I had booze, I'd do a couple of shots. Tone it down, you know? But I don't have booze. They don't let you have booze in here. So, I've been hoarding Nyquil – in a pretty disgusting way, actually. Whenever I can fake a cold to the point where they'll medicate me at night, I sip the dose of Nyquil from the corrugated white paper cup, smile at the nurse, hold it, and eventually spit the dose into a bottle of Snapple that I'd emptied for this specific purpose. It's almost full, the Snapple bottle. But I'd be stoned out of my mind if I knocked back sixteen ounces of Nyquil and my own spit. At least half of it is Nyquil, I imagine. Anyway, I want to be sharp for today. I don't want to be a buffoon.

Today isn't something that I want to get through. Today is something that I want to make happen. I mean I want to be there for it.

Elroy and Severs pick me up, we drive to the church, arrive early. Early enough for me to take an aisle seat, front row. I tell Elroy and Severs to give me some space and they do. Elroy, because he knows I've got something planned. Severs, because he doesn't want to be around me anyway. And the church fills up. A family of four, led by a jacket-and-tie dad, step up to my pew. I stand, nod, smile. I step out and let them into the pew, then take back my spot on the aisle.

A pointy-nosed little woman, brown bun streaked grey, teacher glasses, steps up to the podium. Makes some announcements about what Sunday it is in Ordinary Time, what readings we'll be listening to and such. I don't know if anyone is actually listening to this church lady, don't know why they would. And that pumps me up, reconfirms my intentions, steels my resolve.

Then the procession, formal and weighty. The Introductory Rites, the Act of Penance, where everyone grovels in rote speak, Glory to God in the Highest. The Liturgy of the Word, Old Testament, psalm. The New Testament, a reading from the letter of Saint Paul to the Colossians. That's just perfect. There is a stillness when we "Thanks be to God." Perfunctory, bored, the type of once-a-week gloom that passes for holy these days. I should have worn my lemmings t-shirt, it would fit me now, what with the weight I've lost at the nursing home. And I'm feeling just like I felt in the boys' room, naked, right before I streaked down the hallway of my middle school so many years ago.

Well, I think, here goes...

I step out of the pew, genuflect, march formally up to the hand-microphone on the altar like it's exactly what I'm supposed to be doing. I catch Rory's eye, give him a wink, a thumbs-up. He's not sure whether to get up and say something, or what. I grab the mic from the altar stand, turn and face the congregation. While certainly not the orthodox routine, none of this appears unplanned to anyone in the church.

Aside from Rory. And I'm thinking that I should have recommended the adult diapers when I spoke to him yesterday because it looks like they'd come in handy about now.

"So, I want to start by saying how great it is to be here talking to you on what is shaping up to be a really beautiful Sunday afternoon…"

Elroy

Oh. My. God.

Sally

So, I wake up and Mom's already left the house because it's, like, after ten and she's got such important stuff to do at the church every Sunday. And I think about bailing on church, maybe just watching standard cable all day. But I've been there, done that, too many times. And I think about the amount of stuff that Mom tells me she isn't going to tell me after I do something like skip mass. And the thought of it tortures me into submission. At least, I figure, it will give me a chance to show off my new hairdo.

So, I ride my bike to church, take a seat in the back where there's plenty of space. Mom does the announcements, which is a proud community moment for her that means something to, like, nobody else. And then I zone out. I try to channel Aunt Sadie for a chat, but it's like the reception's not so good in church. Not Aunt Sadie's favorite place, I guess.

I'm half out-of-body after the Gospel, planning to go full on zazen for the Homily, when this guy steps out of the first pew at the front of the church, walks to the altar, picks up the microphone. So, my first thought is, okay, it's like a Knights of Columbus, a Right to Life speech asking for money, or volunteers for a march, or something. But it isn't.

"So, I want to start by saying, how great it is to be here talking to you on what is shaping up to be a really beautiful Sunday afternoon," the guy says into the microphone, beaming at all of us church-going folk. And I look over at Father Mcloughlin, like all his blood was replaced with skim milk, he's that pale. And maybe I'm one of the few people in church right now that figures things may be going off the rails.

"Well, I guess I know most of you from church and stuff, but for anyone that doesn't know me, my name is Frank Johnson. Of the Middletown Johnsons."

I've been coming to this church since baptism and have never seen this guy before in my life. Clever ploy, making it seem like people know him. Ballsy. It should buy him a little time. For what, I have no idea.

"And I was talking to my friend, Rory, yesterday," he points at the altar, "you know, Father Mc…uh, you know what? Let's just keep it to Rory for today, how about that? Because the fact is, people, we're not all friends here. Not really, we're not. And we should be."

And I'm thinking, this could be interesting.

"Maybe we know each other," the guy continues. "Maybe we only know *of* each other. But we're not *really* connected, you know? We should be like family, here. But we're not. And maybe, I don't know, maybe we're not even family with our own families at home. You know what I mean? You know what I mean, I know you do. And that's what me and Rory were talking about yesterday. How that's not the way people should live. How that's not what people who gather as part of a community, like the church, should feel about each other. And we were talking about how we're going to change it. How we're going to fix it, I mean."

He hasn't started shooting anyone yet, which I guess is a good thing.

"What is it that me and Rory were really talking about yesterday? Does anyone want to take a guess?" this guy continues, pacing the aisle like a Baptist preacher. "No? Alright, well, I'll tell you what we were talking about yesterday. We were talking about intimacy. Intimacy, people! I. N. T… ah, I. M…? Anyway, we were talking about closeness. About relationships. Not just standing in the same room with other people, being polite, being socially acceptable. We were talking about relationships with a capital 'R.' And, I hate to say it, but that is something that you don't see too much of, these days. Now I don't want to shake you guys up, I don't want to sound too radical here, but hear me out – because me and Rory, we were talking about the church. And how the church has let us down. Wait a second. Wait a second," he says and pats the air in front of him, calming the nay-sayers, as it were, though no one in the congregation has moved a muscle.

Father Mcloughlin is still in his chair, short scissoring his arms horizontal to the floor, shaking his head side-to-side, as if to say, no, this lunatic and I were not actually having this talk yesterday. But no one in the church is looking at Father Mcloughlin. Except me. And my guess is that everyone still thinks that this was all planned, a visiting speaker, who is eventually going to ask for something on behalf of the church.

"Just wait one second, people. Because me and Rory, we're not blaming anyone. I'll tell you what, if you want to blame someone, then you can blame me. Ah will take full responsibility for the fact that we all don't feel any real intimacy towards each other, even here, in this here Catholic Church!"

Okay, now I'm detecting a Southern drawl, which wasn't there when he started talking.

"Because ah have witnessed it! From the time ah was but a wee child! Ah witnessed our sin of omission on every Sunday of the month! And that sin, what we omitted, people, what we omitted, was intimacy! We come together and stand around each other like statues. And we don't talk. No, we don't. We repeat. We recite. We bow and kneel just like we weren't any more alive than the dust motes all over this dirty floor. Oh, yeah-ya. You heard me. And it's true. Because we all know it's far, far easier to do the expected thing, as opposed to the right thing. So what do ah meen bah that? Huh? Anyone? Well than ahl tell ya wat ah meen…"

Here the guy freezes for a second, maybe hearing himself. Maybe recognizing the fact that he's gone way too far into that deep Southern drawl. That he's starting to talk in a way that would make Foghorn Leghorn sound like a Yankee. And just then, at that moment, that's where he gains my respect. Because just when he realizes that he's gone too far, right when he's so obviously overplayed his hand, well, he just flat-out pretends it never happened. He just corrects it and goes right on with his talk.

Well played, sir.

"What I mean is, we all know it's a lot easier to dress the way you think you should dress, and to repeat the things that you've always been told to say, and to go through the motions of having the appropriate dose of holy in your lives, the way you've been taught since you were kids... It's a lot easier to do all that, isn't it, than it is to really open yourself up and be vulnerable with the people around you. Think about it! Jesus didn't want worship. He wanted intimacy! He wanted vulnerability. He wanted to celebrate the God that's inside every one of us. And by celebrate, ah do not mean to go through some bor-in ritchuall, rah-peat many tahms watchall think yours supposed tah saigh..."

It's been, like, five more sentences and he is deep in the South again. Wow. This is, without a doubt, the best service that I've ever been to. But again, like a hero, he catches himself. Clears his throat. Goes on like the whole drawl thing never happened. Outstanding gamesmanship.

"What I'm saying is... what Rory and I were talking about yesterday... is that it's so much easier to go through the motions, you know, like a train on rails, than it is to recognize that there's something unique and special inside of every one of us. Not just the people around you, but inside of you, yourself, too. Especially inside of yourself. If you don't recognize it inside of yourself, there's no way you're going to be able to recognize it in anyone else. And recognizing what's like God inside yourself, that takes bravery. Because the like-God in you doesn't always look so holy. In fact, mostly, the like-God you've been hiding deep down inside looks a little freaky. It might look weird. Something maybe you're ashamed of, something you'd maybe never show to the world."

I am *so* intrigued with where this is going.

"And this church here, this building we're in, it shouldn't be a place where you hush your voices. Where you repeat prescribed phrases. Where you lip-sync hymns and psalms. This building is where

141

you should feel secure enough to expose yourself, expose all that weird secret Godness inside of you. And it's not like I'm talking about pulling out your junk or flashing your flesh, but you know what? If that's something you want to do it, then go for it! Because, here, this is where you should let what's inside out. This is where you should unfurl that freak flag and let it fly! Because real community – really communing with other people, I mean – it's about knowing yourself and loving yourself and then letting yourself out in a space where you can be vulnerable. Where you can feel vulnerable and at the same time, you can feel accepted. And where the people around you can be vulnerable and accepted, too. Where you can get past what society thinks is right or wrong, and we can all just accept each other the way we really are. Because there is no ugly. And there is no wrong. And perversion is just a word we made up. There is only this God-spark, buried deep in every one of us. And this house, our house, is where we should be able to make it okay – no, we should be able to make it necessary – to expose that little bit of God inside of us, regardless that we're scared of what it will look like. Regardless of what society thinks is normal! Don't pray to Jesus! Be like Jesus! Expose yourself as the freak you are! And be okay with it, here, in your community. Be willing to die for it, even. Because that's what Jesus was all about. That's what he really died for. That's how he tried to save our souls. He tried to save our souls by example. But first, you've got to find your soul to save, and you got to let it all hang out!"

Huh! Some of that actually made some sense. And then I'm thinking, don't ruin it, dude. Just walk off. But he holds the microphone straight out from his body.

"Johnson, out!" and he drops the microphone onto the floor with a resonating clang. Just like a rapper. He looks at Father Mcloughlin. "Captain Rory, you take'em home," he shouts, mic-less, loud enough for me to hear all the way in the back of the church.

And then he walks down the center aisle and out the big wooden doors of the church.

So, I figure, what the hell? I start to clap. I clap and I stand up and I keep clapping. And after a few seconds, maybe about a third of the church joins me, though I'm not sure if it's, like, herd mentality or something. I'm not sure if anyone is really clapping because of what he just said, or if these people are just clapping because they think it's the appropriate response.

Elroy

Oh, my God. That was awesome.

Frank walks straight out the doors at the back of the church, doesn't look at us when he passes. Dr. Severs and I just stare at each other. And Dr. Severs has a look, like, somehow he's going to get in trouble for this. And like, for reals, the RMSOC pretty much did force Frank to go to church. Twice in the past thirty-six hours. And so, now, Frank goes all nut-job preacher on the congregation at Sunday mass. Yeah, that would be the fault of the RMSOC. Pretty cut and dry.

"It wasn't that bad, huh?" Dr. Severs ask me. The priest, up on stage, has mechanically restarted the mass because what else is he going to do at this point? Not even an acknowledgement of what just happened.

"Well, he did tell everyone to ex... ex... expose themselves in church," I whisper. "More than once."

"Yeah, but it totally depends on how you want to interpret that," Dr. Severs whispers back. "And anyway, some people clapped."

"You better sa... sa... say something, like at the end of mass."

"What? I'm not going to say anything. Why would *I* say something?"

"You know, like a di... di... disclaimer. Like, the op... op... opinion expressed by the crazy guy does not re... re... reflect the views of the RMSOC, or something."

"Yeah, man. I mean, I don't really have anything prepared." Obviously.

"Or we could ju... ju... just get out of here," I say.

"Yeah, that's the right idea," Dr. Severs whispers, looking around. "Give things a chance to settle, you know?"

We turn, slip out the back door of the church.

Frank is pacing in the parking lot, flexing his hands from fists to spread fingers, like he's charged up with electricity. And I'm thinking practically—at least on the surface—about how he's going to play this with Dr. Severs. About how he wants me to play this whole thing in front of Dr. Severs. We didn't discuss the fact that he was going to hijack the church service, much less how I am supposed to act in the aftermath. We probably should have talked about it on the phone last night.

But Dr. Severs unexpectedly saves the day. Without a word, he walks right past Frank, opens the driver side front door of the car, gets in.

"I got to run a quick errand, be back in a couple of minutes," Dr. Severs says after rolling down the driver-side window. Then he takes off.

"What's that all about?" Frank asks, still pacing and flexing his hands.

"I don't kn... kn... know. Maybe he's going to dr... dr... drive around the block and smoke pot or something."

Frank stops, shrugs, nods and then goes back to pacing and flexing.

"Okay," Frank says to me mid-pace, "was it too much?"

"No, it was gr... gr... great," I say. "But first, before Dr. Severs gets back, how are we su... su... supposed to act, right now?"

"Oh, yeah, good point," Frank says, stops pacing. "I didn't think about that. God, I'm so pumped up right now. You have to tell me what it was like. I can't even remember anything I said."

"Okay, I wi... wi... will, but before Dr. Severs gets back..."

"Yeah. You're right. Well, you know, I guess we just get back into character. I don't like you and you don't like me, right?"

"Sure," I say. "Then?"

"Then, okay, then you guys drive me back to the home, right? And when you drop me off, you come and sign me in, just like yesterday. So we're setting a precedent, right? God, this adrenaline rush is insane. So, then you let Dr. Severs bring you back home, then you take your new bike back out to the home, okay? You'll be able to sign me out and we'll take it from there," Frank says just as Dr. Severs pulls back into the parking lot.

Severs has rolled down all of the car windows, even the back-seat windows, which must have been some trick because they're all manual and he's only been gone, like, a few minutes. He gets out of the car, stumbles, smiles.

"Sorry, I had to mail something before the post office closes," Dr. Severs says. Neither Frank nor I comment on the fact that it's Sunday. "And anyway," Dr. Severs shakes off his grin, puts on an RMSOC game face, "what in the hell was that all about?!"

"What was what, Moonbeam?"

"That whole…that thing…that, how you…"

"Get it out, Stargazer. You'll feel better when you do."

"That show you put on in church," Dr. Severs says, finally. "What are you thinking? You know you're the responsibility of the RMSOC when you're out with us. Did you even think about how that circus you put on in there is going to reflect on the Club?!"

"No, GrapeNuts, the thought honestly never entered my mind."

"Well, it should have," Dr. Severs says and steps towards Frank and points a finger right in his face.

"I might look skinny, Dreamweaver, but if you don't take that finger out of my face, I'm going to bite it right off your hand. Man, you reek of pot, too."

Dr. Severs pulls his finger back like he touched a hot stove, I think more because of the pot smell than for fear of Frank gnawing it off.

"I do not. That's a hand oil I use. It's made of hemp, so…" Dr. Severs starts to explain.

We see the priest jogging out to the parking lot, ahead of the other people leaving mass. He comes to an abrupt stop in front of the three of us, then it looks like he's not sure what he was planning to do next. But the awkward silence doesn't last two seconds before Frank breaks it.

"Rory!" Frank shouts and steps over and wraps the priest in a big, one-sided embrace. "My man!"

Father McLoughlin stands there, all rigid, doesn't say a word. People from the mass are approaching the parking lot and looking at the priest, all wrapped up in Frank's bear hug.

"Yeah, uh, look, Father," Dr. Severs says, "I'm sorry. That was unacceptable. It was, well, it was the kid's fault..."

"Wh... wh... what?"

"Well, it was," Dr. Severs says. "You're the one that wanted to bring him to church."

What a dick. Frank still hasn't let go of the priest, who is now awkwardly trying to unwind himself from the giant bear hug.

"And anyway," Dr. Severs says to the priest, "maybe the RMSOC isn't the only one that should be apologizing for something. Huh, Father?"

"Excuse me?" the priest says to Dr. Severs. He's finally unwound himself and is holding Frank by the shoulders, at arms-length. Frank is just standing there, smiling huge at him.

"I mean, we've all got stuff to be sorry about, right, Father? We've all got stuff that maybe we wish we didn't do. Maybe stuff we didn't handle in the best way."

Dr. Severs keeps looking from the priest to me. Oh, damn.

"I have no idea what you're talking about," the priest says over Frank's shoulders.

"You have no idea what I'm talking about, huh?" Dr. Severs replies, all snippy-like. "You're a priest, man. Take some responsibility. Because of you, he's like a pedophile waiting to happen." Dr. Severs waits, then makes a face, shakes his head slowly and turns back to the car. "Unbelievable," he says, climbing in the driver's side door, "really unbelievable, Father."

"I have no idea what you're talking about," the priest says, firmer now.

Aside from having no understanding about what Dr. Severs is talking about, it seems like the pedophile comment has kicked-up some instinctive paranoia in the priest, which probably comes with the collar. I take my cue from Dr. Severs, open the passenger side door, lift the seat and start to climb into the back of the car.

"Rory, don't pay any attention to that idiot. Look at me," I hear Frank say as I'm climbing in.

I turn and see Frank put his hands on the priest's sides, under his outstretched arms, so that they look like a couple on a Middle School dance floor.

"I know it was, kind of, rough around the edges. I didn't rehearse. I just felt like I had to let it happen, you know. And that thing with the Southern accent, I know," Frank laughs. "It sometimes happens when I get all wound up in front of a group. It maybe wasn't so elegant, Rory, but we're on to something here. I can feel it."

Father McLoughlin is looking at Frank like he just hit a baby in the face with a rock.

"Ah, do you, uh, need help, my son?" he says to Frank.

"You know I do, Rory. But there will be time for that. And you've got to call me Frank, Rory. Try to remember because it's important here. And now I got to go." Frank pats the priest's sides, leans in and kisses him on the cheek. "But I'll be back, Rory. Don't you worry about that. We'll get this thing off the ground, yet," he says and climbs into the passenger seat of the car.

The priest just stands there, helpless, confused.

"See you around, Casanova," Dr. Severs snarks at the priest and starts the car.

"Keep the faith, Rory!" Frank shouts out the window, waving, as the car pulls out of the parking lot.

Other people are getting into their cars, eyes on the scene we've just made. I notice a ratty-haired girl about my age, standing with her bike on the edge of the parking lot, staring at us. She sees me in the back seat. We lock eyes for a second. She smiles. I quickly look away. Very smooth.

Sally

So, I go get my bike, because there's no way I'm still having my meeting with Father Mcloughlin after what just happened. And as I ride out toward the parking lot there's the weird speaker guy, Frank Johnson, hugging Father Mcloughlin next to a piece of junk car. I'm thinking maybe this guy Johnson actually *is* working something with Father Mcloughlin. But I dismiss that thought quickly because of the way Father Mcloughlin acted after the homily, all shocked and stiff, like he was just anal-probed by aliens or something. So I stop the bike under a tree and watch the scene play out.

Father Mcloughlin is talking to this hippie-teacher type guy over Frank Johnson's hug, and I realize that it's Doctor whatever-his-name-is, the guidance counselor that started at my school last year. And he sucks, so I'm wondering what he's got to do with this Johnson guy because they don't seem like the kind of personalities that would really mesh too good, you know?

And there's this kid I don't know, just kind of standing around. And I think maybe he's just a gawker, but then he gets into the back seat of Doctor whoever's car, so he's obviously part of this, too. Then the Johnson guy kisses Father Mcloughlin. And you couldn't really tell from where I stood but it looks like it was just a peck on the cheek. Then the Johnson guy gets in the car and they drive away. I catch eyes with the kid in the back seat for a second, and then he looks away. More like he's shy than like he's being a jerk.

I don't have anything else to do so I follow the car when it leaves the parking lot. It drives slow through town but then speeds up right after Main Street turns into Route Eighty-Five, and then it gets away from me.

Frank

That went really well, I think. I can't remember everything that I said, but it feels like it went really well. Like I made an impact, I mean. What I want, though, is direct feedback from Elroy. Which I can't get until we ditch Severs.

The adrenaline is drying up and I'm feeling kind of mellow. Severs doesn't try to talk to me, maybe because he's stoned or maybe because he's afraid I'll bring up the pot smell again or maybe both. So, I hang my head out the passenger window and soak up the September sun.

We pull up to the nursing home and I pivot the front seat so that Elroy can climb out. Severs is happy to stay in the car while Elroy signs me back in.

"No detention today, then?" Dr. Severs asks. "What, you don't want to spring for another cab ride home?" he adds, implying that he will not be available to wait around or pick Elroy up if I try to make him read to me again today. Which is perfect.

"I had more than enough of Elroy yesterday. He can sign me back in and then you can take him home. Come on, kid."

Elroy groans and climbs out of the car. We walk into the home, not looking at each other. Hardy is at the front desk again, chatting with the reception nurse. Excellent. I walk by, head slumped, don't look at him, don't say goodbye to Elroy.

"Where's Dr. Severs?" Hardy asks Elroy.

"He's in the ca… ca… car," I hear Elroy reply. "He makes me come in now to sign for Mr. Johnson."

"Good for you. Builds character," Hardy says to Elroy and then shouts at my back, "How was church today, Johnson?!"

I flip him the bird over my shoulder. Back in my room I text Elroy, tell him to call me when he gets home.

Five minutes later, my cell phone rings. I say "Hey" and he says "Hey."

"Look, scope the place out when you come back, okay? Make sure Hardy isn't in the lobby. The desk nurse won't give you any trouble since Hardy was there when you signed me in. But I don't want Hardy to see us taking another excursion. It might make him suspicious. Got it?"

"Yeah," Elroy says.

"Okay, cool. I'll see you in, like, ten minutes," and I hang up.

Elroy

"Okay, cool. I'll see you in, like, ten minutes." Frank says, then he hangs up.

But he's not going to see me in ten minutes. It's going to be, like, twenty or thirty minutes. I grab the bike and carry it down the stairs, out the door of my foster home. It is a really cool bike. I feel self-conscious walking beside it on the sidewalk, because I'm worried someone's going to try and steal it. About a mile from my foster house, maybe halfway to the home, a car pulls up beside me. An older man, grey hair and golf shirt, leans over from the driver's side of his car.

"You got a flat?"

"No," I say, looking at him and then looking back at the road.

"Problem with the chain?"

"No." He continues to drive beside me.

"What's wrong with it?"

"There's no... no... nothing wrong with it," I say.

I can feel him looking me up-and-down. Maybe wondering why a kid dressed like me has a bike this awesome.

"Is that your bike, kid?"

"If I st... st... stole it, do you think I'd be just walking it down the ro... ro... road like this?"

"So why aren't you riding it?"

And I'm getting frustrated stuttering in front of this busybody, when it occurs to me that I might as well get some practice.

"Actually, sir, my father died on a bike, four years ago, today. He was hit by a drunk driver about a mile up the hill. He left my mom and me with pretty much nothing. Nothing except his wrecked bike. So I saved what money I had and I got his bike fixed. Some of it, I paid for. Some of it, I did myself. And every year, on the anniversary of his death, I walk this bike along the same roads where he had his last ride."

The guy is still driving slowly beside me, looking at me.

"That bike looks brand new," the guy says with a cynical look.

"I take really good care of it."

He looks at me as if he doesn't really believe what I'm saying. I look at him as if, whatever, it's none of your business anyway. And he drives away.

About fifteen minutes later, I U-lock the bike to an empty bike stand in front of the nursing home. I hook both the frame and the front wheel into the lock, but think I probably don't have to make the extra effort. It's not like anyone's going to steal it here at the home. And if they did, it would probably just be for a senile joyride, twenty feet and a broken hip. Still, it makes me feel safer knowing that it's properly locked up.

I stick my head in the lobby. No Mr. Hardy. I walk casually up to the front desk.

"You again," the nurse says brightly.

"Me a… a… again," I reply, glum.

"You signing out Mr. Johnson?"

"Unfortunately, yeah."

"Okay, Honey. Just sign here and I'll ring him."

Two minutes later Frank stomps into the lobby. He scans for Mr. Hardy, looks at me.

"Dr. Severs in the car?" he asks grumpily.

"Yeah," I reply.

"Come on, then."

"Bye, bye, Hon," the nurse calls as we slump out the lobby door.

"What took you so long?" Frank asks as we duck through the hedges that line the driveway, out of the sightline of the front windows.

"I got held up at home."

"How's the bike?"

"The bike is awesome."

"Is the seat height okay?"

"Perfect."

"Where's your helmet?"

Oh, right, the helmet.

"I didn't wear it. It's only a couple of miles. I didn't think it would matter."

"Well, wear it. You'll get a ticket if you don't."

"Okay, I'll keep my eye out when I ride home."

"You're really coming along with the stutter, by the way. Did you notice?"

Damnit. It didn't even occur to me I was lying about riding the bike here.

"It co… co… comes and goes. It probably helps when I do… do… don't think about it."

We get to Frank's Camaro, which is parked in the corner of the nursing home lot. He keeps the ragtop on until we're off the grounds, then pushes a button and it automatically retracts. Such a bad ass car.

"Where are we go… go… going?"

"I don't know, really. Away from the nursing home, for one. How late can you stay out?"

"No one would no… no… notice if I didn't ever come home. Se… se… seriously."

"Well, let's not allow your wretched home life to spoil a fantastic Sunday afternoon, huh? I don't have to be back until eight, but let's make sure you're not riding home in the dark."

"I don't mi… mi… mind."

"There's no light on the bike, and you don't have a helmet. Anyway, we've got plenty of time. Are you hungry?"

"Always."

"Then let's go eat and you can tell me how you thought it went at church. You like steak? There's a Ruth's Chris by my old apartment, maybe twenty minutes away. Sound good?"

"Ruth Chris's?"

"Ruth's Chris. It's a chain, but higher-end. Really good meat. They know how to cook it, too. Good wine list. What do you say?"

"Sure."

A part of me wants to make sure that Frank won't be expecting me to pay for my meal, but I'm pretty sure I know the answer and just asking would probably offend him. Plus, I've always wanted to try steak.

Frank

I don't recognize the hostess who's hard eyeballing us as we approach the podium. I'm a little scruffy, but reasonably clean. Jeans and a t-shirt, which has never been a problem for me in here before. But then I take a look at the kid, and it makes some sense. A grungy hipster comes in, not a problem. Lot of grungy hipsters with money these days. But grungy hipster comes in with a kid that looks like he just climbed out of the sewers, I can see how that might be a different story. Maybe tip the scales of perception from bohemian-riche to homeless people of the *please seat us so that we can order an expensive meal and then show you our empty pockets* variety. I get it, don't really blame her.

"Hey, a table for two, please," I say.

She hesitates, looks at the two of us for another second.

"Uh, do you have a reservation?"

"Here? For Sunday lunch? This is a business restaurant. It's pretty much empty today."

"I still need to ask if you have a reservation," the girl says sweetly. She's maybe nineteen. Pretty face, probably not too smart, typical hostess.

"No. No reservation."

She's spinning her wheels, scanning the restaurant for the more senior help. The restaurant must have some kind of policy when it comes to this type of vagrant identification thing. And then the sommelier walks out of the kitchen. Luckily, this Ruth's Chris has historically been my go-to for client lunches and a big part of that history is me ordering very expensive bottles of wine.

"Mr. Johnson, my goodness, it's been a while. Nice to see you again."

And I glance back at the hostess, watch the scales tip back to bohemian-riche.

"Hey, James. Nice to see you, too. I've been working on a project, living out of town for the past six months."

"Back now?" the sommelier asks.

"Soon, I hope, but not yet. Do you have a bottle of two-thousand-thirteen Opus One back there?"

"I do. Shall I bring it to the table now?"

"Let it air out. I'm going to start with a cocktail."

"Mr. Johnson," the hostess says, suddenly bright-eyed and graciously formal. "I can show you to your table now."

Menus in hand, she walks us to a table beside the floor-to-ceiling window. Elroy sits, mouse-like. I put my napkin on my lap and he does the same.

"Hi, Mr. Johnson. Welcome back to Ruth's Chris. I'm Cheryl and I'll be serving you with Enrico today." Cheryl doesn't actually know me, but James must have mentioned my name and the restaurant prides itself in familiarity with the regulars. "Can I start you with something from the bar?"

"Please. A Plymouth Gin martini, up, with the blue cheese olives."

She looks at Elroy.

"Ju... ju... just water, pl... pl... please."

"Still or sparkling?" Cheryl asks. Elroy looks at me.

"Wait a second, kid. You don't want a Coke or something?" Elroy shrugs. "Bring the kid a Coke. Or no, wait. What do they call that drink that's like a Shirley Temple, but the more masculine version?"

"A Roy Rogers? Coke and grenadine, I think?"

"That's it. Bring him one of those. And tap water's fine for the table, thanks."

I'll spend six-hundred dollars on a bottle of wine, but I refuse to pay twelve dollars for a bottle of water as a matter of principle.

Elroy has picked up the huge wooden-handled steak knife and is inspecting it like a museum piece. I've been out to dinner with my niece and nephew before, but only with my brother in tow, and the kids were animals. Totally bad for digestion, eating with children. But

I've never had a one-on-one meal with a kid before in my life. And it's not like I expect Elroy to hop on the chair and start throwing feces or anything, but it's been a while since I've had a solid meal. I don't want anything to ruin it. Some ground rules might be in order here.

"Okay, kid. We'll wait until we get our drinks before we start talking about church. So listen, I expect this isn't really your type of place, huh?" Elroy nods, wide-eyed. "Well, we're going to be here for a while, okay? This is the type of place where you sit back and enjoy a long, leisurely meal. Just take your cues from me. And I know you're always hungry, but just take it easy and slow, okay? We're not in any rush."

Elroy nods as the waiter, Enrico, comes to the table with our drinks. He sets the Roy Rogers in front of Elroy, shakes my martini and pours it into the chilled glass on his tray. When Enrico sets my drink on the table, Elroy is slurping ice at the bottom of his glass.

"Another?" Enrico asks Elroy, who looks at me like a dog that just pooped on the rug.

"Yeah," I say to Enrico, look back at Elroy. "So, about that taking-it-slow thing we just discussed?"

"Sorry. It was so good."

"Don't sweat it. Is there anything left in there?" Elroy shakes the dregs. "There's enough. Cheers," I say, and we clink glasses. "Always look at people when you toast and always take a sip after you clink glasses, even if there's almost nothing left."

"Got it," Elroy says.

"And lose the straw. Straws make the drink go faster. Plus, drinking from the glass is more of a dude thing. Unless you're, like, at McDonalds." I take a sip of my drink, flakes of ice swimming in the glass, sigh. God, is this whole nursing home thing really worth it?

Elroy is watching me. I carefully reach across the table and hand him the martini glass.

"Really?"

"Just a little sip. You need the whole experience."

He nods, puts the rim of the glass to his lips, inhales a little bit of the martini. He involuntarily makes a face like he's got a mouthful of battery acid, but holds it and swallows. Tough little guy.

"It's good," Elroy says.

"Really?"

"No, not re...re... really. But it's very cold. That was kind of nice."

"Good. Well, sip your drink like that. Otherwise we're going to go through eight Roy Rogers and you'll be bouncing off the walls."

Enrico returns with Elroy's second drink. He pulls the straw and takes a small sip. Good boy.

Cheryl comes back and I order each of us a twelve-ounce filet mignon, medium rare. For the table, creamed spinach, cremini mushrooms, grilled asparagus, potatoes au gratin. I tell her to go ahead and bring the wine. When she leaves, I take a sip of my drink, look at Elroy.

"Okay. Let's talk about church this morning," I say, pause. "So talk to me."

"What do you want to know?"

"Well, I mean, what did you think about what I did in there?"

"It was great. Really. I loved it."

"Are you lying?"

"No, why?"

"No stutter."

Elroy looks at me weird, kind of surprised, and I know he isn't lying. He pauses before talking, pensive.

"I guess, I just kind of li... li... like it, here."

"And now it's back," I say, frustrated. "Why?"

"Maybe if you didn't me... me... mention it..."

"Okay, my bad. So, you don't stutter when you're lying. And you don't stutter in expensive steakhouses, as long as I don't mention it. Any other situational non-stutter venues that I should know about?"

"I di... di... didn't know about ex... ex... expensive restaurants until now. Or even about ly... ly... lying, until a couple days ago."

"We should probably explore this whole phenomenon some more. But not right now. So, anyway, did it make sense to you? What I was trying to say at church. No, wait. First, do you think it made sense to anyone? Or was it just a, you know, spectacle or something?"

"It was de... de... definitely a spectacle," Elroy says pensively. "Like the whole Southern accent thing, that was hy... hy... hysterical."

"Hysterical isn't really what I was shooting for."

"No, all the other st... st... stuff was great, too. But, I mean, I do... do... don't ever go to church so I didn't really understand everything you were ta... ta... talking about."

I can tell Elroy feels like he's letting me down. Like I took him out to this expensive restaurant and he isn't carrying his weight with the feedback from the morning. Then he surprises me.

"I mean, I think wh... wh... what you were saying made sense. I think there should be a pl... pl... place where people can really be themselves and not feel, like, ashamed, you know? I would, like, live there if a pl... pl... place like that was really real. And I think people would want to make it ha... ha... happen, too. Not everyone, but some. But, really, I don't think people were ex... ex... expecting it, you know? So it will pr... pr... probably take more than just one speech. But it's a go... go... good start."

He clearly doesn't like to talk for a long time, because of the stutter. Unless he's lying, I suppose. And that was the longest he's ever talked to me.

"I think you're right, Elroy," I say as the waiters bring our food. "Don't touch the plate. It's hot." But he touches it anyway, the skin of his index finger making a brief sizzle sound before he jerks his hand away. "Dude, seriously? The plate's like ten thousand degrees."

He sticks the finger in his mouth.

I dole small amounts of the side dishes onto his plate. He's a disaster with the steak knife. After a few unsuccessful tries at showing him how to cut the steak in a non-abusive way, I give up and just cut a piece for him.

"It's not cooked," Elroy says when he sees the raw red center.

"Trust me, dude."

I hold the piece I've cut in front of his face. He looks at me. I nod and he opens his mouth so that I can put it in. He chews and the look on his face reminds me of my first meeting with Martha, her handless orgasms. It's probably irresponsible for me to get the kid hooked on a really good cut of filet. I mean, it's not the kind of thing that's readily accessible to people without large amounts of excess cash.

But I'm totally digging the fact that he loves this meat so much, getting a real vicarious thrill. He swallows, tries to reach for the knife and fork, but I cut him another piece. Feed it to him. While he's slowly savoring this bit, I cut and eat a piece of my own filet. And it is heaven. I'm still chewing when he swallows, so I hand him my glass of wine.

"Uh, I'm fine," he says. "I've never had wine before."

No stutter. But I don't think it's because he's lying. Mouth full, I make an inch gesture with my thumb and index finger.

"It's not like the martini," I say through my food. "Just try a sip. It kind of detonates what the meat does to your mouth, in a good way. Seriously, it's a six-hundred-dollar bottle of wine, Elroy."

He takes a small sip, swishes it around his mouth, smiles. He gives me the glass and I put it between us on the table. There's hardly anyone in the restaurant and the waiters aren't going to care. And we alternate. I cut him a bite, feed it to him, and he takes a sip of the wine. Then I do the same. About a third of the way through our steaks, I start recommending that he take a mouthful of side dish right after I've fed him his bite. He does the side dish part with his own fork because we don't want this to get any weirder.

He experiments with mixing the tastes, groans with pleasure every time. I pour more wine. I can tell Elroy's thoroughly appreciating how an excellent Cab illumes the pallet after each slightly iron-y bite of meat. We say only a few words, mostly about this alchemy of tastes. The alternating bite and sip cycle slows everything down.

Oddly, it might be the nicest meal I've ever had.

Elroy

I can tell that the hostess doesn't think that someone like me should be at a restaurant like this. It's all white linen napkins and tablecloths, dresses and ties. And even though I'd dug around to find the least shabby t-shirt and jeans for church this morning, the bar is pretty low when it comes to my clothes. And I'm sweaty and dirty from walking the bike to the nursing home. I look at Frank, talking to the hostess. He doesn't look much better than I do. But that's kind of his thing, I think. And by the way the hostess keeps looking at me, I know that I'm the one screwing this up.

But then some guy in a suit recognizes Frank and suddenly we're, like, the most important people in the world. Even though a part of me still feels totally out of place, there's this other part of me that I, like, didn't even know about, which feels really, really good being treated this way. And that part of me is like, hey, we could get used to this. And the other part of me, the careful part, is like, don't get used to anything because that's only going to make it all worse when it goes away.

But this part of me that I don't know, the part that really wants to feel like I belong in this restaurant, it just squashes down the careful part of me and takes the wheel. And inside it feels the way that Spring feels, after a long Winter, when no matter how shabby and worthless you are, you still get to enjoy the same warm air and sunshine that all the better people around you are enjoying.

The drink that Frank ordered me is the best drink ever. It tastes like a cherry Coke, but, like, homemade. It actually has two cherries in it. And even though Frank just told me to take things slow, I unintentionally suck it down without taking my lips off the straw. Wow. Shoot. Pull yourself together. Frank looks at me. My eyes say sorry. He orders me another.

He drinks his drink, savors it, really. And then he hands it to me. I've had a sip of beer before, at my last home, when my foster mom was passed out drunk on the couch. It wasn't good, but it was a lot better than the gin martini Frank lets me taste. I put on the best face I can, swallow, feel the cold nasty burn slide down my throat.

After Frank orders for both of us, we start to talk about what happened at the church. And Frank mentions that I haven't been stuttering. I think maybe this part of me that feels like it belongs here at this fancy restaurant, maybe that part of me doesn't stutter. Just like the part of me that lies doesn't stutter. So, I tell him this and the stutter comes back. I wonder how long I would have gone, not stuttering, if he hadn't mentioned it.

Then we talk about the church, and I feel like he's expecting more from me. Like this whole expensive restaurant thing was just a set up for me giving him something useful about what happened at the church, but I can't think of anything meaningful to say. So, I just tell him what I think, the best I can, and he seems okay with letting it go. Then the waiters bring out our food.

The guy waiter with the Spanish name, he's got a dishtowel around his hand, puts a sizzling white plate in front of me. I touch it just as Frank is telling me not to, burn the hell out of my finger. But I play it cool. I pick up the knife and start to cut into my steak and Frank freaks out a little, like I'm going to ruin it. He tries to explain steak cutting to me, but I keep doing it wrong so then he just reaches over and cuts it for me. Just one piece, one bite. And rather than giving me back the fork, he holds the bite in front of my mouth. I look at the steak on my plate, at the piece on the fork, and figure something went wrong in the kitchen.

"It's not cooked," I say, no stutter, probably because I'm shaken up by the idea of having this piece of raw flesh in my mouth.

"Trust me, dude," he says, and I do. And, oh, my god.

Frank takes a bite of his own steak while I'm still chewing, then takes a sip from his glass of wine. I swallow, reach for the knife and fork, but instead he cuts me another piece. Feeds it to me. And nowhere am I caring that I'm a twelve-year-old being fed in public by a thirty-something man, because the steak is that good. When I swallow the second bite, he hands me his glass of wine. I basically tell him I don't want any and he basically tells me that the bottle of wine costs six-hundred dollars, so what am I crazy, not wanting to try it? So, I take a sip. And he's right. I do not have the words to describe what happens in my mouth, the way the meat and the wine make me feel like the whole world is a good place.

And then we do it again. And it becomes kind of a thing. He cuts me a bite, feeds me, cuts himself a bite, I take a sip of the wine, he takes a sip of the wine and we start all over. After a few bites, he tells me to try some of the creamed spinach, and while it's still in my mouth he feeds me the bite of steak, I let the flavors blend and wonder if I've ever felt this good in my life. So, we do that with the rest of the sides, too – except the cheesy potatoes, because Frank says they're too powerful for the steak and we should eat them on their own. And between each bite, each of us takes a big sip of wine from Frank's glass.

After I don't know how long – long enough for us to finish a second bottle of wine, less expensive but just as good – we finish the steaks. Frank leans back in his chair, unbuttons his jeans, so I do the same.

"Full?" Frank asks. The second bottle of wine is empty on the table. There are scraps of sides left in the serving dishes and I'm so full that I actually let the waiters take them away without finishing last bites.

"Yeah." I'm going to dream about this dinner for the rest of my life.

"Well, man up. Because you've got to try the White Chocolate Bread Pudding."

Frank waves over the waiter. He orders a bread pudding for us to split, a Roy Rogers for me and some kind of after dinner drink for himself. When the dessert comes, we eat it with our own forks. He doesn't feed it to me, I mean. And even though we're both scooping from the same plate, this probably looks a lot more normal to the few other people in the restaurant. Him not feeding me, I mean. Not that I wouldn't let him feed me if he wanted to, for, like, every meal ever.

Between bites of the bread pudding, which is also beyond my ability to describe, Frank lets me take sips of his port wine. And he orders another. I have never understood food and drink before today. I try to sneak a look at the check when Frank signs for it, don't see exactly how much, but do see that there are four figures in front of change. Wow. He gets up, buttons his jeans. I push back the seat, stand up, and remember not anything else.

Frank

Let me just say that no one has ever accused me of having good judgment. I can recognize this flaw, maybe even own it. See, I tend to get caught up in the moment. And this turned out to be a really special dinner. It was. I kind of got lost in it. So much so that it completely escaped my mind that the minority share of two bottles of wine, and maybe of a glass of port, might obliterate a twelve-year-old kid. Especially one that's maybe eighty-pounds, soaking wet. Though, in my defense, we did just finish a pretty heavy meal.

Even so, given all the weight I've lost over the past six months, I was feeling pretty buzzed when I stood up, too. But then, I also had a martini. Gin, which tends to hit me pretty hard. But whatever, I'm not competing with a twelve-year-old in terms of alcohol tolerance, and I'm aware that the majority of this incident is probably my fault.

So anyway, when Elroy topples over like a rag doll at the edge of the table, my adrenaline kicks in. Unfortunately, not fast enough to keep him from hitting the floor. But I'm able to grab him quick, sit him back in his chair, marionette-like. I look around the restaurant, no waiters in sight, which is good. An older couple, dining at a non-adjacent table, obviously noticed that the boy collapsed. I smile at them, give a thumbs-up like everything's fine here, but worry the gesture might be wrongly interpreted as *it's all good, I finally got the kid drunk enough to go rape him in the parking lot.* Especially since they've probably been watching me feed the kid meat and wine for the past two hours. Luckily for me, they don't look like the type of people who would step up, like on one of those primetime "What Would You Do" newsmagazine programs.

I pull Elroy to his feet. He's out of it but takes little walking steps with my arm supporting his weight. I take long strides to the front of the restaurant.

"Bye, Mr. Johnson. Thanks for... Oh, my God. Is he okay?"

"What? Oh, this. It's nothing. He's a necrophiliac."

"He has sex with dead people? Do you mean narcoleptic?" The hostess is a little brighter than I'd thought.

"No, sorry, yeah. Narcoleptic. He just, like, drops off. No big deal. Happens all the time."

"Do you want me to get some help?" she asks, genuinely concerned.

"No. Absolutely not. I mean, I've got it. I'm used to it," I smile, casually. She's cute, maybe I can get some digits. "So, you're new here, right?"

She looks at me like I'm covered in blood or something. Not the appropriate time for flirting. Elroy groans. I give her a desperate smile and hurry out to the parking lot. I walk Elroy two spots down from my car, where he unloads the entire meal onto the blacktop. He's kind of seizing up, like kids do when they puke, so I try to lighten the mood.

"Almost as good coming up as it is going down, huh?" I say, holding his forehead, wine and meat splashing my sneakers.

"Sorry," he says, embarrassed, like a date that got too drunk.

"I'm at least partially to blame, dude. It happens. Shake it off."

He gyrates, literally trying to shake it off. It looks like most of the alcohol is puddled by our feet, so based on my experience, he should be pretty sober in a few minutes. I mean, age and weight aside, it was only wine for Christsakes.

"You okay?" he asks, maybe thinking he got me into some kind of trouble by passing out in the restaurant.

"What do you mean?"

"You dr... dr... drank a lot of wine, too." Offensive, but unintentional, and I am only, like, forty pounds heavier than him.

"And a martini. But I feel great. Maybe a little buzz, but no worries. I'm an excellent drunk driver, anyway." Regurgitated wine and meat drip from his chin, splatter-stain his white t-shirt. "Come on, you'll feel better in a few minutes. We've got to get you cleaned up."

I stick him in the front seat, unfold the ragtop, drive to Main Street. Pull up to a street parking space in front of the Gap. He's resting comfortably, the ride having done some good. I consider going into the store alone to buy him clothes, but leaving a drunk twelve-year-old in the front seat of a totally bitchin open top Camaro seems rife with the potential for bad stuff. And worse, he might throw up in my car.

"Okay, bud. Come on. We need to get you up."

"I'm alright," he says drowsily.

"It's grown-up time, here. You're a little wasted, but it will wear off quick. And in the meantime, I need you to try and act like you're sober. Act like, I mean, there's nothing wrong. Can you do that for me?"

"Sure," he says and struggles to pull himself out of my passenger seat.

We walk up and down the sidewalk, my arm bracing him below the shoulders, but not carrying his weight. What kind of trouble can you get in for walking around with a drunk child, I wonder? He was like this when I found him, officer.

"We're going for normal, here, Elroy. Try and focus. I promise this feeling will be gone in, like, five minutes."

He nods and I remove my arm from his shoulders. He's shaky, but passably sober. We head into the store.

"Welcome to the Gap! Can I help you find anything, today?" Teenage boy, huge smile, way overeager. This kind of super-positive sunshine act might fly with a teenage girl, but with a guy it's just obnoxious. Especially now.

"Bite me, kid," I say and walk past him towards the kids' section. I eye Elroy, pull three different sizes of house brand designer jeans, steer him to the dressing room. I pick out two sizes of vintage t-shirts, the kind I'd buy if I had to shop at Gap, toss them under the dressing room door. I get a belt, because I noticed that he doesn't have a belt. He's in the dressing room a while, but I hear him rustling around, not napping.

"Is it okay?" he asks, swinging the door open.

He knows it's okay. He looks almost like a normal kid. He's obviously got an adrenaline rush from looking at himself in the full-length mirror, which seems to have eradicated most effects of the alcohol, leaving him with maybe just a happy buzz. I nod, smile. He reaches back and starts to gather all of the clothes from the dressing room floor.

"Hold up, kid. Leave the sizes that don't fit on the floor."

"What ab... ab... about these?" he asks, holding his old clothes at arms-length because of the smell.

"Leave them, too. Happy boy up front can take care of it."

I grab two more t-shirts, another pair of jeans, all the right size, walk to the cashier and pay. Across the street is this hipster barber shop I used to go to. It's open until six on Sunday. Hell, anyway, I need a haircut too.

The barber shop is empty, two stylists sweeping hair and topping-off their tonics.

"Julius," I say to the huge, gay, black man who used to cut my hair.

"Frank Johnson, as I live and breathe." It's not like he remembers my head so well, but I always had a tendency to hang around the shop after my haircut, continuing discussions and such. "Forgive me if I say that you look plain awful. What the hell has someone been doing to your hair?"

The barber who comes to the nursing home on Thursdays isn't top notch.

"Long story, Julius. Just fix it. I'll give you the Cliff Notes version."

"And what do you want us to do with that?" Julius asks and points at Elroy, all super gay drama. "Is he a refugee from the same concentration camp?"

"Make him look cool," I sigh, sit down and lean back into the barber chair.

Elroy

Even if Frank dies, I'll still have these clothes. I'll still have this haircut. I'll still have the bike, even though I don't know how to ride it. I'll still have the iPhone, at least until they cut off Frank's credit card, even though I wouldn't have anyone to call. It's morbid, I know, but if I'm being honest, that's what I think about on the drive back to the nursing home.

And I'd still be able to remember today, and all these days. No matter what happens, these days are mine now. Part of me wants him to crash the car, so that there isn't anything more, ever, than this perfect day.

"How're you feeling?" Frank shouts above the wind.

"Great," I shout back.

He pulls the car around the back entrance of the nursing home, parks it in the same spot as before.

"Look, dude. I'm sorry about the whole getting you puke drunk at lunch thing, huh?" He's staring straight ahead.

"This was definitely the be… be… best day I've ever had. Ever," I reply.

He looks at me, smiles, tousles my hair.

"Hey!" I yell, jerking my head away. For the first time in my life, I'm worried about messing up my hair. Frank laughs, calls me a diva.

"It was good, right? Man, there is something about a long, daytime-drinking, bro session at an expensive steak place. Good times." The fact that I'm twelve doesn't seem to enter his mind. "We'll do it again, yeah?"

"Yeah," I say.

"You okay getting home on the bike?"

"Yeah."

"Be careful, because you've got no helmet and there may still be a little alcohol in your system. Needless to say, if you do get stopped by the cops, you did not get drunk with me today, right?" He smiles again.

"I'm fine. Anyway, I wo… wo… wouldn't rat you out."

"Cool. Now, get back into character. I'll see you tomorrow," he says.

We climb out of the car, walk around front, duck through the hedges and go in the front door. We forgot to check on Mr. Hardy, to see if he's in the lobby, I mean. But he isn't, it's just the same nurse at reception. She gives me a pitying look as I sign Frank back in and he walks away without saying goodbye.

I unlock the bike and walk it down the driveway. Walk it down the road, walk it all the way home. I'm starving, which makes sense since I threw up most of the food we ate earlier. I think about making myself a sandwich when I get back to my foster home. Stale Wonder Bread, stale Oscar Meyer Bologna. If I'm lucky, maybe there's a pickle somewhere in the ice box.

Told you, says that careful part of me inside my head. Told you so.

Sally

"Hey, Sally. So, yeah, sorry about your Aunt, you know? I mean, my grandma died two years ago, so like, I can empathize," Dr. Severs says to me as I climb into the backseat of his garbage car.

"Your grandma? What was she, like, a hundred-and-ten years old?"

"She was ninety-three."

"My Aunt Sadie was twenty-five."

"I didn't say it was the same thing, did I? I just said that I could empathize with your loss, that's all," Dr. Severs snaps, then quickly goes back to guidance counselor mode. "You know, it's hard to think about death as something natural. When you lose someone, I mean. And I'm here if you want to talk. I know how difficult it is to get past your own feeling of loss, but it helps if you can focus on honoring your aunt instead of mourning her, you know? Like celebrating whatever nobility there was in her death, instead of hiding from it. Look her death in the eye, so to speak. How did she die?"

"Rectal gangrene," I say solemnly. "She wasn't much of a wiper."

"Oh, ah, that's…" Dr. Severs stumbles.

"Her whole life, she, like, struggled with personal hygiene." I sniffle, short sob. Like I'm going to talk to this pedophile about Aunt Sadie's suicide.

Dr. Severs pauses, then changes the subject.

"So, yeah, well, today you'll be working with Elroy at the Hardy Managed Care facility, reading to elderly people…" then Dr. Severs adds stiffly, "…if he ever gets here."

"So, it's just me and Elroy at the nursing home? Where are the other kids working?"

"Well, it's just… the Club is just starting up, you know? So right now…"

"Me, and this kid, Elroy, are the only ones in the Outreach Club?"

"Just for now, I mean, great things have to start small…"

"How did you ever convince my mother to sign me up for this thing?"

"Your mother is an insightful woman who shares my vision about the importance of the RMSOC and its mission."

"And apparently she's the only one who does. Except this kid Elroy's mom, maybe."

"Elroy's an orphan. He lives in a foster home. Take it easy on him. He's dealing with some difficult stuff, too."

"Like what?"

"Well, like he's an orphan. And he stutters. And he's confused, sexually I mean. He's probably gay and I wouldn't be surprised if he became a pedophile. Also, he just found out that his biological father is actually a priest."

"Whoa," I say. So much for student-counselor confidentiality. This kid, Elroy, sounds more screwed up than me, which is no small feat. I kind of like him already.

"Yeah. Look, you know, I probably shouldn't have just told you all that. I just kind of got caught up in the whole discussion about your Aunt, uh…"

"Dying of bottom rot?"

"Yeah, that, uh, you know, kind of opened me up more than it should have."

"Her, too," I say, snarky.

Then this kid, who's obviously Elroy, opens the car door and climbs in the front seat. I recognize him from the church parking lot, only he doesn't look as homeless as he did yesterday.

"About time," Dr. Severs says nastily. I guess I'm the only one who should be taking it easy on Elroy.

"Hey," I say.

"Hey," he says, not looking at me. He totally ignores Dr. Severs, which is kind of cool. None of us says anything else on the ride to the nursing home.

"You want to show her the ropes, Elroy?" Dr. Severs asks when we pull up in front, like he has no intention of getting out of the car.

"Whatever," Elroy replies and lifts the seat so that I can climb out.

"Hey, Sally, remember. Onday'tay aysay othingnay."

"What the hell is that supposed to mean?"

"It's Pig Latin."

"Huh. So maybe Elroy isn't the only one who's gay in this Club, then?"

"Just don't say anything about our conversation earlier, huh?"

"Fine."

"Great," Dr. Severs says, then shouts out the window. "Do a good job, guys! I'll pick you up at six." He drives off. I catch up with Elroy and we walk side-by-side to the nursing home.

"So, Elroy. Dr. Severs tells me you're gay. And that your birth father is a priest."

Frank

Hardy is roaming around the grounds somewhere, but he isn't in the lobby so we need to make this quick. I'm sitting on the linen couch, grumpy, scanning the bay window, messing with Mrs. Liptenstein about her dead cat, Buttons. But my heart isn't really in it. Messing with Mrs. Liptenstein, I mean. Because I need Elroy to get in here and sign me out before Hardy drops by and effectively grounds our flight for the afternoon.

Bang! Severs drives up in his crap car. Elroy gets out and I lift myself from the couch, amble grouchily towards the reception desk. Elroy sticks his head back in the car, then pulls himself back out and begins walking up the sidewalk. I struggle to maintain my grimace. After being out yesterday, the nursing home has felt like Attica. And I'm about to start grumbling to the desk nurse about unfair treatment and whatnot when I see some skinny guy hop out of the car and catch up with Elroy. No, wait. It's a girl. Bad hair choices. I'm not liking any of this.

The two approach the front door. I scan for Hardy. It's still a go. And then the two of them stop. Turn. Start talking to each other. No, no, no, no. Time is a factor here, kid! And he just keeps talking to this chick.

And they're still talking, like, four minutes later, a whole window of opportunity lost. What the hell, Yoko! You're killing me here. I'm flopped back down on the couch, ignoring Mrs. Liptenstein completely. Watching my afternoon-leave… well, leave. Bros before hoes, little dude! What are you thinking? And of course, right when the two of them decide to finally enter the home, Hardy walks around the corner and into the lobby.

"Where's the little reader, Johnson?"

I look down at my Chuck Taylors, wipe some dirt off of the side of one with the toe of the other. That lousy, rat-hair bitch. I might have to do something substantial, revenge-wise, if I end up stuck in here for the rest of the afternoon.

"Hey, Mr. Ha… Ha… Mr. H," Elroy says.

"Elroy. Whatcha got planned for this afternoon?"

Elroy holds up his copy of *Huckleberry Finn*.

"Great! That will be so nice for Mr. Johnson here. We really appreciate it. And who's this with you?"

The rat girl looks at Elroy, expecting an introduction. After a few awkward seconds, she introduces herself.

"Hello, Mr. Hardy. I'm Sally Berman. I'm here to read to the old… To the people who live here. I'm with the Outreach Club, too," she says in a flat tone.

"Where's Dr. Severs?" Hardy asks.

"Dr. Severs dropped us off. He had to go somewhere, I guess. He told Elroy to show me the ropes."

Elroy doesn't return her look.

"Oh, that's fine. That's just fine. You can read to Mrs. Liptenstein, here."

Hardy steps to a nearby bookshelf, grabs a paperback copy of *This Side of Paradise* and shoves it into Sally's hands. "That will be nice, Mrs. Liptenstein, huh?"

"Have you seen a white cat with a grey hood?" Mrs. Liptenstein asks Hardy.

"Sally, you can read to her right out here, if you want. Or if it gets too noisy, you can go to the kitchen or her room. Whatever you like."

The rat girl lifts her eyebrows, raises the book an inch, and then flops down on the couch next to me. She's looking at me as if she knows me, which is disconcerting. So I get up, grab Elroy by the shoulder, march him out of the lobby and down the hall to my room.

"We had a window of opportunity, man! Hardy was out of the lobby for, like, five minutes while you stood outside talking to that rat-headed chick. What the hell? We were gonna do Sushi this afternoon!"

Elroy is looking at me as if he has no idea what he did wrong. I pull it together. It's not the kid's fault. It's that rat-headed girl who screwed things up.

"It's a be… be… beautiful day," Elroy says.

"I know it's a beautiful day. That's why I'm pissed off."

"So why can't we just tell the desk nurse that we want to re… re… read outside? I can even si… si… sign you out. And then we can sneak around ba… ba… back. They don't know about your ca… ca… car. If anything goes wrong, we can just sa… sa… say Dr. Severs picked us up and took us to ch… ch…church. Mr. Hardy won't kn… kn… know any different."

Huh. Yeah, that could work. Wonder why I didn't think of it. Maybe I'm losing my edge.

"Okay. Good thinking. Sorry I got so riled up, dude."

"It's okay."

"Hair's looking good, by the way."

Elroy smiles. We get into character and march back to the lobby.

Elroy

"So, Elroy. Dr. Severs tells me you're gay. And that your birth father is a priest," this girl, Sally, says.

Stupid. Freaking. Hippie. Stoner. She was in the car with him for what, five minutes before I got there? They ought to take away his license, if you even need a license to be a middle school guidance counselor. I think about going to the principal, telling him how Dr. Severs, like, outed me to another student about the gay thing, which I'm not—and so what, if I was?—and the birth father thing, which also isn't true. But with all the lies involved, telling on Dr. Severs might be a slippery slope.

She lightly grabs my arm, stops me. I turn to face her.

Oh! Sally is the girl from the church parking lot. The one who was watching me and Frank and Dr. Severs and the priest yesterday. The one who smiled at me when we drove away.

"Hey," Sally says, "I get it. You're all messed up. Join the club."

"Yeah," I say.

"My dad killed himself when I was four. And my Aunt Sadie killed herself two weeks ago. And I'm next in line, I think."

"Wow."

"So now we both know embarrassing, shameful stuff about each other – so we're pretty much even. So, we can be friends, right?"

Wow. Many thoughts right now, both weird and good. She wants to be friends. With me. Wow. She's obviously planning to kill herself, so I'm not sure how long I can expect the whole friendship thing to last, but I'll take what I can get. Except now I feel bad because she just dropped some major personal stuff on me, and everything that she thinks is shameful about me is really just a bunch of lies. Maybe not the best way to start a friendship.

"Okay," I say.

"Well, okay, then. So, you're my new friend. Elroy," Sally says, not, like, in direct address, but like she's saying the name of her new friend, me. Which is kind of totally cute.

"Okay," I say again.

I'm feeling super shy and it's hard to look at her eyes. She smiles at me and we turn, walk into the nursing home.

Wow.

Sally

I'm on the couch with *This Side of Paradise* and Mrs. Liptenstein, who keeps interrupting me to ask if I've seen her cat, so it's, like, impossible to read to her. Then I see Elroy and that Frank Johnson come back into the lobby. Frank Johnson being the guy from church yesterday who hijacked the sermon and then kissed Father Mcloughlin in the parking lot. And between Elroy being the secret gay foster-kid offspring of a priest, and the unexpected appearance of "Mr. Expose Yourself in Church" here at the nursing home, this whole Outreach Club thing has gotten a ton more interesting.

And I'm wondering what this Frank Johnson is even doing here, and why Elroy gets to hang out with him instead of reading to old people, and why they seem to hate each other. And while I'm wondering all this, the two of them walk up to the reception desk. So, I tell Mrs. Liptenstein that I need to take a break, but, yes, I will keep an eye out for her cat, and I walk up to the reception desk, too.

"Whatcha doing?" I chirp.

"We're going to read outside," Frank Johnson says curtly. Elroy smiles at me, looks away.

"Read to who, outside?"

"Elroy is going to read to me, outside," Frank Johnson says.

"Why is Elroy reading to you? You can't read? Are you blind, or just illiterate?"

"I can read fine."

"So?"

"So, I'm an inmate here. And Elroy is assigned to read to me. And today we're going to do it outside."

"You *live* here? You're like, forty years old."

"Thirty-three."

"So, I don't get it. Are you, like, a retard?"

"If I were, would that be a nice thing to ask me?"

"Sorry."

"And I'm not retarded. I just live here. And that's all you need to know. Elroy reads to me and takes me on outings with your club. And he has to sign me out when I leave the building, even if we're just going outside to read, like we are now."

"And you're sure you're not, like, special or brain damaged or something? Because, you know, what you just told me, it's, like, not a normal person situation."

Maybe some retarded people don't really know they're retarded?

"No. I'm fully in control of my faculties. It's complicated. So, if you don't mind, we're going to go outside now."

I look at the nurse behind the desk. Awkward smile, shrug.

"Okay, hang on," I say. "We'll come with."

Frank Johnson gives me this look of controlled rage for just a half-second, like I'm totally getting in the way. What the hell? Is he planning some kind of make out session with Elroy in the bushes? But he quickly pulls himself together, pauses to think.

"You both can't read to us at the same time. Mrs. Liptenstein's confused enough. Maybe inside is better for you guys."

"We just started *This Side of Paradise*, so it's no problem to bail. Mrs. Liptenstein wasn't listening anyway. We can take turns reading from whatever Elroy is reading, and we'll read it to the both of you."

The nurse makes a satisfied face, like, that sounds reasonable. Frank Johnson seems to spin his wheels, comes up with nothing.

"Fine. Whatever," he says.

"Is he always this much of a grump?" I ask Elroy and the nurse.

They both nod their heads, yes.

So I go back and gather up Mrs. Liptenstein, bring her to the reception desk. Elroy signs them both out under supervision of the RMSOC because he somehow has that kind of authority here. Mrs. Liptenstein leaves her walker outside, by the front door, leans against my arm for support as we walk down the sidewalk.

"So, where do you guys want to go?" I ask.

"Buzz off, Yoko. We've got stuff to do. Why don't you guys take that bench over there? Me and Elroy will take a walk around back," Frank Johnson says, rudely. "Hey, Mrs. Liptenstein, is that a cat up there by the bench? White, with a grey hood?"

"Buttons?" Mrs. Liptenstein tries to make a break for the bench, but I hang onto her arm. This causes her to swing in a half-circle, lose her footing. I gently go with the momentum until I'm able to lay her delicately onto her side, on the pavement.

"No deal," I say. "One of you guys is gonna tell me what's going on here. Elroy, I thought we were friends?"

Elroy looks at Frank, like, have you ever seen someone do puppy dog eyes that isn't actually trying to do puppy dog eyes? It's so genuine that it's heartbreaking. Frank Johnson looks at Elroy, looks back at the nursing home, rolls his eyes and sighs.

Frank

"So, you decided, as a matter of principle, to imprison yourself in a managed care facility for an entire year of your life?" This girl Sally will not shut up.

"Yeah," I shout towards the back seat.

"Even though you have enough money to afford a car like this? Or did you steal it?"

"It's mine."

"What are you, rich?"

"I do fine," I say.

"So you're, what, like, taking a year off for the nursing home thing?"

"No, I'm still working."

"I thought you couldn't leave without Elroy or they can kick you out?"

"I'm a freelance computer programmer. And I'm good at it, so I'm in high demand. I code at night from the home. And look, what does any of this really matter to you, anyway?"

"Geez, I'm just asking. And another thing," she shouts, "why are you being such a dick?"

Mrs. Liptenstein has rested her bony fingers on top of my hand as I operate the stick shift. She is lolling her head out the passenger window, her body cockeyed in the front seat, her mind God knows where. Elroy is in the back, next to Sally, who is leaning forward between the front seats to talk. Endlessly. This is so not what I had in mind for today.

"Did you just call me a dick? You kiss your mother with that mouth, kid?"

"Ha! I wouldn't kiss my mother with her mouth," she points at Mrs. Liptenstein, "and blame it on you." She pokes my shoulder.

"Trouble at home?" I say in a mean tone.

"You want to hear about it?"

"No."

"You bet you don't. So why the attitude, Mr. Happy?"

"Did it ever occur to you that Elroy and I might have had plans for today? And that you're messing it up?"

"Did it occur to you that this is an RMSOC sponsored outing? And that, as of now, I am fifty-percent of the RMSOC? Plus, I'm easy. You can take me anywhere. And Elroy likes having me around." In the rearview mirror, I see her poke him in the shoulder. She's a poker, this one. "Don't you, Elroy?" He smiles at her, shy, and then gives me an apologetic eye in the rearview.

I consider dropping Sally and Mrs. Liptenstein at my brother's place, just to mess with that bitch Jane. But driving all the way out there and back would cut into too much of our time, so I stick to the original plan and pull into the parking lot of a decent Sushi place a few miles from the home. At least it has a full bar.

We are a raggedy crew, walking into the restaurant. But it's Japanese, so the hostess gives us the same polite smile that she gives the normal people, leads us to a curtained booth in the back. Elroy slides in beside me, Sally beside Mrs. Liptenstein. I ask for green tea, a large hot Sake for myself and another for Mrs. Liptenstein, Cokes for the kids. I'm figuring on drinking the two Sakes myself, or splitting them with Elroy.

"I'll have a Sprite," Sally informs the waitress.

"Uh, I'll have a Sp... Sp... Sprite, too." I give Elroy a Judas look. Sally is all bright-eye smiles as we sit there looking at each other.

"It's been so long since we've had a family dinner," Mrs. Liptenstein says distantly.

"It has, yes," I reply as the waiter sets our drinks on the table.

I pour hot Sake into my little cup, reach across the table and do the same for Mrs. Liptenstein. She bolts it without hesitation. Whoa. Sally, Elroy and I look at each other. I take a small sip of my Sake and it's, like, really hot. What just happened to Mrs. Liptenstein's insides I have no idea. I'm worried we might have to get her to a hospital. But it doesn't seem to faze her at all, so I reach across and fill the cup again. And she shoots the whole thing. Again.

Apparently, Mrs. Liptenstein is something of a drinker and has an esophagus made of asbestos. I hold off on refilling her cup a third time in the interest of preserving however much of her mouth and throat might still be uncharred. I take another sip of my Sake and it's cooled enough for me to drink the whole cup. I refill it, slide it between myself and Elroy. He looks at the cup. Picks it up, smells it, takes a sip.

"Oh, I'm definitely having some, too," Sally says and reaches for Mrs. Liptenstein's carafe and cup.

"Hold up, little lady," I say. "What are you, like, ten?"

"I'm twelve. And you just gave some to Elroy."

"Elroy and I have history. I know how he handles alcohol." Why, just yesterday he was puking red meat and wine all over the parking lot at Ruth's Chris, "Maybe you should stick to your Sprite."

"Yeah, right," Sally says, pouring a cup of Sake, taking a sip, then making a face.

"It's an acquired taste," I say. "In better Japanese restaurants, you always order the expensive Sake cold. The hot stuff is for peasants," I say, a rare teaching moment.

"Gerald, would you order me another brandy?" Mrs. Liptenstein asks, sweetly.

"Sure, hon," I reply, "when the waiter comes back, okay?" Mrs. Liptenstein nods.

"So why are we drinking the hot stuff, then?" Sally asks. I raise my hands, palms up, and spread them towards the motley crew at our table. Sally shrugs, nods. I refill the cups. Mrs. Liptenstein reaches for the one in front of Sally and throws it back.

"What kind of brandy is this, Gerald?" Mrs. Liptenstein asks.

"Rice brandy, dear," I reply.

"I ordered VSOP," she says, snippily. I'm digging the attitude.

"Yes, dear. I'll talk to the waiter when he comes back."

"The little oriental?" she asks distastefully.

"Yes, I'll ask the little oriental man to bring us some VSOP when he comes back."

"Well, say it loud, so he understands."

Seriously, I could listen to politically-incorrect-old-people-speak all day long. I regret not going to a restaurant where there might have been a Black, Latino or overtly gay waiter.

"Quite a performance on Sunday," Sally mentions off-handedly, immediately getting my attention.

"You were there," statement, not a question.

"I was."

"So, what did you think?"

"Well… I think, if you weren't being such a dick to me, I'd ask if you were taking on disciples."

Maybe this whole Sally thing won't be too bad. I look at Elroy. He raises his eyebrows.

Elroy

"Well, there's the grumpy one..." Frank is saying.

"Saint Peter?" Sally asks.

"Yeah, okay. And there was the shy one. And wasn't one of them a doctor?" Frank asks.

"What? Oh, yeah, totally. And one of them was happy and one of them was sleepy and one of them was sneezy and I think the last one was kind of dopey," Sally says, deadpan, "Those aren't the apostles."

"What's the difference? Anyway, they were just a bunch of dudes who dug on what Jesus was all about. There's no margin in knowing all the historical specifics," Frank says, rolling his eyes.

"I'm just saying, if you're going to base this whole 'reinvent the church' thing on what the historical Jesus was actually all about, it might help to have a basic understanding of the people involved. For, like, credibility," Sally argues.

"You're missing the point."

"Then make a point."

These two are going to get along fine.

I'm making an effort to say as little as possible because I don't want to stutter in front of Sally, and I don't really feel like this situation is right for me to break into some elaborate lie. So, Sally and Frank continue to argue about the church thing, and Mrs. Liptenstein drinks her third VSOP brandy, and I think about yesterday at the steak restaurant. The part I can remember, I mean. The part where I felt like I belonged in an expensive place like Ruth's whatever, and I didn't stutter. Until Frank messed it up by mentioning it, I mean.

And I'm realizing that if I could just not feel so much like I don't belong anywhere, then maybe I'd actually stop stuttering. Not like it's going to do me any good, but it's nice to know.

"What I'm saying is, we need to get away from all the history and the top-down God stuff. We need to reverse it completely. Go all inside-out, instead. And to do that, we need to expose ourselves around other people, and they need to expose themselves around us. And each other, obviously. Because you can't go inside-out when you're trying to hide what's inside, right? So, letting it all hang out, that's the first step towards real intimacy. So that's what we've got to focus on, first," Frank says.

"You've got to come up with something other than all this expose yourself stuff. It's too open to misinterpretation," Sally says.

"Yeah, but you know what I mean, right? People can't really know each other when they're hiding a whole bunch of stuff, or when they're all just acting like society says they should, or a church says they should, or anyone else who is telling them how they're supposed to act. Or even worse, when they're trying to be what they think they ought to be, or what they think they ought to want to be. Instead of just being whatever they are. Warts on warts, you know?"

"Oh, no, Gerald! Does Henry have warts again?" Mrs. Liptenstein slurs.

"We're taking care of it, dear."

"Fine. I agree with you," Sally says. "I've got more reasons than anyone to feel like the whole church community thing is a sham. But knowing there's something wrong is different than doing something about it."

"So, let's just figure out how to state the case to anyone who wants to listen, and then we figure out how to give them some kind of alternative. How hard can that be?" Frank suggests.

"They're not going to let you just walk into the church and do your whole improv thing again."

"No, you're probably right. I don't know if Rory is fully committed, to the point of risking his job, I mean. And anyway, I wouldn't want to put him in that position. It's important that we have someone on the inside. A priest, I mean."

"Father O'Farrell showed me his pee-pee one time," Mrs. Liptenstein says distantly. "Father O'Farrell was such a hunky man."

"I think that's enough brandy for you, dear."

"Just one more, Gerald! I always have a final, final."

"Of course, sweetie, we wouldn't think of denying you your final, final," Frank says, waves down the waiter, indicates another round.

The sushi is pretty much gone. It wasn't as good as the filet mignon, but Frank showed me how to use chop sticks and I really liked the California Roll and the Eel-Avocado Roll. And I got used to the Sake pretty quick, too. So did Sally.

"Well, if you can't talk to people in the church, maybe we can find a way to divert some of them, like, when they're walking into Mass. And you could talk to them, like, outside somewhere?" Sally suggests.

"Sounds like a plan, kid," Frank says, and I'm not at all jealous about how he's taken a liking to Sally.

"Glad Buttons is dead," Mrs. Liptenstein muddles. "Daddy got it for 'sponsibilty of me. So dirty. I thought that cat would never die."

She leans over the table and tries to kiss Frank on the lips. He leans over and puts his hands on her shoulders, briefly giving me the impression that he's going make out with her, but instead he just lowers her gently back into her seat beside Sally.

"Yes, dear, we all hated Buttons," Frank says, kindly, lifting his cup. "To Buttons!"

Mrs. Liptenstein lifts her glass, nods, and drinks the last of her brandy. Sally and I share the other small cup.

"Good times," Frank says. "Now, let's finish up, people. We need to be getting back to prison before the guards realize that we're out."

Sally

Elroy doesn't say a word at the sushi restaurant, and I'm wondering if it's because of me. Or, maybe, he and Frank Johnson just sit there drinking and eating in silence, whenever they go out. But I think it was because of me. Like, maybe Elroy's ashamed of his stutter or being gay or something. Anyway, it definitely wasn't because of Mrs. Liptenstein.

Frank Johnson drives us back to the home, parks in the back. Says his good-byes to me and Elroy and Mrs. Liptenstein in the parking lot, like he's going to go back into the home without us. But then I realize that it's just because he and Elroy need to go back into this whole "we hate each other" shtick that they do to fool the guy that owns the nursing home, Mr. Hardy, Frank Johnson's arch nemesis.

So Frank Johnson looks at Elroy for a second. Then he nods, takes Elroy by the shoulder and marches him back around the home. In through the front door. I follow with a stumbling drunk Mrs. Liptenstein.

Frank Johnson leaves Elroy at the desk and walks out of the lobby without saying anything to anyone. I drag Mrs. Liptenstein over to the couch, pulling her walker along behind us, sit her down. She immediately falls asleep with her head draped over the back cushion, mouth open, snoring loudly.

"Looks like you wore her out," Mr. Hardy says, appearing from nowhere. Or so it seems. Maybe I'm a little drunk from the Sake. "Did you guys go for a walk?"

"A short one," I reply. "It's such a beautiful day."

Mrs. Liptenstein coughs up a wad of phlegm and it rolls down her chin. Mr. Hardy winces. You'd think, running an old people's home, he'd have seen a lot worse.

Elroy gives me a wave and I say bye to Mr. Hardy, follow Elroy out the front door. We stand at the end of the sidewalk, waiting for Dr. Severs.

"Do you feel drunk?" I ask Elroy. He shrugs.

"Not as mu... mu... much as yesterday. You?" he asks, and I'm wondering if going out drinking with a twelve-year-old kid is a regular thing for Frank Johnson. Thinking, if this is what Jesus was like, I could get into it.

"I don't know, really. I never had alcohol before."

"Oh. Me neither. Before ye... ye... yesterday, I mean."

"By the way, you don't have to worry about the stuttering thing," I say. "It doesn't bother me."

"Thanks," Elroy says. "Hey, do you th... th... think we can try and get Dr. Severs to let us ride our bikes out here to... to... tomorrow?"

"Yeah, that's a good idea," I say. "I mean, if outreach with Frank Johnson is going to be anything like today, then it's probably better to remove Dr. Severs from the picture as much as possible." Then I add, "Hey, anyway, is it okay with you that I came along? I kind of just barged in with you guys. And I know I have a habit of, like, taking over the conversation sometimes."

"Yeah. I li... li... like it. It's even better with you," Elroy says, then goes into a full-on blush, which is sweet. And I realize that I haven't thought about killing myself or thought about Mom, or even Aunt Sadie, this whole afternoon.

"And the whole gay thing, that's fine with me, too. And it's totally cool if you ever want to talk about it. I mean, GBF's are, like, all the rage right now, anyway."

Elroy's blush deepens.

"GBF?"

"Gay best friend."

"Oh," he sighs. "Dr. Severs just thinks I'm ga... ga... gay. It's not, like, a definite thing."

"Either way, it's fine with me. Why does he think you're gay?"

Elroy looks at the ground for a few seconds, like he's making a decision. Then he looks me in the eye.

"It's because I once to... to... told him that I was wearing my foster mom's underpants."

Whoa. Complicated kid.

"Were you, really? No judgments."

"No."

"So why would you tell him that? Is it because you want to wear your foster mom's underwear?"

"No, gross. I was just te... te... testing something."

"Oh, now I'm intrigued. So, what could you be testing that would involve you telling the school guidance counselor that you were wearing your foster mom's underpants?"

"It's this th... th... thing that happens. Where I don't st... st... stutter, if I'm lying."

"Fascinating! So, if you're telling a lie, then the stutter goes away?"

"Yeah."

"Cool. So, lie to me."

"I don't th... th... think it works if you know I'm lying."

"So, try it."

"OK. So, my bi... bi... birth father is that priest. That guy, Father Mc... Mc... Mcloughlin, he's my real father. See? It doesn't work when you know I'm ly... ly... lying."

"Wait a second. So, your birth father isn't a priest? And Father Mcloughlin? Hold it. Did you tell Dr. Severs that Father Mcloughlin is your biological father? Oh, my god, that's classic! You are awesome, Elroy."

He smiles huge.

"Thanks. But Dr. Severs didn't seem to have any problem sharing this information with you. Probably with other people, too. So how long before this whole gay thing gets out at school and makes my life even more miserable than it already is?"

"You realize you didn't stutter when you just said that, right?"

"Sometimes I don't st... st... stutter, like, when I feel okay about myself."

"So why did you start stuttering again?"

"Because you brought it up. That I didn't st... st... stutter just then, I mean."

"Oh. Okay, sorry."

"It's alright."

"You know," I say, "we can work on that if you want."

Elroy

"You know," Sally says, "we can work on that if you want."

And I'm not sure if she means my stutter, or me feeling okay about myself. But I don't take it any further. Instead, while we wait outside the home, Sally and I try to quickly come up with an elaborate plan to trick Dr. Severs into not dropping us off at the home tomorrow and instead letting us ride our bikes.

We agree that Dr. Severs is nosy and suspicious, so if he gets the idea that this is something we want, he'll block it. And maybe it would even put at risk the flexibility we have now. So, Sally suggests we tell Dr. Severs that we're working on a science project together. And that, for the next couple of weeks, we'll need to make stops at the library and at her house after reading to the old people. So, it would be easier if we have our bikes with us at the nursing home. And Sally's big twist is, then we ask Dr. Severs if he can put the bikes into his trunk at school and tote them out here. Because, she says, a selfish prick like Dr. Severs is definitely going to tell us to just ride them here ourselves.

"So, we've got to talk deets about the experiment in front of him, like we're really into it, you know? We've got to talk about it so much that he doesn't want to hear about it anymore," Sally says, and she starts to teach me some of the stuff that she learned in lab class last year.

So, we finally land on a science topic that we think will pass the Dr. Severs believability test, and she gives me just enough information to fake it on the ride home. We kind of rehearse improv the discussion just once, and as we finish Dr. Severs pulls up in his garbage car.

"So, Dr. Severs," Sally says, climbing into the backseat.

"Me first, okay, Sally?" Dr. Severs interrupts. "Look, you two are almost teenagers, right? And I'm getting a little tired of being, like, the RMSOC chauffer. I mean, I've got projects to plan and important stuff to do. And, well, carting you guys back and forth is kind of a waste of my time, you know?"

I exchange looks with Sally. This could work, too.

"I guess we co… co… could ride our bikes out here, if you want."

"Done!" Dr. Severs says, "Okay, Sally, what did you want to talk about?"

"Whatever. Nothing," Sally says, bitter because Dr. Severs is getting something that he wants, despite the fact that we're getting something that we want, or maybe just because there's no longer any deception involved.

"How'd it go, Sally, on your first day?" Dr. Severs asks her.

"Fine."

"How'd she do, Elroy?"

"Fine," I say.

I want to say that she did awesome. And I want to say that the RMSOC is awesome. I want to say that, in less than a week, the RMSOC has landed me two new friends, a bike, a phone and, literally, the three best days of my life. I want to say that the RMSOC is the best thing that ever happened to me. But Dr. Severs is such a dick. He's totally coincident to any of this good stuff that's happened to me, and he probably would have found a way to block it if he had the chance.

Plus, he told Sally I'm gay. And that Father Mcloughlin is my birth father. Both of which were supposed to be confidential, regardless of the fact that they were lies. So, there's no way that I'll ever give him any positive feedback about anything.

"Come on, guys! Let's get a little more pumped, here. We're getting triple credit for community service hours here at the nursing home. We're putting the RMSOC on the map, and we're helping people. I want to see you put your hearts into it, okay?"

"Fine," Sally and I say, both flat, almost in unison. Dr. Severs gives us an exasperated growl and no one says anything else until he's back in the school parking lot.

"You're dropping us here?" Sally asks.

"Yeah. I picked you up here, remember? Plus, Elroy lives, like, right over there." Dr. Severs points in the general vicinity of my foster house.

"You're not even going to offer to drive me home?"

"Where do you live?" Dr. Severs asks, sighing.

"It's only a few blocks from here."

"So, do you want me to drive you home then?"

"No, I've got my bike," Sally says. "It's locked up in the rack over there. I just wanted to see if you were going to offer."

"I was gonna offer, Sally."

"Easy to say, after the fact."

"Whatever. So you guys will head over to the nursing home on your own tomorrow, right? You're not going to wait for me before you go, correct?"

"Wait, are you offering to drive us?" Sally asks, "We could put our bikes in your trunk."

"Do you want me to drive you?"

"Are you offering?"

"No," Dr. Severs says after having thought about it for a second.

"Then I guess you'll never know if we wanted you to drive us. All you'll ever know about any of it is that you're a selfish person." Sally says and climbs out of the backseat.

"Whatever, Sally. Grow up. I'm the one that created the RMSOC in the first place. How can I be a selfish…"

And Sally slams the passenger door, mid-sentence.

"So, meet here tomorrow after school?" she asks me.

"Can I me… me… meet you at the nursing home? I've got a co… co… couple things to do after school and don't know how long it will take."

Sally looks at me funny.

"Sure," she says. "So. Good day, right?"

"Right. Good day. See you to… to… tomorrow," I say and walk towards my foster home.

I look back a couple of times, just to make sure Sally gets her bike unlocked and rides off okay.

Frank

Disciples? Why not? Disciples. Yeah, that could work.

Sally

~ *Sally, honey, I'm not asking you for an explanation. I'm happy you had a good day.*

~ I'm not trying to give you an explanation. I'm just saying that it doesn't have anything to do with my plans to kill myself. Once I figure out how I'm gonna do it, I mean.

~ *How about you stop with all these absolutes and just take it day-by-day. You're alive, right? So just live. You're only twelve-years-old.*

~ And you were only twenty-five.

~ *You're not me.*

~ No, that's the thing. I am you. And I am Dad. And I'm living in the same hot mess that made you guys decide to punch out early, so you can't expect me to just look on the bright side.

~ *So fine, I'm not trying to convince you not to kill yourself, either. I'm not real, you know. You're just arguing with yourself, crazy girl.*

~ You're real to me. You're one of the only things that's real to me, no matter how crazy that makes me sound.

~ *So, fine. You really want to know what I think?*

~ Of course I do.

~ *Well, if you're going to kill yourself anyway, then I'd say you've got a free pass to do whatever you want to do right up until the end. So, if you're really going to do it, then you might as well go out with a bang, you know? Because you're in the unique position of having absolutely nothing to lose. And this whole Frank Johnson thing, and this kid, Elroy? I mean, it sounds like there's some potential for a lot of fireworks there. If it were me, I'd make the most of that kind of send-off.*

~ It would give us something to talk about. After, I mean. You know I love you, Aunt Sadie, right?

~ *I love you too, Lambchop.*

Elroy

So, another day without running into the Jew Crew at school, which is good. But I'm getting worried about what will happen when I eventually do run into them, because it's bound to happen. Me being so obviously the reason that they all had detention for the first week of school. And I have a feeling they're not going to let that slide.

I did pass Saul Lipski in the hall today, the big one, the one that could pulverize me. But the other two weren't with him. He was all alone, like me, in the crowded hallway. He gave me a quick stink-eye, but then he looked away just as fast. Like he didn't want anything developing, just the two of us. So maybe he's just a thirteen-year-old kid when he's all alone. But knowing that isn't going to help me much when I run into him with the other two.

I also saw Sally at the end of the hallway, when we were switching classes after lunch. She waved and I waved back. But then she ducked into a classroom before I had a chance to talk to her. I'm going to ask her about her class schedule, casual like, so maybe I can find a way to run into her more often during the day.

After dismissal I hang back in the Social Studies classroom for a few minutes, give everyone else a chance to take off. Then I dart to my foster home, grab my bike, remember to bring my helmet and the giant lock, start walking to the nursing home.

I'm about a block from my foster home, approaching the school, when I see them. In the school parking lot, hanging out under the basketball hoop. And what's worse, they see me. I'm walking this bike, carrying the helmet and oversized lock, so running isn't really an option. And I'd only be putting off the inevitable. And by now my spine has turned to ice. I actually start to dry heave some, because what am I going to say to Frank if they take my bike?

"El-roy, El-roy, El-roy! Jew Crew in da'house, just hanging and talkin, when alls a sudden we sees a dead man walkin!" Saul Lipski raps.

Part of me is thinking how right I was about the whole gang mentality thing. Congratulations, Dr. Freud. And I just keep moving, step after step. Throwing up in my mouth and swallowing it. Praying for a miracle.

"Welllll… Jay-field, getting ready to drop the mic, cause stutter-boy bringin me a bran new bike!" Jacob Hirschfield raps.

They start on a path to intercept me. And there's nothing at all I can do about it. Isaac Rothstein, the weird little guy, is a step behind them, doing all kinds of flexed-finger arm scissors. I could probably beat Isaac to death with the lock, but I don't have any chance with the other two.

"Sup, stranger?" Sally shouts, pulling up behind me on her bike and scaring me so much that I pee myself a little. Maybe Frank has a point about the diapers. Sally is all smiles, not yet registering the two brutes and midget, walking this way, ready to beat me to death. I guess, if Frank were here, my humiliation could be complete.

"Hey," I say to Sally as she pulls to a stop beside me.

"What're you doing?"

"That's a ha… ha… hard question to answer," I say, looking at the Jew Crew, who are, like, ten feet away by now. Sally follows my eyes.

"What the hell do you losers want?" Sally asks the Jew Crew, tough girl like, getting off her bike.

"Stutter-boy gots my bike," Jacob Hirschfield says.

He folds his arms high on his chest. Sally opens her eyes wide at him, cocks her head.

"That so?" she says.

"Yea-yah," Hirschfield says.

Sally nods, like maybe she agrees with him. And then she tucks her chin down into her chest and winds up like a lion getting ready to roar.

"RAAAAAAAAAPE!" Sally screams in a voice that sounds like what death must sound like. "RAAAAAAAAPE! HEEELP! HELP! ME! THEY'RE TRYING TO RAPE ME! RAAAAAAAPE!"

And the Jew Crew just stops, dead in their tracks, all standing there with their mouths hanging open and no blood in their faces. Sally stops for a second to take a breath, and she actually smirks at them. And then she drops to her knees, arms spread at her sides, like Willem Dafoe in that Vietnam movie when the helicopters were flying away, and goes at it again.

"RAAAAAAAAAAAAAAAPE! RAAAAAAAAAAAAAAPE!"

There are, like, six or seven adults doing different things in a fifty-yard radius around the school parking lot, and by now they are all looking this way. I mean, how could you not?

And this second roar, it totally breaks the Jew Crew's inertia. They scramble, bump into each other, spin around in an every-man-for-himself panicked get away. Three Stooges style, only supercharged on meth or acid or one of those drugs that make people pop.

I don't know for sure, I've never tried these drugs. I've only heard about them, and my last foster mom only smoked pot.

And just like that, the Jew Crew is gone. This, I think, is what an eerie silence sounds like. And Sally gets up, brushes off her knees, smiles at me, then waves a "We're okay" to the adults around the parking lot.

"So why are you walking your bike?" she asks, as if nothing had just happened.

Frank

Maybe they got in trouble because I let them drink yesterday. Or maybe Mrs. Liptenstein is dead. I haven't seen her in the lobby at all today. Something is definitely wrong. But there's Hardy, chatting up the desk nurse, not a care in the world. Looking over at me every once in a while, all kinds of sinister, but really no different than usual. He's setting me up.

After about an hour, he walks over to the couch where I'm sitting, stands in front of me. I look out the window at the sunny day that I'm missing.

"We can end this, you know," Hardy says to the side of my face. I still can't figure out his angle.

"It's like I hear a voice," I say, glancing around the room, "but it's not really there."

"Maybe we can work out a compromise, Johnson. This whole charade isn't doing either of us any good."

"There it is again," I say, wistfully.

"Look, I'm ready to split the difference. I'll refund you three months of the six you have left if you get the hell out of here, by tomorrow. I've got this school club coming every day for the next couple of months, you know. You're not going to have a moment to yourself."

"Maybe the television is turned up too loud in one of the rooms?" I muse. "I should ask maintenance to have a look."

"Three months or nothing. I'm not going to just fold," Hardy says calmly. "Last chance. Going once. Going twice. Ah, it looks like your reader is finally here!"

And there are Elroy and Sally, walking in the front door, looking like they've spent the past two hours being dragged behind a field plow. I feign exasperation for Hardy's sake, stomp off to my room. There better be a good reason. From the look of them, I figure there is.

"Sally, hi!" I hear Hardy say feebly as I walk away. There's a brief indecision in his voice about whether to bring up the fact that she and Elroy look like tumbleweeds, which seems quickly followed by his decision to just ignore it. "Mrs. Liptenstein is under the weather today, so you'll be reading to Colonel Adams. Elroy, you know the drill."

I hear Elroy marching behind me.

Sally

"Jesus, Elroy! Pedal! Pedal!"

I'm running behind his bike, my hand clutching the seat and pulling hard to the right because the whole scrawny weight of him is listing to the left.

And... I lose it. He falls. Luckily, we're on the grass slope next to the school because he lands on his face. For the third time.

"Is the bi... bi... bike okay?" he mumbles, fingers still locked on the handlebars, face buried in turf and dirt.

"The bike's fine. It's like titanium or something. How's your face?"

"Fine."

"Look, dude. You've got to trust the fact that when you pedal, the bike will stay up. You only have to make this leap of faith once. When it happens, you'll believe it and everything will be apple pie. But you got to believe it! I mean, think about it. Do you know how many idiots can ride a bike?"

Maybe motivational speaking is not in the cards for me.

"Let's go ba... ba... back up to the top," Elroy says.

He lifts up the bike, walks up the hill again. When we get to the top, he mounts, feet on the ground straddling the bike, bracing himself.

"Okay, I got the bike," I say. "I'll hold you up. You just focus on staying centered and pedaling."

"You said that the la... la... last three times," Elroy says.

I think he might be making a joke.

"And you said you'd pedal the last three times! And instead you just turn the pedals once and then stand on them in a slow lean into the dirt! Come on, man – you've got this. Just forget about falling and let go. Trust the Force!"

And he exhales, inhales, grimaces and launches himself down the hill with me sprinting behind. And after maybe twenty feet he buries his face in the dirt. Again.

On about the twentieth time down the hill, he gets it. And it's brilliant. I'm sprinting behind him, holding the seat, thinking about shoving him over myself because that's how frustrated I am, when he finally starts to pedal. I mean, he'd pedaled before, but then he'd stand on the pedals and tilt over.

This time he pedals with both feet, like he means it. And I'm running beside him, whooping like a maniac, telling him to keep pedaling because it's all him, because I'm not holding on anymore. And I can only see the back of his head, but somehow I know what his face looks like, all dirt and grass-stained and full of joy. And, this is weird, because I'm suddenly thinking about how I can't wait to have kids someday. Even though I, like, won't be around someday to have kids because I'm going to kill myself.

But it's not like I'm making any decisions right now. The two thoughts are side-by-side in my head and even though they contradict, it's okay. Because I am as happy as I have been in a very long time. And I'm laughing hysterical and breathless when Elroy face plants at the bottom of the hill because he doesn't know how to turn and would have gone off the grass and into the street otherwise.

By the time I get down to him, he's on his feet, and I have never seen a smile that big. I jump right into his arms, wrap my legs around his waist, dropping him like a sack of potatoes. Slam, flat onto his back. I probably weigh more than he does and there was a lot of momentum, what with me running at him downhill.

I probably should have thought that through, because I'm hoping I just knocked the wind out of him as he rolls around gasping for air like a dying person. But even though I'm kind of worried, it doesn't kill my mood at all. Because we did it! And I can't even remember the last time I did anything with anyone else!

Finally, Elroy starts to breathe again, and the O of his mouth goes right back to the smile he was wearing right before I sacked him. He coughs, and a little blood comes out, but right now neither of us wants to worry about something like that.

"I get it! I get it," Elroy says. "Let's go to the flat part of the parking lot so I can figure out how to turn. Can you hold onto the seat while I get started?"

I don't say a word about the fact that he didn't just stutter.

Joe Barrett

Elroy

So, yeah, I can ride a bike. I! Can ride! A bike!
You know, it's easy. No big deal.

Frank

"I'm not sure if I even want to know," I say.

Elroy is beaming. Like he just had sex for the first time. And I wonder if he did just have sex for the first time. With Sally.

They were both all dirty and beat up when they walked into the lobby. Kind of rough sex, it would have to be, but who knows what kids are into these days. Jesus, they're not even teenagers yet. What kind of world are we living in? Elroy can't stop smiling and I'm getting a little grossed out.

So then Sally walks into my room with Colonel Adams. And she points at my bed, tells him to sit, the way you'd talk to a collie dog.

"Would you happen to have a cigarette?" Colonel Adams asks Sally.

"Yeah, I'm twelve-years-old, but sure, you can have one of my cigarettes. Is menthol okay?" Sally replies, rummaging through an imaginary purse, smiling like an idiot.

She and Elroy definitely had sex. Oh, my god. This can't be my fault?

"That would be fine," Colonel Adams says eagerly.

"Oh, sorry. I must have left them in my other purse. No, wait, here they are!" Sally says and holds her thumb and forefinger a centimeter apart. She hands the Colonel a little piece of air. Which he takes from her.

Then the Colonel pulls a real Zippo lighter from his vest pocket. He flares the lighter in front of his fingers, then proceeds to make smoking gestures, sighing with great satisfaction. Roll the laugh-track, because there have got to be hidden cameras on us right now.

"Excuse me, Colonel, could we have a moment?" I ask respectfully of the old man smoking an imaginary menthol cigarette on my bed, and he nods.

"Now look," I say to Elroy and Sally, "I don't want to be the adult in the room, here. No offense, Colonel." The Colonel inhales deeply, flicks his fingers, palm down, indicating that I can go on, "But don't you think you guys are a little young for this type of thing?"

"Uh, it's not a real cigarette, Mr. Johnson," Sally says.

"Jesus, Sally. You can call me Frank. we were drinking together yesterday. And I'm not talking about the cigarette..." I look at the Colonel. He blows imaginary smoke at me, "...about the, whatever's happening over there. I'm talking about what's going on with you two."

"What do you mean, what's going on with us two?" Sally asks.

"Your big smiles, the fact that you're both all dirty..."

"What, I just taught Elroy how to..."

"Yahahaaaa," I interrupt and wave my hands in her face. "I don't want the details!"

"I just taught Elroy how to ride a bike," she says flatly, chin lowered, eyebrows raised. Ugh. Awkward.

But wait a second.

"You didn't know how to ride a bike?" I ask Elroy.

"Nope," Elroy says. "But I do now. I rode all the way out here."

"Why didn't you tell me you didn't know how to ride a bike?"

"I don't know. I was embarrassed, I guess. Anyway, how would I have ever learned how to ride a bike? I mean, it's not something you're born knowing how to do. And I never had a bike before. Or a friend to teach me."

"You cut me deep, Elroy."

"Aw, come on, Frank. I'm sorry. I would definitely have let you teach me how to ride the bike. But you were just so excited about getting it for me, and I didn't want to disappoint you by not knowing how to ride it."

"Hey, are you lying?" I ask.

Sally steps behind Elroy, starts waving me off like I'm a swarm of killer bees. What's her problem?

"What?" Elroy asks, "Why would I lie about something like that? Oh, right."

"Are you freaking kidding me?!" Sally screams at me. "He hasn't stuttered once since he learned how to ride that bike! And you go and blow it! Wake up, man!"

Damn.

"Okay, okay, I'm sorry. My bad. Totally. Don't say anything Elroy. Maybe you can get it back."

The Colonel looks at me like I am something that he scraped off the bottom of his shoe and I wonder what's going on in his head right now. He takes another drag of the space between his two fingers.

"And what were you talking about, about us two, when I came in?" Sally asks me pointedly.

"Nothing. Forget it. Misunderstanding."

"You are not inspiring a whole lot of confidence right now, you know. If we're going to try and make some kind of alternative church group, you're going have to pull yourself together. Otherwise you're wasting our time, here."

Sassy little thing.

"Whoa, easy, Lambchop. I got confused. It happens."

"What did you call me?" Sally asks, and I think she kind of sobs at the question mark.

"What?"

"What did you just call me?"

"What? Lambchop? Why?"

"Why would you call me that?"

"I don't know. it just came out. Sorry," I say, and Sally's eyes fill with tears.

Seriously, what the hell did I just do?

"My Aunt Sadie calls me Lambchop," Sally says, full-on sobbing now.

"Okay, okay. I'm sorry. Don't… get upset. Ah, I'm sorry. Ah, what am I sorry about?"

"You're disgusting," the Colonel says to me, nose in the air.

Screw you, old man.

"Look, Sally, I'm really sorry, but I honestly don't know what's going on here. Just, don't get upset, alright? I mean, you can get upset if you want, but…"

"I think her Aunt Sadie died a couple weeks ago," Elroy says. He looks at Sally, who nods, sobs.

For the love of God, seriously?

"I'm, ah, I'm really sorry, Sally. How did she die?"

"I think she killed herself," Elroy answers, looks at Sally, she nods again, sobs again.

Are you freaking kidding me? How in the world was I supposed to know that her aunt, who killed herself just two weeks ago, used to call her Lambchop? Who the hell calls a kid Lambchop? Though I guess I just did. Weird. But anyway. And I don't mention that Elroy didn't stutter just then, for several reasons.

"It's okay," Sally says finally. "How would you have known that she called me that."

I know, right? And then Sally smiles, big, like she's imprinting on me or something. I've got to get out more.

The Colonel turns towards me again. I raise an open palm and hold it in front of his face.

"One word, old man, and I'm going to put that cigarette out in your eye!" At this point, why not?

"I could kill you with a spoon, Butterhead," the Colonel replies calmly, looks back out the window.

Oddly, I'm familiar with the slang. It's how my own grandad used to refer to Japanese soldiers when he was talking about the war, because of their butter-colored skin. We are totally in the bizzaro world right now.

"Can we all just take a minute, guys? I think things have kind of unraveled here," I say.

And everyone takes a few breaths. I look out the window and there's probably only an hour or two of sunlight left. So, in terms of getting out, this day is pretty much shot.

Sally

So, okay, I'm not crazy here. I mean, sure, I'm totally planning to kill myself and everything, but I'm not, like, out of touch with reality. And there's no way I can believe that Frank calling me Lambchop was just some random thing. There are, like, a zillion casual terms of endearment out there. And Lambchop wouldn't even be in the top million.

So, I'm thinking, it has to be a sign.

~ So, was it you?

~ *What do you think?*

~ I don't know. That's why I'm asking.

~ *Does anyone else ever call you Lambchop?*

~ No. But no one else ever really calls me anything. Is it, like, a New Jersey thing? Something popular around here to call girls when you were growing up? I assume Frank's from New Jersey. I mean, where else would someone like him be from?

~ *There was a TV show with a puppet named Lambchop when I was a kid. Maybe he saw the same show.*

~ See? How can you say that you're just a voice in my head? How would I have known that there was a TV show with a puppet named Lambchop when you were a kid? Only you would know that.

~ *I've been calling you Lambchop since you were a baby. Maybe I told you why one time. I think I even got you a puppet like the one named Lambchop when you were little.*

~ Don't ruin it, Aunt Sadie.

~ *If you want to think it was a sign, then think it was a sign. A sign of what, anyway?*

~ I don't know. Maybe what he was talking about with the Church? What's wrong with it, how it needs to change?

~ A religious sign? Seriously? Don't make me say that you're reminding me of your mother. I don't want to offend you, here in your own head.

~ No, not a religious sign. Anyway, he's not talking about religion. He's talking about people opening up and letting each other in. So, like, Lambchop could be a sign from you letting me know that it's okay to open up to him. And to Elroy. To, you know, embrace the whole thing, not hold back.

~ But isn't Frank, like, insane?

~ Oh, definitely. He's hanging on by a thread. But aren't we all? I mean, I'm having a conversation with my favorite Aunt, who recently ended her own life.

~ Fair point.

~ So, I'm still going to kill myself and everything. That plan hasn't changed. But in the meantime, I'm going to take this Lambchop thing as a sign from you that it's okay to really dive in with this whole Frank and Elroy thing. Are you good with that?

~ Whatever you want, Lambchop.

~ Maybe you could be a little more definitive for me?

~ I would, if you'd let me.

~ Fine. I love you, Aunt Sadie.

~ I love you, too, Lambchop.

"Hey, Sally? You with us here?" Frank asks.

He's been asking a few times already, maybe. We're all still in his room. Frank, Elroy, Colonel Adams and me. I took a bit of a powder, I guess.

"Yeah," I say, "I'm with you guys."

"We good? You and me, I mean," Frank asks.

"We're good."

"Okay, so it's Tuesday, which gives us four days to figure out how to divert church traffic to our own little outdoor soiree on Sunday," Frank says. "So here's what I'm thinking…"

"Hey, Frank?" I say.

"Yeah?"

"It's okay if you want to call me Lambchop. I mean, you don't have to. But it's okay if you want to. You, too, Elroy. If you ever want to, even though I know that might be weird, you can call me Lambchop, too," I say, and my eyes sting a little. "But not you, Colonel. You can only call me Sally."

The old man looks at me, shrugs, continues to smoke his imaginary cigarette and stare out the window.

Elroy

So that careful part of me, you know, the one that tells me not to get too attached to anything good? I think it must have fallen down a well or something, because I can kind of hear it yelling in an echo, like a faraway voice, but I can't hear anything that it's trying to tell me.

Of course, I know what it's trying to tell me. I've lived with it for, like, twelve years. But you know what? I think I'm done listening to it. Because, not only do I know how to ride a bike, my own bike, but my two best friends are also my two biggest heroes. How often does that happen? And they like me. Both of them do. There, I said it, and I didn't get struck by lightning and the sky didn't fall on my head.

I mean, can you believe it? Put aside the whole teaching me how to ride a bike, thing. Is anyone going to say anything about what Sally did to the Jew Crew? Probably not, I guess, unless I do. Sally didn't even seem to think twice about it. What the hell is this girl made of? And why is she friends with me? Frank, too. I mean, I have no idea what they see in me, but I want to see it, too. Or at least believe it's there, whatever it is.

"Hey, Elroy. Bring it back, huh?" Frank says, however much time it is after he tells us all to take a minute. "What is with everyone today?"

"Sorry. I zoned out," I say.

"Sally?" Frank says, "Hey, Sally?"

Sally's eyes are open and she's staring out the window through the Colonel's imaginary smoke rings. Frank looks at me, as if I might know what to do.

"Should I shake her or something?" I ask.

"I don't know," Frank says. "Isn't there something about how you shouldn't startle a sleepwalker because it will, like, give them a heart attack or something?"

"I don't know. Maybe we shouldn't mess with her," I say.

"Sally?" Frank says again. "Hey, Sally? You with us, here?"

And she comes out of it.

"Yeah," Sally says, "I'm with you guys."

Frank asks if everything's okay between them, because of the whole Lambchop thing I guess, and she tells him everything's good.

"Okay, so it's Tuesday, which gives us four days to figure out how to divert church traffic to our own little outdoor soiree on Sunday," Frank says. "So here's what I'm thinking…"

But Sally interrupts him, says it's okay for him to call her Lambchop, if he wants to. Then she tells me that it's okay for me to call her Lambchop, too. And I think I love Sally. Like maybe I'm actually totally and completely in love with her.

But I don't think I could pull off calling her Lambchop.

"Okay, Lambchop," Frank says, gently. Obviously, he can pull it off. "So how about we talk about how we're going to let people know that there's an alternative to boring old Sunday Mass in a few days?"

We decide that the best way to make this happen is to carpet bomb the church with signs and flyers about fifteen minutes before noon Mass on Sunday.

And we—meaning Frank—all decide that it all has to have a parochial feel, so that normal church-goers don't get scared away by the idea of some kind of hippie love-in, in Frank's words. And then Franks sets about assigning tasks to everyone. And he proceeds to assign all of the main tasks to himself, which he will execute on his computer. Messaging for the main sign, messaging for the secondary signs, messaging for the flyers, design of the main sign, design of the secondary signs, design of the flyers.

And this is fine with Sally and me, because this whole thing is kind of Frank's gig. Obviously.

And then Frank talks about the actual get together that we're going to have with the people we can divert from Sunday Mass. And he wants to have a real spread, as he calls it. You know, like Jesus would have wanted, he keeps saying. Which I think is maybe starting to get a little sacrilegious and I'm not even a Christian, but he's all jacked up so Sally and I just go with it.

"So, screw the whole loaves-and-fishes thing. Let's talk treats," Frank says. "Imagine you're some poor sap getting ready to be bored to death for an hour of your weekend, standing up, kneeling down, listening to stuff you don't understand, reciting responses that you don't really mean, eating a single stale cracker and taking a sip of bad wine… And then, here we are. Behind door number two! What would blow your mind?!" And then Frank proceeds to answer his own question. "I'll tell you what would blow your mind. Water ice. Everyone loves water ice. We can get, like, five different flavors, all gourmet-style, like cucumber-lychee and cherry-lime. And we can get scoopers and little paper cups, and we can serve it to them. That would beat the crap out of those little crackers, especially on a hot day."

"Water ice?" Sally asks me.

"It's like Italian ice, same thing," I say. A little fact I picked up living in a South Jersey foster home, outside of Philadelphia.

"And sticky buns," Frank continues, ignoring our aside, "because who knows if everyone's had breakfast? And even if they have, who wouldn't want a sticky bun? And we'll have those individual hand-wipes, because we're that considerate. And what else? I'll tell you what else. Sangria, that's what. It's still the season. And we can make a lot of it and everyone can have as much as they want. And maybe we can add a bottle or two of Everclear, which is basically moonshine, to give it a little kick, you know? And limeade for the kids. Not lemonade. Limeade. Because it's different, it's special. Just like everyone who chooses to join our meeting. Are you guys feeling me?"

Sally and I both nod, encouragingly, even though he's getting a little manic. And I think Frank's rant is making both of us feel better, because for a while it felt like we were the only crazy ones in the room. Aside from the Colonel.

So, tomorrow or Thursday, whenever Frank gets through with the signs and flyers, we've got to go to Kinko's and pick up the materials that he'll order online. And then, latest Saturday, we've got to buy the booze and make the Sangria, which means we've got to get Frank out of the nursing home at least once this week. And Frank's going to work on ordering the shaved ice and sticky buns, and all the necessary wares and utensils, for delivery on Sunday morning around eleven-fifteen.

When it comes to Sally and me, we just have to find a good spot for the alternative Sunday gathering, somewhere on the church grounds. Not so far from the front door that we can't be seen by everyone entering the church. And we've got to make sure that Dr. Severs can bring Frank to the church, because how else would he get there since no one knows that he's got a car in the lot.

And so, we've got a plan.

"But what are you going to talk about when we get everyone to the spot? Are we just going to give them some food and drink and see what happens?" Sally asks, reasonably, I think.

"Bah! Don't worry about that, Lambchop," Frank says sweetly. "Just leave it to me."

And ten minutes later, after we've all thumbs-up'd the plan, after we've said our good-byes, carted the Colonel back to the lobby and signed ourselves out, Sally and I are riding our bikes home just as the sun is starting to set. And even though I just learned to ride a bike today, we're going fast. Too fast. Sally is yelling at me to be careful, but I'm wearing my helmet so what can really happen? I keep pulling ahead, making her keep up. Because it feels like I'm flying.

It feels like I'm actually flying.

Frank

I'm on the lower part of the church roof where it comes all the way down, almost to the ground. It's maybe just six feet high where I am. And I'm on my stomach, flat on the shingles, reaching down to grab this giant rock from Elroy because we need it for what we're doing. And the rock is like half as big as Elroy, must weigh twice as much as he weighs. And this time there are some roots or thick vine-like things wrapped around the huge rock.

And I've gripped the vines firmly with both hands, and I'm pulling it up onto the roof as Elroy lifts it from underneath. Lifts it until the giant stone is right over his head. And just as I pull this giant rock away from his reaching fingertips, the vine unravels. And the rock drops. I'm backwards on the roof from the momentum of the vine breaking free, so I can't see what happens.

I scream, "Elroy!" Scramble to the side of the roof, look down. And he is totally underneath the rock. Wile E. Coyote style, like in the Roadrunner cartoons. He's not screaming or crying, just groaning quietly, like he's mostly asleep.

I drop head-first from the roof and kind of roll next to him and pull the rock straight up off of his chest. And there's no blood, but it's bad. It's like his chest has flattened by about four inches, way too much to be a "shake it off" kind of hurt. I'm screaming for help, not sure if I should try to move him or if that would only make it worse, when I sit straight up. Wide awake.

This is, like, the fifteenth time I've had the dream tonight. The vine thing was an interesting variation. I think it helped me dream about a bigger rock.

I don't usually go all Jung on dreams, but this one seems kind of obvious even though I don't totally get it. What's also weird is, Sally doesn't show up in any of these recurring night terrors. It's just Elroy helping me in a way that gets him, like, destroyed. Always something that crushes this huge cavity into his chest. But there's never any blood, it's just like he deflates.

And always this recurring dénouement moment just before I wake up, this feeling that maybe none of it would have happened if I'd thought things through a little better, beforehand.

But maybe I'm making too big a deal of it. It doesn't have to mean anything. I'm just exhausted from designing all of the signage, then coding until after three a.m. I wouldn't let anything hurt Elroy. Not that I'm doing anything to intentionally hurt Elroy in my dream, in my dozen-plus recurring night terrors, which are happening more times each night, getting progressively worse since the first dream last Saturday.

And he always gets crushed because we are working together, because he is trying to help me with my plan. Like he's collateral damage. And that thought hits me like a brick in the face, squeezes my heart into a cold little black ball, makes me feel criminally irresponsible, like I've carelessly set a crowded movie theater on fire.

But I'm probably making too big a deal out of it. That's why I try not to over-analyze dreams. I usually don't remember my dreams in the morning, anyway, so how important can they be?

Sally

"And tell me about Dr. Severs? He's great, isn't he? He reminds me so much of you. Of what you could be, I mean. Of what you could do with your life."

"Dr. Severs is fine, Mom."

"Did he say anything about me?"

"Dr. Severs? Why would he say anything about you?"

"Well, I wouldn't expect him to," Mom says.

"Why wouldn't you expect him to say something about you?"

"I guess he wouldn't mention that the whole Rudolphsville Middle School Outreach Club was really my idea? That's okay. I really don't want any credit. I'm just so happy that it's happening. I'll get my reward in heaven."

"*You* came up with the idea for the RMSOC?"

"Yes. Well, me and Dr. Severs. Mostly me. He made an appointment to meet with me last year when he first started at your school, because I'm involved in so many things where the Church crosses over with the community. And he had this idea to start a club where kids at your school could do service work in the community."

"Okay. That's pretty much all the RMSOC is, in a nutshell. So where do you fit in then? I mean, how was it your idea?"

"You're developing a very cynical and bitter shell, Sally. And it's making you ugly to talk to," Mom says, not answering my question.

"Sorry, my favorite person in the world just died." That's going to hurt her. "I haven't gotten over it yet. So anyway, about the RMSOC being your idea?"

"So, Dr. Severs came to me with a concept. Anyone can have a concept. Concepts grow on trees. I was the one that shaped it for him. I pretty much came up with all of what he put on his slides for the school board. The virtuous cycle that can develop between the neighborhood youth and the businesses in town. And how that will affect the status of the neighborhood, how it will affect Main Street and housing values, all of that," Mom says, making an effort not to brag.

"But none of that stuff is actually happening, Mom."

"Not yet. But it *can* happen."

"I suppose it *can* happen," I say, "just like anything *can* happen. But there's nothing about what's going on right now in the RMSOC that would actually *make it* happen. If anything, the RMSOC probably has a lower chance of making that kind of virtuous cycle happen than, say, a bus station full of random people."

"It's because of Dr. Severs, isn't it? He's a good man, but he's young. I was afraid he wouldn't have the practical chops that it would take to turn my vision into a reality. But there is no way that I can take over the RMSOC myself, I've just got too much going on."

"Whoa. No one was asking you to take over the RMSOC. I wasn't even implying that you get involved."

Holy crap. Mom getting involved in the RMSOC, even peripherally, would seriously accelerate my plans to commit suicide. And I've got stuff to do right now. And the RMSOC is actually a pretty big part of it, albeit unintentionally.

"Look, it's going great," I say. "On my first day Dr. Severs actually told me that you contributed so much to the RMSOC. And things start small, right? But I think you set Dr. Severs up right. And I think he knows it. And I think he can get us there. Okay?"

"Alright, Sally. If you say so. It's nice that Dr. Severs even mentioned my contributions, I guess, though I'm sure he wouldn't have gone into the extent of them."

"But I think he knows, Mom."

"Really?"

"Yeah."

Frank

For some reason that dream I had about Elroy last night, like fifteen times, won't leave me alone all day. And it's not like I'm going to talk to him about it or anything, so I'm not sure why I'm so anxious for him to get here this afternoon. Maybe just so I can see that he's alive, that his chest hasn't been caved in by a huge rock. But that's ridiculous, like, what are the chances?

Or maybe it's because he was late yesterday and we didn't get to sneak out to the car and drive off the grounds. That's probably it. Because we're right at the start of our Indian Summer and I want to ride around with my top down, preferably a few drinks in me, as much as possible before Winter gets here. So, it makes sense that I'm anxious for Elroy to arrive.

At three-twenty on the nose, Elroy and Sally walk in the front door. I scan the lobby. No Hardy in sight. I've got my laptop bag with me so I'm all ready to walk out. And no Hardy in the lobby means Sally doesn't need to take any old person luggage, who we'd have to drag around, like Mrs. Liptenstein, that lush. Or the Colonel, who turned out to be kind of a snob and even more of a dick. So, it's shaping up to be a pretty good day when Elroy signs me out, without issue, at the front desk.

"What do you know about dreams?" I ask Sally, sitting beside me in the front seat at Elroy's insistence.

"Everything," Sally replies.

"Really?"

"No. Sorry. Snarky is like an instinct with me," she says and actually sounds sincere above the wind of the moving car.

"I get it," I say. "Not a problem. Just reign it in, you know?"

She nods, smiles.

"Why do you want to know about dreams?" she asks.

"It's nothing. It was just a general question."

"Really? Like, you could have just as easily asked me, what do I know about horses?"

"I've just been having some weird dreams, lately."

"Like what, are you torturing family members to death or something?"

"Really? Is that what having weird dreams means to you?" I ask.

"I wouldn't worry about it. I mean, we're talking about taking a stab at right-setting the Catholic Church. Going into direct competition, so to speak. And even though it's not, like, on a grand scale or anything, that stuff is deep. It can bring up a lot of feelings, especially for someone that was brought up Catholic," Sally says.

I look in the rearview mirror. Elroy isn't following our conversation. Between the back speakers and the wind, he can't hear what we're saying up front.

"It's not about the Church thing. I've got no qualms about trying to put together an alternative to the Church. I mean, we're not hurting anyone. And if we can build some intimacy, maybe help some people and help ourselves, then great. That's not what I'm dreaming about," I say, glance in the rearview. "I'm dreaming about Elroy."

"No way. Sex dreams?"

"What? No! Why would you even say that?"

"I don't know. An older man having dreams about a younger boy. You do the math." She's smiling, like she's only messing with me. "What about Elroy, then?"

"He dies."

"You're having dreams about killing Elroy?"

"No, I'm not having dreams about killing Elroy," I say. "Not directly, I mean. But in the dreams he's, like, helping me. Maybe he's doing something that I should know better than to ask him to do. And then, there's an accident. And I don't actually see him die, and he's always still breathing when I wake up, but usually his chest is caved in. From whatever accident happened. A lot of times it's something that falls on him. In one version, my car rolls into him while he's sitting on a sidewalk, crushes him against a brick wall. But it only crushes his chest. You think I'm just making something out of nothing?"

"How many times have you had these types of dreams? Like, two or three?" Sally asks.

"I woke up from this dream at least fifteen times last night."

"Whoa! Seriously?"

"Yeah. But it's just a dream, right?" I say. "I mean, you can always read so many different things into dreams. Like tea leaves or a Rorschach blot, right?"

"Yeah, but I'm not so sure there are, like, too many ways to interpret that one, Frank."

"So, what do you think it means?" I ask.

"What do you think it means?" she asks back.

"I don't know. I don't think you're supposed to take dreams literally. Like death, in a dream, might actually mean a good thing."

"I can't really see a lot of positive ways to interpret Elroy's chest being accidentally crushed by some kind of blunt force, repeatedly."

"But you don't think I should be worried about it, do you? Like, you don't think something's going to happen to Elroy, right?"

"Do I think that you're actually dreaming about the literal future and should be worried that something's going to happen to Elroy? No, I don't think that. Do I think you should be worried about waking up from variations on the same dream of Elroy dying because of some partial fault of yours, with increasing frequency for the past few nights? Yeah, maybe just a little bit, you should worry about that," Sally says and holds her thumb and index finger an inch apart.

Elroy

Frank pulls into the parking lot of a Mexican place only a couple blocks from my foster house. We walk into the restaurant and are led to a high-backed wooden booth in the rear. Frank sits facing the front of the restaurant. Sally and I sit side-by-side, facing Frank. Whatever they were talking about in the car is apparently over now. The waitress, a pretty, black-haired lady about Frank's age brings us menus, asks what we'd like to drink.

"You two want Sprites?" Frank asks us and we nod. "Two Sprites and a pitcher of margaritas, classic, rocks. And can you have the bartender make it with Hornitos if you've got it, if not, something of the same grade?"

The waitress looks at Frank, then looks at Sally and me. Hesitates.

"You want a pitcher of margaritas?"

"Yeah. What?"

The waitress looks at Sally and me again.

"A whole pitcher?"

"Yes, and it probably won't be the last one. I like margaritas. Is that a problem?"

"Just for you, right?"

"Just one glass," Frank says. "Are you implying that I might be tempted to share some of my margaritas with these tweens, here?" The waitress doesn't say anything. "They're twelve-years-old, for Christsakes. We're getting dangerously close to impacting your tip here, honey."

"Two Sprites, pitcher of classic margaritas, Hornitos, rocks," the waitress says, skeptically. "Salt on the glass?"

"Do I look like a peasant?"

"Salt on the glass," she repeats as a statement, walks back towards the bar.

"Careful with the drinks, guys. I think the waitress is on to us."

"You picked up on that, huh?" Sally says. "Nothing gets by you."

"Easy, Lambchop. You guys can just take sips from my glass. I don't think we want to risk filling a separate glass for each of you."

"So, what's this all about, Frank?" Sally asks. "Why such a liberal attitude towards pre-teen drinking?"

"I've been cooped up for six months. Elroy – and now, you and Elroy – are necessary accomplices in my efforts to sneak out for some daylight, without compromising my position with Hardy. So, in my mind, it justifies a celebration. It's not really about pre-teen drinking, per se, as much as it is about me not wanting to drink alone. Plus, it's safer for you guys to experiment with me than it is for you to sneak off into the woods and experiment by yourselves, don't you think?"

"So, with you we won't overdo it, then?" Sally asks.

"I wouldn't go so far as to say that." Frank's probably remembering me, throwing up in the steak place parking lot three days ago. "Let's just say that few situations are beyond my capabilities to handle. So, at the very least, you'll be safe with me."

"Says our designated driver before he drinks his first pitcher of margaritas."

"Sally, you're safer in the car with me when I'm drunk than you are when I'm sober."

"How so?"

"When I'm drinking, I pull it back a little. I don't drive so fast. I don't trust my super sharp reflexes as much. And I assume that my judgment is slightly impaired, which is something that I do not typically assume when I'm sober. Take now, for example, where sober me is totally comfortable arguing the merits of drunk driving to a twelve-year-old."

"You make an excellent point," Sally says as the waitress walks up to the table with our drinks. She sets the Sprites in front of Sally and me. She sets the pitcher squarely in front of Frank, in the middle of his placemat, and puts the salted glass where glasses usually go.

"I'm sensing something," Frank says to the waitress.

"You're sensing me, concerned that you are going to give these children alcohol, and worried that I am somehow going to lose my job because of it," she says.

"Utter nonsense. You have nothing to worry about. Ah, we're going to need a few minutes," Frank says and pulls out his laptop, opens it in front of the waitress, and makes a show of scrolling through designs for our signs and flyers. "We're working on a Church project."

Sally

So, let me start by saying that Frank is definitely a crazy person. The fact that he seems to have a good heart doesn't make him any more sane than a bedbug. I mean, I'm a twelve-year-old girl, drinking tequila with him, at four o'clock on a Wednesday. So, you know, do the math. But he's got a few valid points.

First, I agree with Frank that most people just go through the motions when it comes to religion. I mean, I definitely don't connect with anything that goes on at Mass.

Second, I also agree with Frank that we'd be better off looking inside ourselves instead of praying to a God that's "out there" somewhere. It's just a lot simpler to look at God from the inside-out perspective because we can actually try to figure out the inside part.

Third, I think he has a point when he says that people can't really reach deep and relate to each other when they're all kinds of loaded down with shame. So, this idea of exposing yourself to get past the shame and start creating some real intimacy with other people, that also makes sense to me.

And I guess I'm on board with his idea that the best way for anyone to drop their guard enough to expose themselves is to have a party. A real party. Like, to make sure people are really enjoying themselves. Talking deep, yeah. Being vulnerable, yeah. But doing it because they're not taking themselves too seriously. So, mixing it all up with food and drink and good times. Frank says that's what Jesus was trying to do in the first place.

And, oh, side note. Frank's fully convinced that he's got this total 'bro' relationship with the person who was actually Jesus. The historical person, I mean. More like he's the only one who really gets Jesus these days. And it's not, like, a real-time relationship, the kind I have with Aunt Sadie in my head. It's more like the type of relationship you'd have with a favorite author who's dead, like Charles Dickens or Ernest Hemingway.

So, even though I don't think Frank is at all mentally stable, I agree with a lot of what he's trying to do when it comes to hijacking community from the Church and hitting the reset button.

I guess it's the idea that he actually believes he can pull this off, on any scale, is what makes him crazy.

And all of this is what's going through my head very clearly, like I can really see it all. And then I kind of ride this wave down into a fuzzy hole. We should not have ordered that third pitcher of margaritas.

Elroy

So, Sally's just sitting there, drinking Frank's margarita, kind of listening and kind of lost in thought. And Frank keeps talking about what's wrong with the Church and the whole idea of worship and how people don't really relate to themselves or to other people. And he's really getting riled up, like he does when he talks about this stuff. So, then he stops for a second to, like, kind of check in with Sally. And Sally closes her eyes, looks like she's about to say something very wise.

But instead she throws up. Like, huge. Like a fire hydrant when you knock the valve off, the kind of liquid pressure that you wouldn't think a small body like hers could possibly produce. And all of it hits Frank square in the chest, continuously, for like a couple of seconds, easy. And it splashes all over the rest of Frank and all over the booth and the table and me. And when it finally stops, Frank and I are just frozen, looking at each other for I don't know how long.

"We shoul nothav ordereded tha thir picture uh magatitas," Sally slurs, and this kick-starts Frank back into action.

"Run. Out. Now," Frank says in whisper-shout. He pulls out his wallet and throws all this money on the table. There are, like, hundred dollar bills in there. And I scramble out of the booth just as Frank reaches in to grab Sally. Then I'm running to the front door and Frank's right on my heels, Sally like a sack of potatoes under his arm, his laptop bag swinging from his shoulder. And after we burst through the front door, Frank overtakes me, does a kind of shake-and-bake in the harsh sunlight, darts into a little alley between the restaurant and a dry cleaner. And I'm right behind him.

"What about your car?!" I scream, thinking he's, like, going to let them have the car, too?

"They won't know it's mine!" he shouts over his shoulder and crosses the street behind the restaurant and ducks into another alley. I can hear shouts coming from the front of the building.

"Where are we going?!"

"Away from here!" Frank yells. "Far as we can get! Look, we just need to lay low for an hour or two! Come on, keep up!"

He's somehow maneuvered Sally's limp body over his shoulder as we duck-and-run through another block of alleyways. We dart to the left and I see my school, just two blocks ahead of us.

"No! This way!" I scream and run the alley dumpster route behind the buildings until we end up on the backside of the closed soup kitchen that Dr. Severs and I were supposed to work at last Thursday. Was that really less than a week ago?

"Stop!" Frank shouts, chest heaving. "We've got to stop! Stop here."

He uses what looks like his last bit of strength to lay Sally gently on the pavement, her back against the concrete wall of the soup kitchen building. And then he turns and flops down next to her at the edge of the building, struggling to catch his breath. Sally looks like a rag doll, but she's got this peaceful smile on her face like somewhere in there is a small part of her that's aware, that thinks all of this is amusing. She definitely doesn't look sick.

"We can't stay out here in the open," Frank pants. "We need cover. A safe house, until things settle down."

I smile.

"It's fine," I say, catching my own breath. "I know where we can go."

"What? Where?"

"My house."

"Your house?"

"My foster house."

"Sober up, dude. How are we going to get to your foster house?"

"Look," I say and pull his shoulder so that he can twist around to see up the alley. "It's right over there. The grey house."

"Seriously?"

"Yeah," I say, and Frank smiles, like maybe he might start to enjoy this whole adventure again.

Frank

"Come on in," Elroy says and steps through his front door.

And even with everything else going on, it's hard for me not to notice what a freakshow this place is. Like a low-budget horror movie set from the eighties. Like, interior design by Mrs. Havisham on acid, or what the inside of a conspiracy theorist's head must look like. And the smell. I duck my head and inhale Sally's puke reek because it's better than the heavy ammonia hang of whatever smells like boiled cabbage and clearly isn't.

Elroy actually lives here?

And then this little troll lady, maybe a hundred-and-forty years old, steps into the living room and looks at us like we're daylight bandits or something.

"Hey, Mrs. Jones. It's just me," Elroy says, to no response. "Uh... Elroy," he adds and still no response. "The foster kid? I live here."

The light finally goes on.

"Of course you do, Roy!" the ancient lady says.

The poor kid does actually live here.

"Uh, these are my friends," Elroy says and extends his arm towards us.

And I try to put myself in the old lady's shoes for a second, so that I can, you know, gauge what kind of reaction is coming next. Because she's looking at her twelve-year-old foster kid standing next to his thirty-three-year-old male friend, who's got a passed-out, pre-teen girl thrown over his shoulder, caveman style. And of course, we're all covered in vomit, reeking of tequila. I mean, how could you not call nine-one-one right now?

But she just smiles at us.

"I know..." the old lady says and breaks a silence that is so the least awkward thing happening right now. "...I'll bake a cake!"

"Uh, thanks, Mrs. Jones. We'll be up in my room," Elroy says.

And I'm thinking, seriously? Okay. She's old. She's got a bit of the dementia, obviously. But the fact that Elroy's adult male friend is carrying this passed out twelve-year-old girl up to his bedroom should trigger some kind of atavistic response in her. But there's nothing there. And what's really pissing me off right now is that the State of New Jersey assigned this person to be Elroy's primary caregiver.

"Is Mr. Jones home?" Elroy asks as he leads us up the stairs.

The old lady stops, turns.

"Oh, no, Ray. Mr. Jones won't be home for another two weeks. He's on another hunting trip." She winks when she says it, which is, like, totally creepy.

"Um, I don't think so, Mrs. Jones. I mean, I saw him this morning."

"Oh?" she says, and then claps her wrinkled hands. "That's right, he's at the urologist."

Either way, I get the impression that Mr. Jones isn't going to get in the way of us holing up here for an hour or so.

"It's going to be a lemon cake," the old lady says, more to herself than to us, as she skitters back into the kitchen.

"Watch your step, there, Frank," Elroy says.

I know that I'm not really at my best right now, like I am in no position to be appalled by anything, but there is a giant hole in the third step. Like half the step is missing. This place is literally a death trap.

"Your foster parents, their bedroom is on the first floor, I presume?"

"Yeah," Elroy says. "The upstairs is pretty much mine."

I skip the third step entirely, not trusting the weight bearing capacity of the remaining half to support both me and Sally. At the top of the stairs, I take a breath.

"Been a while since you guys have put the recycling out," I say, wedging myself through a hallway lined with stacks and stacks of old newspapers... oh, just like Elroy's bedroom is, too.

"They don't have recycling trucks in this town. You have to take stuff to the dump yourself. And who's gonna make that drive?" Elroy explains sheepishly, but I don't really buy it.

His room is half the size of a prison cell. I have to turn sideways and shutter-step between the bed and the floor-to-ceiling stacks of newspapers before I'm able to flop Sally onto his mattress.

"This is nice," I say, incredulous, nodding, but I can't even maintain that sarcasm. "Elroy, you live in squalor."

"It's not so ba... ba...bad," he replies.

And I think that's the first time he's stuttered all day. So now I feel bad. Or worse. Worse is what I feel.

"What's in the other rooms?" I ask.

I'm thinking maybe we can set him up somewhere else. There must be two or three other bedrooms up here. I saw doorframes above the newspaper stacks.

"This is the be... be... best one, believe me."

"So, move some of these newspapers out of here, then."

"No room."

"Elroy, man, this is no good."

"Don't worry ab... ab... about it. There's a shower in the bathroom up here. No sh... sh... shampoo, but there's soap. And I can get you some of Mr. Jones' clothes if you want to ch... ch... change."

I look at Sally, passed out on the prison mattress. Probably best not to try and wake her. Given the fact that I'm wearing most of the alcohol that she drank at the restaurant, I figure she ought to be right in about an hour. For a second it crosses my mind to reconsider this whole juvenile drinking buddy thing I've got going on. And not just because they're pukers.

I decide to stick a pin in that thought, address it later. For now, since I've got some time, I might as well get cleaned up.

"Sure, dude. A shower would be great. Do you, ah, have a towel?" I ask, saying it less like, can you get me a towel, and more like, do you own a towel?

"Just the one," Elroy says, "but it's dr... dr... dry."

"I don't suppose you have a washing machine?"

"Yeah, but no dryer. We hang the cl... cl... clothes on a rack in the basement to dry. It usually takes a day or two. I'll fi... fi... find you something from Mr. Jones' closet."

Listening to Elroy stutter, in this living environment, makes me want to slit my wrists.

Sally

"How are you fe… fe… feeling?"

My eyes are open. Elroy is sitting on top of a little wooden desk by my feet. I look around the room.

"Were we, like, kidnapped by human traffickers or something?"

"You're in my ro… ro… room."

"What the hell, man?" I say. I reach out and touch a stack of yellow newspapers that is, like, a foot from the cot I'm lying on. "You actually sleep here?"

"Yeah," he says.

I think I'm embarrassing him, so I try to pull myself together.

"Where's Frank?"

"He's in the sh… sh… shower."

"What happened?"

"You threw up and we had to, like, fl… fl… flee the restaurant. We left Frank's car there. We have to lie low here for a little wh… wh… while before we can go back and get it."

"So we got here, and, what? Frank decided to take a shower?"

Frank is so weird.

"You th… th… threw up on him. Like all over him. Someday we'll laugh ab… ab… about it," Elroy says, smiles.

"You're stuttering again," I say.

"Yeah."

"You weren't stuttering earlier today. The part I can remember, I mean."

"You guys are my fi… fi… first house guests," Elroy says and looks at his feet.

Frank opens the door, stands outside in the hallway, dressed like Harpo Marx.

"Not a word," Frank says.

And so we're silent, for like three seconds. And then Elroy cracks up. And the next thing I know we're all hysterical laughing. And it's like, post-trauma laughing. It's like, we're right in the flashpoint center of the bizzaro world, laughing. And I think the fact that we're laughing so hard is because we're together in it. Like, togetherness laughing. And I can't believe I just met these two idiots, like, three days ago.

Frank

"No, come on. This is perfect," Elroy says. "Anyway, we can't wait until dark because that would mean getting you back to the nursing home too late. Dressed like that, you look nothing like what the people at the Mexican place would ever even recognize."

Our laughing jag has obviously fixed his stutter again, but it's not like I'm going to mention it.

"So, I'm just going to look like your average homeless person, getting into a Chevy Camaro ZL1 convertible, triple black with oversized quad pipes, and just driving away. That won't be at all conspicuous."

"Come on, Elroy's right. Just play it cool," Sally advises me. "It's not like anyone is really going to be looking for you. I mean, how much money did you leave at the restaurant, anyway?"

"I have no idea. Maybe four hundred dollars."

"Why would anyone walk around with that much cash?" Sally asks again.

"I always carry a lot of cash. It's one of my things."

"Okay. Well, anyway, if you left that much money, then I seriously doubt that the restaurant did anything like call the police. I mean, we made a mess, but you paid for the meal..."

"You made the mess," I say to Sally.

"You let me drink a whole bunch of tequila, so share some of the responsibility," she replies.

"That's fair," I say. "And I did pay, like, five times the cost of the meal. Anyway, I highly doubt that they would call the police even if we skipped out on the check entirely. I mean, what would they say to the cops? This thirty-something dude got a twelve-year-old girl so drunk in my restaurant that she projectile vomited all over the place? You think they want to open that can of worms?"

"Exactly," Elroy says. "No one is even going to be looking for you."

"The guy who owns the restaurant might want to beat me up some."

"Okay, but he doesn't know your car is still there, so it's not like he'll be waiting for you outside or anything. And as long as you're not planning to go back in and ask for some of your money back, you should be able to just walk up, get in the car and drive away."

"Fine. I'll pick you guys up out front as soon as I can. Stay in the house until you see me pull up. If anything happens and I don't make it, just get yourselves back to the nursing home, get your bikes, and forget you ever saw me today. Okay? Okay. So, wish me luck."

"Good luck," Elroy says.

"Seriously?" Sally rolls her eyes, like we're making way too big a deal out of this.

And Sally's right. Five minutes later, without incident, I pull up in front of Elroy's foster home and they climb into the car. Five minutes after that, we're pulling into the back entrance of my nursing home.

"You guys both okay?" I ask before we get back into character. "Sally? You feeling better?"

"I'm fine," she says.

"Sorry about not keeping a better eye on you and those margaritas."

"They tasted a little too good, I guess."

"Next time we'll be more careful," I say, then look at Elroy.

"That was actually a lot of fun," Elroy says, brightly, "like a spy movie or something."

"Dude, we've got to talk about that rat hole you're living in," I say. "I mean, there has to be someone who you can call to shut that thing down as a foster home. Seriously, it's not healthy for the Joneses to be living there, much less you."

"And wh… wh… what? Let the foster system mo… mo… move me somewhere else? Like, to another town?"

Right. I hadn't thought about that.

"Alright, but this conversation isn't over. It's late, so let's get back into character," I say.

Which we do, and then we walk around to the front of the nursing home. And I walk straight to my room without scanning the lobby for Hardy, without saying goodbye to Elroy and Sally while they're signing me back in.

Elroy

Even though I live so close, I decide to take my bike to school on Thursday morning so I can lock it up next to Sally's and we can leave together for the nursing home right after dismissal.

I'm crouched down, working the big lock around the front wheel and bike frame, when Saul Lipski pulls into the rack. Three slots down from me, no bikes in between. And he doesn't notice that it's me until he gets off his bike and grabs his own lock from its clip under the seat. And when he does notice, well, it would be awkward even if Sally hadn't saved my life two days ago by screaming rape like a maniac and scaring the living hell out of Saul and the rest of the Jew Crew. So, now, it's like, uber-awkward.

"Hey," I say, because we're obviously not strangers, in the normal sense of the word, and saying "Hey" seems a lot less awkward than just not saying anything at all. And Saul glances around, scanning the parking lot for his friends. Man, if these cliquey kids ever knew what it was like to be really alone, all the time, I don't think they would ever be so mean to me.

I don't think they'd ever be so mean to anyone, really.

So Saul looks at me, because I've kind of forced his hand. I mean, right now both he and I know that that if he doesn't say anything to me, it will look like he's not secure enough to be a total dick unless his friends are around. Which is obviously true, but not something that Saul would want to, like, shine a spotlight on.

"Where's your psycho girlfriend, loser?" he says after a couple of seconds.

"What, no rhymes, Mike D?" Whoa, where did that come from?

"What did you just say?"

"I mean… I mean, what? You can't bust rhymes unless you've got your friends to back you up?"

I'm just letting the momentum carry me, not really thinking about what I'm saying, having maybe never stood up for myself before in my whole life.

"Wait, what?" And Saul is legitimately trying to get his arms around whatever it is I'm saying. "You want me to rap for you?" Said in the same way he might ask, you want me to give you a hernia test?

"No," I say quickly. "Why, do you want to rap for me?"

"No, I do not want to rap for you," he says with finality.

"Good, because I don't want you to rap for me. I was just saying, whenever you're with that Jew Crew, ah, crew, you always talk in rap rhymes. I mean, when you're with those two kids, it's like that's the only way you know how to talk is all, like, gangsta rap. So, I was just saying, why don't you talk like that when you're alone?"

"Look, loser. I'm a Jew. I've been dealing with psychologists for half my life. You're not going to get anywhere with this type of talk."

He scans the parking lot for his friends again.

"I was just pointing out the obvious. Like, what's obvious to everyone else, I mean. That you're, like, nobody unless your friends are around."

And maybe I let the momentum take me one step too far. Because Saul throws his lock on the ground and puts on this berserker face and I'm pretty sure he's about to crush my skull with his huge, bare hands. But right at that perfect moment, right when I'm getting ready to die at the hands of an enormous eighth grade rapper wannabe, Sally comes to my rescue. Again.

"Hey, Hebrew Crew! You messing with my friend?!" Sally shouts and crashes her bike full speed into the slot between Saul's bike and mine. I don't know what it's like for girls, but if a boy was in that kind of hard stop, bike-rack collision, he'd be rolling on the ground, bent in half, right now. But Sally is still straddling her bike, feet on the ground, like a fence standing between Saul and me, holding back much bodily harm.

"It's *Jew Crew*," Saul says, automatically, wincing the same way I'm wincing at the thought of a crotch of any gender stopping a bike that way.

And I don't know if she's channeling the pain into her anger about Saul bullying me or what, but she just steps off her bike and right up into Saul's face.

"Let me give you a message that you can pass on to your stupid, nineteen-nineties rapper wannabe buddies." Sally spits the words at his face, maybe because she's angry, or maybe because she's actually in a lot of pain. I mean, she hit that rack really hard. "If I find out that you, or either of those retro-loser rap idiots you hang out with, even look sideways at my friend Elroy here," she reaches backwards with her right arm, clumsily cups my cheek in her palm, "I'll tell you exactly what I'm going to do! I'm going to go, first to the Church and then to the police. No, actually, I'm going to let the Church take me to the police. Because I'm going to tell them that the three of you totally assaulted me, sexually. And I'm not talking about normal rape, because they can test for that. I'm talking about broomstick, baseball bat, Catholic-hate-crime gang rape. And I'm willing to do whatever it takes to make it look real. And if you think I don't know how to self-inflict defensive bruises, then you better think again."

Here Sally bangs the inside of her forearm against the top of the bike-rack with a sickening amount of force. She holds the inside of her arm in front of Saul's face with no more pause than when she crotch-smashed the bike-rack. And I can't see the inside of her arm, because her back is to me, but I imagine there's a pretty sick mark there.

"So, even if only one of you messes with Elroy, I'm going to drag all three of you into some very public, very nasty, very hate-crime sexual assault charges. And you better believe I'm gonna make sure it sticks. So even if just one of you idiots decides to go ahead and screw with Elroy, you're all going to be on the news. And you're all gonna to go to jail, where you're each gonna get gang-raped by a bunch of white-supremacist, Jew-hating, Nazi wannabe's... so, like, at least you'll be able to identify with the wannabe part," Sally snarks, briefly interrupting her rant. "And then, if any of you somehow makes it through prison without taking your own life, when you do get out, you're each going to have to register as a sex offender, anywhere you go. And neighborhoods will put up flyers when you try to move in, telling everyone to keep their kids away from you. And the best job that any one of you will ever get will be, maybe, pumping gas, if you're lucky, because what company would ever want to hire a sex offender? So, each of you will probably end up killing yourself after prison anyway, wondering why you waited so long, because the only thing it bought you was a few more years of pain and suffering. And there won't be anyone to say goodbye to because your parents would have obviously killed themselves years before because they couldn't handle the shame, because they expected a little more from their sons than being gas-pumping, ex-con, ass-raped, registered sex offenders. Are you feeling me, here, Jew Crew boy?"

Sally takes a deep breath, the first in a while. Saul looks like everything liquid has been sucked from his body. He actually looks physically smaller, by, like, a full size or two. Which is impossible, I know.

"Okay. Yeah. Okay. I feel you. I mean, I understand," he says.

This will probably be the most aggressive encounter that Saul will ever have in his entire life.

"Yeah, well, you better feel me. Because you can play gangsta-rap all you want. You can pretend you're freaking Bugsy Segal in the playground for the whole rest of the school. But if any one of you crosses the line with Elroy, any single one of you, then it's a major life decision for all of you."

"Okay. Geeze. We were only fooling around," Saul says, quietly now.

"Don't test me, *Jew Crew*," Sally says, just as quietly, and grabs his collar. "I've got absolutely nothing to lose." She releases his collar, taps his cheek with her open palm, and whispers loud, "Don't forget to tell your friends."

Whoa. She totally went Khaleesi on his ass.

Sally turns back to me, smiles, rolls her eyes and waits. Saul is still standing there, not sure of anything in terms of moving on from this. I kind of feel the same way.

"He's still there?" Sally asks me, in a normal voice, and I nod. "Tell him if he doesn't leave I'm going to start screaming rape."

"Ah. Hey, Saul. I think we're done here," I say.

I give him a look like, sorry, I had no idea what a sociopath my friend is. So, he backs off slowly, the way you would from a rabid dog or a suspicious backpack at a bus station, then he turns and walks stiffly to the school. Sally listens to his footsteps, still looking at me.

"Gone?" She asks.

I wait until he's walked in the door.

"Yeah."

"Oh, my god," she moans, grabbing herself between the legs. "I think I broke something down there."

She's bent over, one hand between her thighs and the other on the bike rack, taking deep breaths, like she's about to give birth.

"Sally..." I say, still in shock from the whole scene, but aware of tears on my cheeks.

"Ah, ah, ah-ah, ah..." she says and holds up a palm to my face from her bent-over position. "Don't!"

"Just listen," I say, crying, but in a way that's kind of secondary to what I have to say. "No one has ever cared enough about me to, well... No one has ever cared about me at all. Other than Frank, I mean. And what you just did ..."

"Please, stop, you'll ruin it. No big deal, seriously..."

"What you just did would have spooked, like, Keyser Soze. It would have given Hitler nightmares," I say, changing direction because this whole gratitude thing isn't being well received. "It was the darkest thing that I've ever seen in my life. And I'm an orphan, living in foster homes, so I set the bar pretty high when it comes to dark. Seriously, Sally, you took badass to a whole other level there."

"You think?"

"You have no idea," and there are still tears, but they don't really have anything to do with what I'm saying. And Sally doesn't seem to mind because I'm just talking about how bad-assed she is. "So, like, thank you," I say, pause. "You know I would, like, do anything for you, right?"

"I guess I do, now," Sally says, smiling. And then she reaches up from her bent over position to punch me in the chest. "Man, I could use a drink right now. You?"

"Four o'clock can't get here fast enough," I say.

"Word," Sally says, unbends herself, stands.

She takes the hand that was clutching the bike-rack and flops it over my shoulder, leans her head against my chest for a second, and then we walk into school, together.

Frank

"Okay," I explain, "we're set with fifteen gallons of water ice, three flavors, cucumber-lime, lychee-celery and blood orange, which is being delivered by Ice Ice Baby, this hipster shave ice place in Brooklyn that's supposed to be awesome. And we've also got two-hundred Honeydew Bakery sticky buns, ten trays of twenty, which will be baked that same morning, so they should still be warm by the time they're delivered. And ten gallons of limeade from GreenerGrass Markets. And a few hundred paper cups and plates and spoons from Costco. And all of this is being delivered to the church address, attention 'Picnic Committee,' Sunday at eleven-fifteen. Are you guys writing this down?"

"No," Sally says.

"Well, write it down. Because you guys have to do all the receiving and set-up."

"And we've also got to carpet bomb the church with posters and flyers a half-hour before Mass," Sally says. "Tell me again how is this is a fair distribution of work?"

I think Sally is grumpy because she assumed we were going off-site today. Truth is, we all assumed so. But unfortunately, Hardy was in the lobby when Elroy and Sally arrived. And, obviously knowing nothing of our ulterior motives, Hardy stuck Sally with one Mrs. Chong, a small lady of indeterminate Asian origins who is confined to a wheelchair and, as far as we can tell, speaks no English. And there is no way that I was going to take that kind of luggage on another drinking spree with the kids, especially after what happened yesterday.

So, we're confined to my room, walking through the logistics for our rapidly approaching Sunday meet-up. On the bright side, if we have to have a fourth, Mrs. Chong is perfect – like a pet rock in a wheelchair, staring out the window. Much lower maintenance than Mrs. Liptenstein or the Colonel.

"First of all, Lambchop, I'm paying for all of this. Second, I'm the one who's going to be doing all the work once we gather a crowd on Sunday. And finally, you know I'm not independently mobile. I've got to wait for Dr. Severs to pick me up, so I won't be showing up at the church yard until almost noon. I didn't ask for these constraints. I'm just working around them as best I can. So, if you're in this thing, you'll have to pull your weight where you're needed most. Unless you're gonna bail, which is fine, because Elroy and I can handle it ourselves."

That was mean talk. Like, respect the talent, roadie. When did I turn into such a diva?

"Fine. Sorry," Sally says. "So other than the stuff you just went through, we pick up the signage from Kinko's tomorrow, and that's everything then?"

"Really? That's everything?" I ask, dramatically, like she's missing the powdered sugar in a frosting recipe, and I'm the one that's trusting her to make my wedding cake.

"The sa… sa… sangria," Elroy says.

"Zackly!" I shout and point at Elroy like he wins the better student prize. And then I pause. "Why the stutter, dude?"

"It's no… no… nothing."

"Seriously," I say.

"It's st… st… stupid."

"Wait, you feel like it's too stupid to share with *us*?" Sally asks him, incredulously. "Come on. Spill."

"Whatever. It's Mrs. Ch… Ch… Chong. She makes me ne… ne… nervous."

I look at him as if he's lost his mind.

"That potato over there makes you nervous. Why, what do you know? Do you think she understands English, like she's a snitch or something?" I ask.

Sally rolls her eyes.

"No, nothing like that. It's just, I lived with a Korean foster fa... fa... family for six months, back when I was seven. It was kind of an ab... ab... abusive situation. I don't want to go into it," Elroy says. "But she, Mrs. Chong, looks ju... ju... just like the grandmother who, you know, kind of terrorized me. And it sorta of fr... fr... freaks me out."

"Okay, Elroy, let's stop this right here. Because every Asian person over the age of eighty looks exactly the same, men and women alike. And you're gonna have to conquer this phobia, because it will haunt you again and again – do you know how many Asians there are in the world right now? And every day, they're getting older and older. So, here's what you do. Just put this plastic bag over her head," I say and pull the liner out of my empty wastepaper basket and hand it to him. "Believe me, she's not even going to know it's happening."

"That's okay," Elroy says, shaking his head, not taking the plastic liner.

"Go ahead, do it," I say. "We'll pull it off in twenty-minutes, slip it back into the wastepaper basket, and none will be any the wiser. I mean, she's so freaking old, who's going to question how or why she died, anyway. So, it's the perfect crime. Sally, you'll have to hold her arms down, okay?"

Elroy still doesn't take the plastic bag.

"Stop being so creepo, Frank," Sally says. "I mean, she's sitting right there."

"Creepo? I don't think so," I say and start pacing the room like an Agatha Christie detective. "First off, we've totally confirmed that she doesn't understand English because otherwise she'd be trying like crazy to bust out of that chair right now. And that means she isn't a spy."

"I totally don't get who you think would be spying on us in the first place?" Sally says, and I wave her off.

"And secondly – Elroy, how do you feel right now? Knowing you could have ended her life and totally gotten away with it? And that *you* made the conscious decision not to suffocate her. You were in complete control. So how does that make you feel? And how do you think your decision not to kill Mrs. Generic Old Asian will make you feel from now on? When you happen to be around the random, generic Asian old person, I mean?"

"Better, I guess?" Elroy says.

"Bang!" I shout. "So you're on the road to recovery. In that specific area, at least."

"I cannot believe that you're the one leading this movement of ours," Sally says, pinching the bridge of her nose, "So anyway, we were talking about the sangria?"

"Right, the sangria! One of the most important parts of our meal. I mean, we've got the bread, but we still need the wine, right?"

"It's like having Jesus right here in the room with us," Sally says.

I decide to take that as a compliment, even though it was leaning pretty heavy in the other direction.

"Right on, Lambchop," I say. "Now, Elroy. Did I not notice two large chest freezers in the basement of your foster home yesterday?!"

"No, you did not!" Elroy shouts back, enthusiastically.

Wait, what?

"Whaddaya mean?" I ask.

"What do you mean?" Elroy asks me back.

"Two deep freezes, in your basement? Big white boxes, like refrigerators lying on their sides? That you open from the top? There are two of them in your basement, right?"

"Ah, no," Elroy replies.

"Are you sure?"

"Yes. And you never even went do… do… down to my basement yesterday."

And he's right. I'm remembering last night's recurring nightmare. A dream where Elroy and I were stirring up two big vats of fruit and grain alcohol in a couple of ancient freezer chests in the basement of his foster home. A dream where it was easier for him to stir the sangria mix by standing in the freezer chest and straddling the vat. A dream where he slipped on ice or fruit, fell onto his back, and the lid of the deep freeze snapped shut from the impact. A dream where I spent way, way too long trying to find some kind of tool to pry off the lock of the freezer chest, and by the time I did it was too late. Because when I eventually did pry off the lock and open the lid of the freezer chest, Elroy was on his back, taking his final breath. And his chest was caved in, just like the other dreams.

I had this same dream maybe twenty times last night. So, okay, no freezers in Elroy's basement, then.

"What?" Elroy asks, pulling me back into the present.

"Nothing. You're right. My bad," I reply. I've got to do something about these night terrors.

"So... the sangria?" Sally asks, exasperated now.

"Right. So, I don't suppose you have a deep freeze in your basement?"

"No," Sally replies. "Why do we need a deep freeze, anyway?"

"Because we're going to take a fifty-gallon cooler and we're going to fill it with about twenty pounds of fresh fruit. And then we're going to pour two bottles of grain alcohol into it and mix it up so that the fruit absorbs the alcohol. And then we're going to mash it up and stick the cooler in a deep freeze for at least twenty-four hours. And on Sunday, right before our meet, we're going to pour twelve bottles of Tempranillo on top of the fruit-alcohol mash."

"Temprillo?" Elroy asks.

"Tempranillo," I say. "The only wine that should *ever* be used to make sangria. And then, bang! Stand back, my friends, because it's gonna be epic."

"So, what? Are you just going to buy a deep freeze that can fit a fifty-gallon cooler?" Sally asks.

"Not enough time," I say. "And where would we put it? No, I'm going to have to call in a favor."

"From who?" Elroy asks, evidently assuming that he and Sally are my only friends in the world.

Sally

I shouldn't be so grumpy about the fact that we're stuck in the nursing home all afternoon.

I mean, if the RMSOC were actually legit, we'd be stuck doing boring stuff in nursing homes and other charity spots all afternoon, every afternoon. I mean, we haven't even seen Dr. Severs since he dropped us back at school on Monday, so that's something I can be thankful for. And even though we're confined to Frank's room, the conversation, while deranged, is at least entertaining. It's funny how entitlement works, how your expectations can amp up so quickly.

So, Frank makes a phone call to his brother, Johnny, convincing him to let us use his deep freeze on Saturday. Telling Johnny that he's having a bunch of fruit and booze delivered to his house on Saturday morning, that someone will need to be there to sign for it. And from the sound of it, Johnny's not too enthusiastic with the idea of lending his deep freeze or accepting Frank's deliveries.

"Dude, man up! It's your house," Frank says into the phone. "What's she going to do, ground you? Grow a set." Frank pauses to listen. "Yeah, well it's happening. Get her a spa day, I'll pay for it." Frank pauses to listen. "Yes, seriously. I'll buy it online right now. Tell her it's an early birthday gift. What? Then tell her it's a late birthday gift." Frank pauses to listen. "Okay, well it doesn't really matter because both me and the deliveries are going to be at your house on Saturday morning, so there's going to be a scene regardless. What? No, late morning. When have you known me to do anything in the early morning?" Frank pauses to listen. "Johnny, we've danced this dance before, right? It's going to be so much easier for both of us if you just get on board and help me out. What? Because it's happening, that's why, and if you try to push back, it's only going to make things worse. Okay? Okay. I'll see you Saturday morning. Yes, I'll send you a link to the spa pass. Okay, thanks. What? That doesn't mean I can't thank you, does it? Whatever. See you on Saturday."

Frank hangs up his phone, turns to me and Elroy says, "Okay, we're all set."

"Sounds like Frank's brother is pretty eager to help us out," I say to Elroy as Frank goes to his computer and orders a spa package for his brother's wife.

"It's a co... co... complicated relationship," Elroy replies. "Frank's brother's wife hates him. Hates Frank, I mean. I'm not completely sure why."

"There could be so many reasons," I say.

Elroy

So, on Friday, I don't see Frank at all. And it's only the second time I haven't seen him for a whole day since we met last Wednesday. So, okay.

Sally and I have to go to Kinko's to pick up our signs and flyers at four p.m. and bring them to her house, because it's closest to the church, and by the time we're done it will be too late to head to the nursing home. And I'm sure Frank isn't all weird about it, so there's no reason that I should be. It's only one day, anyway. And I'll be with Sally. So, no big deal.

But there's that careful part of me, shouting from the bottom of a well somewhere inside my head, telling me that maybe I ought to watch my step with how attached I'm getting.

Sally and I walk to Kinko's from the school, because it's only a few blocks away and we're going to have to carry the signs and stuff another few blocks to her house, which would be hard to do on our bikes. I haven't said anything about her mind-raping Saul Lipski since I told her how bad-assed she was yesterday morning, and I can't figure out a way to work it into the conversation as we walk to Kinko's.

"Did you ca… ca… call Dr. Severs?" I ask her.

"Yeah, he was kind of pissed," Sally says. "But I told him we'd make up the time on Saturday, so it's fine. I also talked to him about picking up Frank on Sunday morning and taking him to church. That's fine, too. I mean, he complained about it, but I told him that the RMSOC was his Club and if he forced Frank to go to Church last Sunday, he couldn't really cut him off the following week. And since Frank doesn't have a car, and you and me don't drive, how else is he gonna get to the church?"

I say "Cool" and we keep walking.

Frank paid for the signs and material online with his credit card, so we don't have any problem at Kinko's.

"You think he went a little overboard?" Sally asks as we're hauling the stuff to her house.

Frank ordered one big foam-core sign, which we're going to put on this stand thing by the front doors of the church. He also ordered two poster-size signs, which we're going to tape to the back and side doors. And that much seems pretty reasonable. But where he might have gone overboard is with the filers, because he ordered five-hundred of them. And they've got Sunday's date on them, so it's not like we'll be able to re-use them for another event… if there is another event.

And I'm not really sure what we're supposed to do with five-hundred flyers in the thirty minutes before Sunday noon Mass. I don't think more than a hundred people even go to noon Mass.

"Maybe a little overboard," I say.

"We're right up there, the white one," Sally says.

"Wow. Your house is awesome."

"It's actually pretty normal, Elroy."

"Not compared to where I live."

"True, but sad." Sally makes a pout face at me and I'm pretty sure she's not being sarcastic. "Let's get this stuff up to my room before my mom comes home and busts us."

We go straight up the stairs and stick all of the signs and flyers into her closet. I'm not going to describe Sally's room, especially how it smells, because I'm afraid it would get kind of creepy, how much I love it.

"Oh, crap!" Sally says.

"What?"

"My mom's home."

I look out the window as a white Prius pulls into the driveway.

"Oh," I say. Sally's wearing an odd expression. "Is that a problem?"

"You mean is it a problem that I'm with a boy, in my room, when no one else is home? Yes, that's a pretty huge problem, as far as my mom's concerned."

I'm worried and all, don't get me wrong, but to be honest, when she says that stuff about being alone with a boy in her room – and the fact that I'm that same boy – well, my heart kind of goes a little crazy in my chest. And not just my heart. I quickly take off my jacket, drape it over my arm and hold it in front of my jeans. I don't think Sally notices anything unusual.

"It's hot in here," I say. "Are you hot?"

"No," Sally says, looking at me funny for a second. "Come on, we've got to figure something out."

"Should I hide, maybe?"

You'd think I'd be stuttering right now. But whatever kind of nervous energy is in the room right now, it's not the kind that makes me stutter.

"No, that would just make it so much worse if something went wrong. We need a way to deal with this head-on." We hear the front door open, and Sally's eyes light up. She reaches up and messes my hair. "Look, Elroy, I'm really sorry that I have to ask you to do this, okay?"

"Do what?"

"I think we can convince my mom that you've got, like, pretty severe special needs," Sally says with a pleading look.

"Wow," I whisper.

She says this thing about me having severe special needs like it's not going to be too much of a stretch. And, I mean, that was the first idea that popped into her head? Whatever bubble of young boy-girl crush that was in the room just before bursts, like it was never there at all. I don't need to hold my draped jacket in front of my jeans anymore, so I put it back on.

Sally

"Hey, Mom," I say, jogging down the steps.

"Sally? I thought you had RMSOC today?" Mom says.

"I do," I say. "Elroy! Come on, boy!"

I shouldn't be calling him like he's a dog. I feel so bad doing this, already.

"Who is upstairs?" Mom says in a very heavy tone.

"Elroy. Come on down, Elroy!"

"There's a boy? Upstairs?"

Elroy steps very slowly down the stairs.

"It's not a boy, Mom. It's Elroy. He's what I was doing today with the RMSOC. We were working with the Special Talents Academy, over by the church? You know it. And I took Elroy for a walk, and well, he had to use the bathroom, so we came here."

"So why didn't he use the downstairs bathroom, young lady?"

"Mom," I whisper out the side of my mouth, jerk my head to the right, and we both take two steps away from Elroy, where he can totally still hear us. "He doesn't use downstairs bathrooms. Don't embarrass him."

"Why doesn't he use downstairs bathrooms?" Mom whispers out the side of her mouth, just like I was doing, and I know I've totally, like, Jedi mind-hooked her.

"How would I know," I whisper out the side of my mouth. "He's the one with special needs."

Mom nods her face in a knowing way. Game over.

"Hello. Elroy. It's. Nice. To. Meet. You." Mom says, and I find it hard to believe right now that she does so much work with the Catholic Church, helping people, because she's that awkward.

"He doesn't talk!" I shout, just as Elroy is opening his mouth.

I step over, pull my sleeve onto the heel of my hand, wipe some imaginary drool from his chin. Elroy looks at the floor. Shakes his leg the way a dog would when you rub its belly and it thinks it's scratching itself. Very nice touch.

"Well, I guess we'd better be getting back!" I tell Mom. "I'll be home around six or seven."

"I've got a meeting with the youth group leaders tonight, Sally, so you'll have to fix yourself dinner." And then Mom steps up to Elroy, puts her hands on his arms, right below the shoulders, leans towards him until her face is maybe six inches from his, looks him straight in the eye. "We are all God's children, each special in our own way," Mom says slowly. "Thank you for visiting us today."

Elroy looks at her, wide eyed, and a long string of drool runs down his chin and onto the front of his shirt. I grab him by the sleeve and lead him out the front door.

"I am soooo sorry," I say as he and I walk away from the house.

"It's okay," Elroy says.

"Really, Elroy. It's the only thing I could think of. And it's not because of the stutter or anything." Elroy gives me a quick look of serious pain. So, that was not a good thing to say. "I mean, it's not anything about you at all, what made me think we could convince my mom that you're retarded." I'm making this worse. "It's my mom. She... She's afraid of special needs people."

"No, sh... sh... she isn't."

"Well, I mean, she's not afraid, but she gets uncomfortable around them."

"Who do... do... doesn't?"

I've got to fix this.

I stop, grab Elroy's arm, turn him so that he's facing me. And I'm about to tell him that he's, like, one of my favorite people ever and I would never do anything to hurt his feelings. I'm about to tell him that, but instead of saying it, I lean in and kiss him, right on the lips.

It's not like a make-out movie kiss where we use our tongues and glom all over each other. But still, it's a real kiss. For, like, three or four seconds, we kiss. And it's the first time I've ever kissed a boy. And he kisses me back. But when I pull away, he just stands there, like he's catatonic or something. So, I punch him in the shoulder with the heel of my hand.

"Don't go getting weird on me about this," I say harshly, and he totally bursts into a smile. So I hit him again. "I mean it."

Elroy

"All my instincts, they return
And the grand facade, so soon will burn
Without a noise, without my pride,
I reach out from the inside..."

I feel ya, Peter.

Frank

"Martha, you've got to keep him out of here until, like, ten-thirty, tomorrow morning."

"Why ten-thirty?"

"Because that's my window."

"Ten-thirty isn't a window. It's a line."

"Okay, how about this? I don't want to get up before nine-thirty, so I told Elroy to sign me out no earlier than nine-forty-five, no later than ten-fifteen. So, window, okay?"

"Well, I'll try."

"You'll try? Martha, when have I ever asked for your help?"

"All the time."

"Well, this is important. Think about all the good times I've been able to give to you over the past six months."

And Martha sighs, thinking about just that.

"Fine, I'll make sure he's held up until after ten-thirty," she says, then pauses. "Hey, Frank?"

"Yes, my dear?"

"You know, you've only got six months left here. And that's the outside bet, assuming you or Ed doesn't break before then."

"I do know that, yes."

"Well, and this has nothing to do with how great it's been having you here, because it has. You've changed my life. But I'm just wondering, when you do leave, I mean…"

"My media server and all of the associated accounts are on auto-pay, and the credit card won't expire for another ten years. And when it does I'll renew the auto-pay on the same accounts. So, you can bank on your soaps for as long as I'm alive, and for at least a month after I'm dead, if anything were to happen."

"You're an angel, Frank."

"Yeah, well, let's not go making a big deal of it."

Elroy

When we pull up to Frank's brother's house, Johnny opens the front door, walks across the lawn to meet us.

"Jane is out till two. The stuff is in the garage. Just do what you have to do and get out of here."

"Hey, I'm great! Thanks for asking!" Frank says brightly. "You remember Elroy? This is Sally."

"Hey," Johnny says to me. "And nice to meet you, Sally. Where'd Frank find you?"

"Goodwill," Sally replies.

Wendy is standing in the front door.

"Cousin Elroy! Are you still broken?" she shouts. Sally gives me a look.

"You still play Air Hockey?" I say, holding up my iPhone, happy that I didn't stutter.

"You still my bits?" Wendy shouts back.

"Wendy! What did I say about that word?!" Johnny yells.

"Sorry," Wendy says in a littler voice. I give Frank a pleading look.

"Make it quick," Frank says to me.

I nod, jog to the house as Johnny, Frank and Sally walk across the lawn to the open garage. Wendy and I sit on the couch in the living room, where I totally annihilate her at iPhone Air Hockey. Six straight games.

Who's your bits, now, Wendy?

I haven't been thinking about what happened with Sally because if I think about it, I'm going to act weird around her. But what I really want to do is walk around behind her, holding a giant boom-box over my head, playing ballads by Peter Gabriel and Journey. That's what I would do if I did what I was feeling like.

So, after we parked our bikes at the nursing home this morning, she laced her fingers through mine when we were walking to the front door. And I looked down at our hands and then looked into her eyes and smiled at her and she punched me in the chest with her free hand. So now I figure I'll just kind of play it cool and let her take the lead with how we're supposed to act around each other.

I walk into the garage after humiliating Frank's five-year-old niece. Frank looks over at me, I give him a single nod and he smiles. Sally is dumping cartons of raspberries, blackberries and blueberries into a big rectangular cooler, the kind that has a push-button nozzle near the bottom for filling cups.

"Don't you need to wash those?" Johnny asks Frank.

Frank scrunches the side of his face into a look like, you're such a loser. When all of the fruit is in the tub, Frank dumps in three cartons of orange juice, one bottle of cranberry juice and two bottles of something called Everclear, which, Frank has explained to us, is pure grain alcohol.

"You ought to go easy on that grain, dude. People go blind," Johnny says.

"That's totally a myth," Frank says and takes an empty bottle by the neck and begins to mash and stir the witch's brew that he's concocted.

"Seriously, man," Johnny continues, "we used to make garbage pail punch in college and we only used one bottle of Everclear. People got messed up. You can't even taste the alcohol."

"This isn't garbage pail punch, Pollyanna. It's sangria and I know what I'm doing."

"Have you ever considered looking back on your long string of bad life choices and trying to use them as a, kind of, going-forward reference?"

"I've considered it," Frank replies, still churning the mixture, "but I was worried that type of introspection might suck all the life out of me. You know, turn me into something horrible, like an insurance salesman."

"Right. Why would you want to be a responsible male provider when just being a part of the male anatomy is working out so well for you."

"Good one," Frank grunts. "Now help me dump this into the cooler. Then we need to get this thing into the deep freeze."

"What about the Temprolino?" I say, looking at the cases of wine.

"Tempranillo," Frank corrects me. "And that goes in tomorrow, once this stuff is frozen."

"So how do we get the cooler to the church tomorrow?" Sally asks.

Frank looks at her, then stares at nothing for a second.

"Man, I knew there was something," Frank says. A few minutes later the cooler is freezing in the garage and we're in Johnny's kitchen drinking tiny green boxes of apple juice.

"It's a Church picnic, dude. Bring the family, meet some new people. It will be fun," Frank says, a pleading tone in his voice that isn't doing his leverage with Johnny any good.

"You want me to bring my family to some kind of garbage pail punch frat picnic at Church? Absolutely not. You have got to be out of your mind."

"Stop calling it garbage pail punch. It's sangria. And I've got a ten-gallon Igloo full of limeade for the kids. Shave ice. Sticky buns. Come on, man, it's a Sunday Church thing, for Christsakes. A family affair. There'll be priests there. How bad could it possibly get?"

"Stop. You're just making it sound weirder. I'm out. No, actually, I was never in. And I'm not going to be in. Figure it out on your own, Frank," Johnny says, like the discussion is over.

Then we hear the front door open.

"Nice, Johnny!" Frank's brother's wife shouts, and we hear her walking towards the kitchen. "I drive all the way out there to find out that you booked the spa appointment for next month instead of... oh! You have got to be kidding me."

"Janie!" Frank shouts. "I was worried we were gonna miss you!"

Frank

"He just stopped by."

"He didn't just stop by."

"What's the difference, anyway? He's my brother. What, like he's not allowed to come over to the house?"

"The difference is that you intentionally tried to get me out of the house, for whatever this is, and you couldn't even get that right. That was deceptive. So, don't try to tell me that there isn't something going on here. Because there's no way in the world that I'm going to believe that you just happened to gift me a spa package on the same morning that he just shows up here for no reason, with his weird little friends."

"We're right here, you know," Sally says.

"Who is that one, anyway?" Jane barks at Johnny.

"That's Sally, my child bride," I reply before Johnny does. What was he going to say, anyway? "We're planning to adopt cousin Elroy and wanted to see if you two would be the godparents."

I put my arm around Sally, squeeze her to my side. Elroy looks at me sidelong.

"Congratulations. I knew one day you'd find an intellectual and emotional peer," Jane says coldly.

Why do I feel like she just insulted Sally?

"Just like you did," I say, which is just as cruel because both Jane and Johnny take it as an insult. And that's kind of a low blow...to Johnny, I mean. I don't feel so great about it.

"Can we just, take a step back, here?" Johnny says.

"No," Jane replies, all fired up with righteous indignation.

I don't know how my brother can live with this person. I look at him, and something tells me he might be thinking the same thing.

"No?" Johnny asks.

"No."

"Okay, so let me get this straight..." Johnny says, dropping all emotion from his face like actors who play psychopaths in movies sometimes do, but I think this is for real.

He stares at Jane, like he's seeing her for the first time. And then suddenly he's all cock of the yard, looking around his house and nodding, like, yeah, I paid for this and it's mine and no one is going to make me feel like a lodger in my own home. Looking like he might walk over and strangle the life out of Jane with his bare hands. And I'm not sure what I'm feeling, but it's not as good as I thought I would feel at a moment like this.

"Hey, Johnny, it's fine," I interrupt. "We've got to be heading..."

"No, it isn't fine."

He turns back to Jane, who's still holding her ground, but in the corners of her eyes you can see this look creeping in, like maybe she took it a wee step too far, here.

"Get over it, Jane! Get over it or get out. Frank might be the world's biggest idiot, but he's my brother. And I love him. And he'll be here, in this house, whenever he wants to be here. And when he is here, you're gonna drop this whole whatever it is you've got going on and you're going to treat him like family. And you're going to treat Elroy and... and..."

"Sally," Sally offers.

"...my child bride," I say weakly.

Upstairs, Timmy wakes from his nap and starts to cry.

"Sally, right, sorry," Johnny says. "And you're going to treat Elroy and Sally like guests, too, because they've obviously got enough problems without you making them feel bad about being here. So, whatever grudge you've got with Frank, which is like a decade old anyway, it ends right now. And you make the decision to join this family, which he's a part of, or you don't. It's your call. And I am deadly serious right now, so think before you talk."

Would anyone like a thick slice of awkward silence?

"Okay," Jane finally says, meekly, looking towards the sound of Timmy crying upstairs.

"Okay, what?"

"Okay, I'll be nice to Frank. And his... people." Jane glances at me, smiles kind of sorry and kind of hopeful.

I lift my palm to her face and look away, like, way too soon.

"Jesus, Frank!" Johnny shouts.

"Okay, fine!" I shout back at him, walk over and give Jane a hug.

A real hug, like she's my sister-in-law and part of the family, not just some acid bitch that ruined my brother's life. And it feels good. Really good. I mean, it's been a long time since I've actually hugged a woman for real. I might even be getting a little turned on, here. And maybe Jane picks up on the fact that this hug has gone on one heartbeat too long because she pushes me away.

"Friends?" Jane asks softly.

"Don't be gay," I reply, just as softly.

And then she walks over to Johnny and presses her body against him, gives him a long, slow kiss. Like maybe I wasn't the only one who was getting turned on in this here kitchen. Johnny should have manned-up a long time ago.

I glance over at Sally and Elroy. She's holding his hand. When did that happen?

"I like it when you take control," Jane says to Johnny in a low tone.

"You better get used to it," Johnny replies, same low tone. Yuck.

"Oh, I will," Jane says and kisses him long and slow again.

"Uh, we're still right here," Sally says to them, then turns to me. "You know, you Johnsons are weird people."

"Go easy on your soon-to-be adopted son, there, Lambchop," I say. "We're still above the Mason-Dixon line."

Sally quickly lets go of Elroy's hand. Elroy gives me a look, like, come on, man! Johnny and Jane ignore the lot of us for another fifteen or twenty seconds of smooching.

"I'm going to go get Timmy, stick him on the couch with Wendy and put on *The Little Mermaid,*" Jane says, her hand on Johnny's chest. "The extended cut."

"Really," Johnny says, not like a question.

If this keeps up I might have to start calling him John. But, no, he'll always be a little bitch to me.

"Show your brother and his friends out, meet me upstairs," Jane says and separates from Johnny. "Nice meeting you Sally. Bye, Elroy. Frank, we'll see you soon?"

I look at Johnny.

"We'll see him tomorrow," Johnny says. Yes! Mental fist pumps!

"Tomorrow?" Jane asks, catching herself before she slips back into full-on bitch mode.

"Yeah, we're taking the family to a Church picnic."

Sally

~ He's not my boyfriend. Did you even see where he lives?

~ *I never said he was your boyfriend.*

~ You were thinking it.

~ *And why wouldn't I?*

~ He is very sweet though, right? I mean, if I wasn't going to kill myself, it would be nice to just, kind of, keep hanging out with him. And Frank, too, I guess. I mean, they are so not normal. But, I actually have fun when I'm with them. They're like...

~ *Like family?*

~ Jesus, Aunt Sadie, I met them, like, a week ago. Less than. And anyway, how long before Frank gets himself arrested for something stupid? And Elroy's lifestyle has got dysentery written all over it. So, it's not like these two are a real long-term solution.

~ *Because everything that you love always goes away?*

~ You know, that would sound a lot deeper if you hadn't killed yourself a few weeks ago. Anyway, it's not like I'm going to be hanging around much longer either, and I'm probably better off without the luggage.

~ *Life is short, Lambchop. It's weird and it's unpredictable and it's erratic – like Cirque du Soleil run amuck, when you're really living it, I mean. It's this big, wonderful mess of weirdness and violence and fear and sometimes beauty. And sometimes love. And you can't get any of the good stuff without all the mess. So why don't you stop looking for an exit and stop trying to predict the ending and just be. Just be. No plans. No future. Just now.*

~ I wish you'd followed your own advice.

~ *I had terminal cancer, Lambchop, and I didn't want to die a slow painful death.*

~ Wait. Really?

~ *No, not really. I just tried to carry too much stuff and it got too heavy and I finally took the easy way out instead of trying to untangle myself from all of it. I guess I'm a lot more noble in your head than I was in real life. But you don't want to end up like me.*

~ Dead?

~ *Well, that. But I'm talking about how I was before I died. Like a homeless lady with a broken-wheel shopping cart, just dragging and collecting and loading, every step heavier than the last one. You don't have to be like that. You can choose to stop. Stop expecting good things because that will only let you down. Stop expecting bad things, because that's only gonna weigh you down. Stop judging people like their bad choices are some kind of burden that you have to personally bear. Just make the decision to ignore before and after, and just be, here and now.*

~ Where do you come up with this stuff?

~ *It's all in here, Lambchop. It's all right in here with me.*

Elroy

"Be there at eleven-fifteen, okay?" Frank says to Johnny from the driver's seat.

"Yeah, sure," Johnny replies, still kind of glowing, looking back at the house.

"Hey, Johnny," Frank says. Johnny looks back at him. "Go crush that bitch."

"You're talking about my wife, Frank," Johnny sighs.

"Okay. How about... go tame that filly, cowboy."

"Better, but still."

"Fine. How about I'll just see you tomorrow, little brother."

"I'll see you tomorrow, big brother," Johnny says, winks at me, walks back towards his house as we drive off.

"So, was that pretty much normal family time with the Johnsons?" Sally asks from the back seat.

"That was better than most, actually," Frank says.

"I'm definitely coming over for Thanksgiving," Sally jokes.

But when she says it I just think, whoa, could you imagine how awesome that would be. And I'm there in the front seat, the wind and sun beating on my closed eyes, imagining a real holiday with, like, a fire and home-cooked food and Sally and Frank and all of his people. It's this really clear picture in my head, like an awesome memory even though it never actually happened, and it doesn't matter that it never happened because just having this thought is enough. Like, I can keep this thought with me, always, and that will be enough. And in that careful part of me, trapped deep down in a well so far away inside of me, I can hear that tiny voice screaming, like it's being tortured or something.

"You awake?" Frank nudges me.

"Yeah."

"What's wrong?"

"Nothing. I was just thinking."

"Are you worried about tomorrow?" Frank is looking directly into my eyes, which always makes me super nervous, especially with Sally in the car, because he's driving like a maniac.

"Why would I be nervous about tomorrow?" I ask.

I look out the passenger window in the hopes that Frank will turn his eyes back to the road. But I give him a quick glance and he looks hurt by what I said. Maybe that I'm not taking tomorrow seriously enough, I don't know. So, I reach over and put my hand on his shoulder, say, "There isn't anything for me to be nervous about, I mean. You're gonna be awesome."

"You think?" Frank asks, smiling.

"You're always awesome," I say.

"Thanks, E. You're pretty awesome, too."

"What are you two talking about up here?" Sally asks and sticks her head between the front seats.

Even with the wind from the drive, I can still smell her shampoo. Talk about awesome.

"What, no booze? It's not even a school night," Sally says as we pull up to a diner in Johnny's home town.

"It's more important than a school night. Plus, I love this place. I used to come here when I was your age, on like, dates and stuff," Frank says.

"You went on dates when you were our age?" I ask, picturing the title sequence of *Happy Days*. But I can't picture Frank as, like, The Fonz or Richie Cunningham or Potsie Weber. If anything, I picture him as a kind of Charlie Sheen type character, circa *Two and a Half Men*, who sits around Arnold's and makes snarky comments about how everyone is dressed, about how Fonzie's office is the Men's Room.

"Not really date dates," Frank says. "But, like, a bunch of guys would meet a bunch of girls here at the diner, and we'd just hang out. Eat french-fries, drink cokes, that kind of thing. People in your school don't do that?"

"I have no idea," I say. "Maybe they do."

"Kids mostly just text each other these days," Sally says. "And plus, everyone's got so many extracurriculars, there isn't a lot of time to just hang out."

"Your generation sucks," Frank says.

"Amen," Sally replies, quickly adds, "Not you, Elroy."

I smile small so that she doesn't punch me.

A waitress sits us at a booth by the window, Frank on one side, Sally and me on the other. Frank studies the menu, which is enormous. I'm thinking Sally might reach for my hand and hold it on the seat between us, where Frank can't see. But she doesn't. So, I think about how Johnny stepped-up back at his house and I decide, screw it. I reach over and thread my fingers through hers, breathing so heavy that I'm worried about hyperventilating.

Sally raises her eyebrows and looks at me with no expression. Then she smiles, squeezes my hand, doesn't pull away. I feel like my heart is going to beat out of my chest.

"What's up with you?" Frank says, lowering the menu, looking at me like I'm having a stroke or something.

"Nothing," I pant.

"Are you guys holding hands?"

"What of it?" Sally asks aggressively, and I'm worried she's somehow going to lay into Frank. I mean, after seeing her in action with the Jew Crew and later Saul, I know that nothing good could possibly come of her going all psycho on Frank.

"Nothing. It's nice," Franks says. "It's just making me kind of nostalgic, is all."

"It's no big deal, Frank," Sally says, and my heart drops. But she doesn't let go of my hand. Which is good. Trying to understand Sally makes my mind hurt.

"I'm gonna hit the Men's Room, get me a Diet Coke if the waitress comes back," Frank says, gets up and walks to the back of the diner.

"It's kind of a big deal," Sally whispers to me.

Then she glances left, right and behind her. Then she leans over and kisses me on the lips. Again! And I just want to pull her onto my lap and kiss her for the rest of the day. But I don't say anything. I just smile, because I can't help it, and I look at her.

"We're going to have to practice that," Sally says, sweetly. My heart drops again.

"Was I doing it wrong?" I ask, but, I'm thinking, it couldn't have been wrong because it was, like, the best kiss ever. All of them. That couldn't have been just me.

"No, Elroy. You are an amazing kisser."

"Have you kissed a boy, other one, ever, else?" I gibber awkwardly, my heart a pinball in my chest.

"Nope, you're my first and only," she says.

"So why do I need to practice?"

"First, *we* need to practice because I really like kissing you. Second, *we* need you to get used to kissing me a little more so that it doesn't look like you just saw the sun explode every time it happens."

That's fair. I wonder when is it okay to tell a girl that you love her? Definitely not now. Way too soon.

Maybe sometime tomorrow.

We all order breakfast for lunch, talk a lot about nothing important for, like, a couple of hours. It's probably a lot like what Frank used to do when he was our age. Except he probably never had a thirty-something adult at the table with him and his friends. But it's not like Frank really counts as an adult, anyway.

Then Frank takes us back to the nursing home. We sign him in. Sally and I ride our bikes back to town. We don't speed this time. We ride kind of slow so that we can talk to each other. And we don't really say anything that I can remember but, like at the diner, it was kind of the best conversation ever.

When we arrive at the school, Sally gets off her bike. I foot-slide my kickstand into place, walk to her, reach my palms up to cradle her face and I kiss her. *I* kiss *her* this time. And this time, we kiss more than just once. This time we kiss, like, three separate times.

Frank

"What's in the bag?" Severs asks as I climb into his putrid little car.

"Don't get too excited, Moonbeam. It's not weed." He ignores the reference.

"So, how'd it go with the kids this week?"

"Same sadistic torture as last week, thanks."

"And now back to Sunday Mass."

"Yup."

"So, ah, look, Mr. Johnson," Severs says, haltingly, "I'm glad you're kind of digging Church and all, and I'm really glad the RMSOC could help to make it happen, you know…"

"You look, BranFlakes. I'm a thirty-three-year-old man living in a nursing home in order to prove a point. And your only contribution has been to help Hardy try and browbeat me into submission so that I'll blow the joint. Let's not make this into something that it isn't."

Severs tightens his hands on the wheel, looks straight ahead.

"I'm just saying that we don't want another scene at Mass like last week, because, you know, the RMSOC is, like, involved with you being at church and all. Whatever you've got going on with Mr. Hardy is your business. We're just doing outreach, trying to help where we can. The RMSOC is going to do the world a lot of good, and the Hardy Managed Care Facility is just helping to get us started. So, I'm just asking you to respect the RMSOC's involvement here. And, you know, behave accordingly."

"Well, if that's all you're asking, Honeydew, then you've got nothing to worry about."

Sally

"I can't believe he got actual glassware for this thing," Elroy says after we've set up the tables and are arranging the vats of water ice, trays of sticky buns and the Igloo cooler of limeade, all for easy access. I am truly amazed that no one from the Church has come over to ask what we think we're doing. I mean, we couldn't be more visible. The front door of the church is only, like, twenty-yards away. Which is kind of the point, I guess.

So, by eleven-thirty the whole spread is set. We've stacked cups by the water ice and limeade, laid out a dozen rows of these short-stemmed, wide mouth poco-grande glasses that are made of real glass. Frank clearly doesn't believe in low-balling his events.

"There's Johnny," Elroy says, pointing to a white Escalade pulling to the curb about thirty-yards off the lawn where we've set-up. We walk down to meet him.

"This is legit," Johnny says and climbs out of the massive vehicle, eyeing our spread.

"In a manner," I say offhandedly.

"And they let you have alcohol at this thing?" Johnny asks, incredulous but not at all suspicious.

"Yeah," Elroy replies. "For the adults, I mean."

"Your parish is a lot more progressive than ours," Jane says.

She pulls their son from his car seat. The little girl has already bolted from the car and is running up the slight hill to our camp.

Elroy helps Johnny pull the cooler out of the trunk. I try to take one of the cases of wine, but Johnny waves me off, tells me that he'll come back for them.

"So, what is this, anyway?" Jane asks as we walk up the hill.

"I don't know," I say. "Just kind of a different way to bring the community together, I guess."

I wish that Frank would get here. I mean, I can hold it together, but this whole performance art piece is his brainchild, so I'm not going to know what to do if people start asking real questions. Johnny is emptying a case of wine into the sangria cooler while Elroy stirs it with this giant wooden spoon that was delivered with the rest of the stuff.

I look at my phone and it's eleven-forty. Still no one from the Church has showed up to ask what the hell we're doing. It probably helps that there are grown-ups with us now.

"We need to fill the glasses," Elroy says to Johnny after they've shut the lid on the cooler, now filled to the brim.

Johnny shrugs, works the tap while Elroy exchanges empties for fulls and lines them up on the table. After they fill maybe half the glasses, I lift the side of the cooler and it's still, like, totally full. Okay, last steps.

"So, now what?" Johnny asks and looks at me.

"So now we just need to do the signs and flyers."

I ask Johnny to put the main sign up on the stairs of the church, to the left of the big doors. Elroy takes the two poster signs for the back-side doors. I give a stack of flyers to each of the kids, hand-outs for the people arriving at the church. Jane takes the stack from her son, who is only, like, three or four, gives him back just a few and walks to the front of the church with both kids. I only met Johnny's wife yesterday so I don't really know what she was like before, but today she's all-in with the family Church picnic thing, and I'm figuring it's because of that whole scene at Johnny's house yesterday.

Johnny joins his wife and kids at the bottom of the church steps after he's set up the sign at the doors, takes some of the flyers from Wendy. And they're smiling and talking like a happy church-going family. It occurs to me that, if you ever want to pull off some covert, underhanded plan, the best way to do it is to try and involve people that are totally oblivious as to what they're actually doing.

I'm feeling a weird mix of pride and shame when Elroy gets back to the tables.

"All set?" I ask.

"All set," he replies. "Now what?"

"Well, now we hand out drinks to whoever comes up here. Otherwise, I have no idea. In Frank we trust, right?"

Elroy smiles and I kind of want to kiss him, for luck. Or maybe just because I kind of want to give him a kiss.

Elroy

Johnny, Jane and the kids are handing out flyers to the first people arriving at the church. And it looks like the people are asking what's this all about, Johnny and Jane replying with shrugs and smiles, probably saying that they're not from here and are just helping out. Or something like that.

Right now it's all mostly old people who just smile, ignore them and head into the church anyway. But I see families coming from the parking lot. And part of me is super nervous, the stuttering kind of nervous, because we're about to create, like, a public spectacle in this new town where I live. And I'm also worried that we'll screw it up before Frank even gets here, because where is he anyway?

"Thank God," Sally says.

She points to Dr. Severs' piece of garbage Honda, which slows down in front of the church, speeds up, and then jerks to a stop when Frank opens the front door. Dr. Severs lets Frank out and continues on, passing the parking lot, probably driving around the block so that he can smoke some pot. That's good, I think, because he's probably going to need it a lot more than he figures.

"Kids!" Frank shouts.

He walks up the hill in his jeans and a black Def Leppard concert t-shirt. He goes straight to the table, picks up a glass of sangria, bolts it. Then he refills from the cooler tap, bolts it again, rubs the bridge of his nose like it gave him a brain-freeze. He refills a third time, takes a normal sip.

"A little stage fright," he says. "Damn, this stuff came out good." He walks over to the table with the limeade, grabs two paper cups, fills them from the sangria tap, hands one to each of us. "This is a party, remember? You're supposed to be having a good time!"

Sally and I look at each other, like, both wondering why we didn't start drinking before Frank showed up. I take a big sip and it tastes really great, not heavy like the wine I hardly remember at the Ruth's steak place last week, more like the kind of drink you get in a juice box. Sally's already done with her cup, refills it from the cooler tap before anyone else shows up.

And I wonder, since we're kind of seeing each other, should we maybe have a talk about her drinking problem? But instead I decide to play catch up, finish my cup, refill it. Down the hill I can see Johnny, Jane and the kids starting to divert some of the crowd in our direction.

I feel Frank's hand on my shoulder.

"Okay, so the first few minutes of any party is always the most awkward," Frank says to Sally and me. "So you've got to make sure that everyone has a drink, like pronto. That's rule number one. Hand the glasses to the adults, point the kids to the limeade and water ice and sticky buns. Make everyone feel welcome, but don't get too caught up in any one conversation. Your main job is just to make sure that everyone gets super hydrated. And to smile, really big. That's important, remember to always be smiling. No matter what happens."

He grabs three glasses of sangria and walks out to meet a young couple with two toddlers, who are walking up the hill towards our camp. Sally and I look at each other, bolt our paper cups of sangria, each take two full glasses from the table, and follow Frank down towards the family groups making their way up our hill.

Sally and I mostly just greet people, jog back and forth to the drinks table for more sangria. And we watch Frank. Because he is on fire. Like an amped-up social butterfly. No, actually, more like a manic social hummingbird. He's everywhere at once, slapping backs, hugging women, picking up children, pulling families together to kick-start a conversation before teleporting somewhere else. And I'm pretty sure he doesn't know a single one of these people. But his enthusiasm is infectious and it's starting to spread like electricity through the little groups.

It doesn't hurt that all of these people probably still believe that they're at a Church sanctioned event. But I don't want to take anything away from Frank's performance, which is, like, on the same level as professional athletes or superheroes. He just keeps sparking these little fires of casual intimacy at strategic points around the crowd, fanning the flames through conversation and drink and appropriate touching, with a blind faith that the whole thing will eventually flare up and burn on its own.

There are about a hundred or so people standing around our camp when Johnny and his family walk back up the hill. They're beaming, laughing and goofing in the warm sun, having fun like the type of family you see in a pharmaceutical ad while a legal spokesperson talks in a low voice about how the whatever drug could harm or even kill you.

Frank sees Johnny and family, breaks away from a small group and walks over to give him a hug, to give them all hugs, kids included. And then he walks them over and introduces them to another young family.

Frank catches my eye, waves me over behind our drinks table. When I get there, he's opening a cardboard carton, inside of which is a nineteen-eighties style boom-box, a plug-in microphone and a whole bunch of batteries.

"Hey, bud. Load these up for me, okay? I'll meet you back here in about three minutes. Got to keep mixing the cement!" he says.

Before I can answer, he busts back into the crowd like a stage diver at a mosh pit. So I load up the electronics, test the microphone on the boom-box with a tap of my fingers at low volume. Then I grab another sangria for myself, also one for Sally, and I scan the crowd. I finally see her, making a really good effort to imitate Frank, looking for conversations to resuscitate, drinks that need refilling, stiffening people who need a smile or welcome hug.

And she's a hundred times better at this whole thing than me. But, just keeping it real, she's not even in the same ballpark as Frank. He's like the Michael Jordan of party-starting. Sally catches my eye and I wave her over.

"Did you see Frank?" Sally asks. "He's like a kung fu master fluffer out there." She's breathless and points at the electronics. "Where'd all this come from?"

Before I can answer, Frank gently nudges her out of the way, grabs the microphone, cranks the volume on the boom-box to max.

I hand Sally her paper cup of sangria.

Sally

So, here we go, then. I brace myself with a swallow of sangria. Then I drink the whole cup. Frank was right, this stuff is awesome. I take a step closer to Elroy, wrap my fingers around his for a second. And then, as Frank starts talking, Elroy and I begin filling empty glasses from the cooler tap.

"So, yeah, well thanks, everyone, for coming out, you know! Isn't this great? I mean, how nice is it to see so many friendly faces, right? Yeah, I'm talking to you, Dr. Phillips – where are those hands? Right, Mrs. Phillips? Ha ha."

Frank is pointing vaguely into the crowd. I've never heard of any Dr. Phillips who goes to our church, but the crowd just eats it up. The balls on this dude. Elroy and I have filled up the remaining empty glasses, set them on the table in rows.

"But seriously, it's really awesome to see so many people step out to try something new. I mean, I don't know how many of you caught my sermon a week ago, but this is exactly what Rory and I were talking about. Getting out of the church – and I mean that both literally and figuratively – and creating an intimate environment that will help us connect as real people. And I think the good Lord likes the idea, too, because, let's hear it for the day we've got here, huh? Hallelujah!"

Frank spreads his arms wide in the sunshine, then passes the mic in front of the hooting crowd. While Frank talks, Elroy and I are running back-and-forth to the cooler behind him and refilling drinks for the crowd with two big glass pitchers.

"Hallelujah! And what we're doing here today, people, isn't just enjoying ah taste of the wurld's finest sangria, enjoyin frozen treats with the kiddiez hea in the sunshine! What we doin is askin queschins! An it's allllllll right to be askin them queschins, too!"

Walking back to the cooler, I subtly give Frank a sharp kick in the ankle.

"Hey, thar!" he shouts at me, into the mic.

"Southern accent," I mouth wordlessly. Frank nods thanks. Bizarre. I go back to refilling drinks in the crowd.

"What I'm saying is, it's okay to stop every once in a while and ask ourselves what we expect from this community that we call the Church. I mean, hell, Rory and I – oh, that's Father Maculkin to most of you,"—actually, it's Father Mcloughlin, but close enough—"we were asking ourselves these same questions just a week ago Saturday. And what we came up with is that we all deserve more than what this Church is giving us. Because, I'm sorry to say it, but the Church isn't treating us like people. And we're all real people with hearts and souls, right?! So, then why does the Church treat us like robots? Because what do robots do? They recite and repeat! Just like we do every Sunday at Mass. But we're not robots! And you know what makes us different from robots? It's that, way deep down, beneath all the stuff that looks the same as everyone else, there's something unique inside each of us. Something that makes us each different, you know? And, maybe, this unique part of each of us might just be what God is all about. I think, maybe, that's what my homie, Jesus, was trying to teach us in the first place!"

Again, the crowd hoots its approval, clearly still believing that our picnic is actually a Church-sponsored event. Luckily, they're also all still drinking as fast as Elroy and I can pour.

"But instead of helping nurture that unique self inside of us, the Church just lets us keep it buried under a big, stinking pile of shame. Because we're all loaded up with guilt and shame, friends, every single one of us. And you know how I know that? Because we're Catholics, that's how I know it. So instead of encouraging us to help each other find that unique self under all that shame, the Church asks us to recite and repeat like robots. And, well, Rory and I think that's just plain wrong. The Church should be about individual expression, not conformity! The Church should be about compassion, not judgment! And that's what we're trying to kick-start here today. That's what we want to bring back to the Church. Because, Rory and me, that's what we think Jesus was really talking about. So, let's do it together, huh? Let's all try to build a better Church, from the inside out!"

The crowd hoots and cheers. And then I see Father Mcloughlin, walking up the hill towards us, carrying the large sign that Johnny had set up beside the church doors. And, oh great, Mom is walking right beside him.

"Now, hold on! Let's just take a second, friends! Because I want you all to give it up for a great man of vision, without whom, none of this would have been possible! My friend, my partner in crime, let's give it up for Rory!" Frank shouts, points down the hill, adds in a low tone, "That's Father Rory Maculkin to most of you."

The crowd turns. And there he is, walking up the hill, carrying our big sign like a sandwich board advertisement. Father Mcloughlin freezes as the crowd turns, erupts into cheers.

What a shit show.

Elroy

"So, here's what we're gonna do, friends!" Frank shouts, turning the crowd's attention from Father Mcloughlin back to himself. "We're talking about having the courage to share what's different about yourself, making other people comfortable enough to share their own selves, too. Well, I don't just want to talk about it! I want to practice it! I want everyone to close their eyes, spin around, and then open your lids and walk up to the first person that meets your eyes. And I mean the first person, whoever that is. And we all know when we meet someone's eyes, so don't try to cheat! Just trust the process. Walk up to this person, tell them something that's buried deep inside yourself! Make them feel like it's okay to tell you something that's buried in themselves! Because the church we want to create, it's not a passive-participation type of church. It's about active participation! And I know that's scary. But what have you really got to lose? Just shout Geronimo and dive head-first into intimacy. Shock treatment style. Now, do you think you can do that for me? I think you can! Oh, and bottoms-up!" Frank shouts.

He drains his glass and holds it upside down in front of the crowd. And the crowd does the same while Frank looks around for anyone whose glass isn't drained and upside down.

"That should help loosen things up," Frank says to Sally and me.

We're now standing behind him at the drinks table. He puts the microphone on the table, refills his glass at the cooler tap, grabs another full glass from the table rows, and cuts through the crowds in a b-line for Father Mcloughlin. Sally looks at me and shrugs. We pick up our glass pitchers of sangria and follow Frank through the crowd of closed-eye, spinning people.

We refill glasses as we go.

"Rory!" Frank shouts and knocks the sign from Father Mcloughlin's hands, wraps him in a huge embrace. "We're doing it, Rory! It's small, but it's a start!"

This poor priest clearly has no idea what to say or do here.

"Mr. uh, Johnson," Father Mcloughlin finally says, weakly.

Frank pulls back from the embrace, his hands still on the priest's shoulders, gives him some kind of a weird look.

"Sorry. I mean Frank," the priest says. "Frank, what you're doing here… it's not okay, with the Church, I mean."

"Oh, I know, Rory. That's why we're doing it *outside* the church."

"Yes, but, you're still on Church property. And you put these signs up to, kind of, hijack the people going into the church," Father Mcloughlin says and pulls the big sign in between himself and Frank. "And you made people believe that this was something that the Church endorsed."

"We never actually said that, Rory. It was only implied," Frank says.

"Mr. uh, Frank, I think you need, uh, help," Father Mcloughlin says, slowly.

"I do need help, Rory. I'm going to need a lot of help. But all in good time, right?" Frank says earnestly to the priest.

Father Mcloughlin shakes his head, like, that's definitely not the kind of help he was talking about.

"Sally?!" Sally's mom shouts after noticing me and Sally standing behind Frank.

Sally's still holding my hand.

"Hi, Mom!"

"Sally, what in God's name are you doing here?"

"I'm helping Frank. He's, like, one of my best friends."

"Oh, is this your mother?" Frank perks. "It's so nice to meet you, Mrs. uh…"

"Berman. My last name is Berman, Frank. Geeze. Her name is Edna," Sally says.

"Mrs. Berman! Edna!" Frank shouts, boldly, and walks towards her with open arms.

Sally's mom shrinks backwards, like Frank's covered with killer bees or something.

"It's kind of an RMSOC thing," Sally says to her mom.

Frank shrugs, turns back to Father Mcloughlin.

"It is not an RMSOC thing!" I hear.

Whoa. Where did Dr. Severs come from?

"What is an RMSC?" Father Mcloughlin asks, looking at Frank, then at Dr. Severs.

"RMSOC." Dr. Severs corrects him while struggling to maintain his clarity through an obvious marijuana daze. "It's the Rudolphsville Middle School Outreach Club, and it has nothing to do with this circus here."

"And why are you holding hands with that retarded boy?!" Sally's mom shouts. She looks at me like I'm a pile of worms.

"Special needs, Edna," Dr. Severs says to Sally's mom. "And Elroy isn't retarded. I mean, he doesn't have special needs. He's just a twelve-year-old cross dresser who's probably going to end up a pedophile. No thanks to you!" Dr. Severs points at Father Mcloughlin, who's like, what?

"I beg your pardon?!" Father Mcloughlin says to Dr. Severs.

"You can beg all you want, Romeo. But tell me something. Because I can see how you'd have to abandon Elroy, being a priest and all, but what about his mother? What did you do with Elroy's mother?!" Dr. Severs shouts.

I guess marijuana does make you all paranoid. Sally's mom's face looks like she's about to give birth.

"I've never seen this young man before in my life," Father Mcloughlin shouts, wide eyed and arm-waving, more to Sally's mom than to Dr. Severs.

"You saw him just last week after Confession, Father! When are the lies going to stop?! Take some responsibility!" Dr. Severs screams, like a girl.

Frank just stands there, observing the small group, thoroughly interested in the dialog. Sally is still holding my hand. This whole thing is about to go totally off the rails.

I gently unwrap my hand from Sally's, turn around and walk back up the hill. As I cut through the crowd, it's clear that Frank's plan is badly in need of some gas. People are talking to each other, but you could cut the awkwardness with a knife. I get to the drinks table, bolt a glass of sangria, pick up the microphone.

"Uh, hey, everybody. My name is Elroy," I say into the mic. "I'm an orphan, a foster kid. And I have a pretty bad stutter, and I'm ashamed of it," the crowd stops what it's doing, turns to look at me, maybe confused because there isn't a trace of stutter in my voice. "And I just want to say that I'm not retarded. And I don't wear old lady's underpants. And I'm not gay. Not like I think there's something wrong with being gay," I clarify, "...it's just that, I'm not. And Father Mcloughlin isn't my biological father." That sends a pretty serious ripple through the crowd. "And I've never felt like I was anything but garbage, until I met Frank. And Sally. Oh, and I'm in love with Sally, too."

I look at Sally as she breaks through the crowd. She rolls her eyes and collapses her shoulders in a body-sigh, like she's saying, "Way too soon, dude." But I can tell she's smiling underneath it all, and I figure my own face is beaming like a sunrise.

So, Sally walks up to me, takes the mic from my hand, kisses me on my lips and punches me in the chest. Punches me, like, a little harder than I think she needed to, because it feels like my heart stops for a second.

"Okay. My name is Sally Berman. And for a while now, I've been trying to figure out how to kill myself. Just like my Dad did when I was little. Just like my Aunt Sadie did a couple of weeks ago. You maybe see a pattern here, Mom?!" Sally shouts, bobbing her head to look through the crowd and catch eyes with her mom. "And just like a lot of you here, I've been a member of this congregation my whole life, but it never felt like I was really a part of anything. So, I think we should listen to Frank. Maybe see if we can change that. I mean, wherever we end up, it isn't going to be any worse than where we started, right? Oh, and even though I think he's moving way too fast, I guess I love Elroy, too."

"You say you'll give me
Eyes in a moon of blindness
A river in a time of dryness
A harbor in the tempest
  But all the promises we make
From the cradle to the grave
When all I want is you…"

I feel ya, Bono. Think Sally does too.

Frank

"And I think most of you already know who I am," I say after taking the mic from Sally. Freaking brilliant, what these two are doing. I glance at Elroy, who looks like he's been shot full of morphine, then continue. "My name is Frank Johnson. And my Grandad died last year, right before he was supposed to move into a managed care facility. And that facility wouldn't refund my money, so I've been living at a nursing home for the past six months. As a matter of principle. I know, at my age, right? And maybe I get too caught up in the principle of things sometimes. Seriously, I'm wearing adult diapers right now. But I really don't think the diapers thing is so much principle any more. It's really about comfort and convenience. I mean, am I the only one not even looking for a bathroom right now, or what? But I digress. It's possible that I have some problems. Maybe undiagnosed Manic-Asperger's or something, if that's even a thing. And I've been spending my days getting drunk with a couple of twelve-year-olds lately, so there's that. But that's who I am. That's who you can get to know, right here. And it's not someone you'd ever get to know in that building over there that we call a church. And I think getting to know each other on an intimate level is so much more important than sitting and standing and kneeling and praying like robots, in that same building over there. And you know who would agree with me? Jesus, that's who! The real Jesus who drank too much and liked to party weird with his posse. If anything, Jesus would think that the Church actually gets in the way of us being intimate as a community. And if Jesus were here right now, do you know what I think he'd say? I think he'd say exactly what Rory and I would say. I think he'd say Fuck! The! Church!"

Too much?

Sally

"I think he'd say Fuck! The! Church!" Frank shouts.

Whoa!

So, I'm pretty sure that this crowd just figured out that our picnic isn't a Church-sanctioned event. And nobody moves or says anything. They're, like, frozen. Because that was pretty damn sacrilegious, even for a crazy person. I see people with glasses at their lips, not drinking, afraid, maybe—I don't know—that everyone is about to be struck by lightning or something. And this goes on for, like, lots and lots of seconds. Then, finally, this young dad to our left breaks the deadlock of awkward silence.

"Yeah! Fuck the Church!" he shouts, right in front of his wife and toddler.

And, like, most of the crowd just erupts with cheers. Not all, but most. And that young dad who just yelled "Fuck the Church!" he walks up and grabs the microphone right out of Frank's hands.

"My name is Norman Sullivan, and I haven't gotten a spontaneous erection in almost three years!"

"Norm!?" the young wife shouts.

"We're almost bankrupt, I've been taking so much Viagra. It's been so long since I've felt like a man. Am I supposed to keep this bottled up forever?" Norm whines, and then some other guy walks up and gently takes the microphone from his hand.

"My name is Mike Harrison, and I lost my job six weeks ago!" There's a gasp from a single person in the crowd. Mrs. Harrison, I presume? "I've been lying to my wife, my kids, every single day for the past six weeks. And I've been coming to Church every Sunday and it doesn't make a god damned bit of difference…"

Holy cow.

And I laugh. Not at these guys, Mike and Norm, because obviously this type of cathartic release isn't what anyone would think is funny. But I guess I'm laughing at the whole situation we've got here. And I laugh so hard that the world spins and I fall down onto my side. And that's when I realize that I am, like, totally wasted. Like, single uncle at the wedding drunk. And it just hits me, all at once. That sangria was definitely a lot stronger than it tasted, I think, and close my eyes for a second.

And as I take a little rest, I hear some lady on the mic talking about her three abortions in high school.

Elroy

"I think he'd say Fuck! The! Church!" Frank shouts.

Seriously, Frank? Even I know better.

I look over at Frank's brother Johnny, whose mouth has literally dropped wide open. Total panic shock. Like finding out that your helpful neighbor babysitter is actually a registered sex offender, that kind of shock. Same with his wife, Jane. But Jane comes out of it pretty quick. I see her turn slowly, close her fist and punch Johnny right in his open mouth. So, maybe one step forward and two steps backwards as far as Johnny's empowered home life is concerned.

But nobody notices Jane punch Johnny because before she actually hits him, some guy in the crowd shouts "Fuck the Church!" and a whole lot of people start to cheer. And this same guy takes the microphone from Frank and outs himself about erectile dysfunction to his wife and the whole crowd. And then another guy confesses to having lost his job and lying about it. And as this goes on I notice that Sally is, like, passed out on the grass by the drinks table.

And I'm thinking, hey, a little nap might feel pretty good right now.

Frank

I open my eyes and it takes some time for them to adjust to the light. And it's not because I'm drunk, it's because everything is white. And that's, like, a total drag when you're massively hung over. My head is like a balloon about to pop. And, oh, Martha Hardy is sitting next to my white sheet bed, napping in a chair. I grunt and she startles awake.

"Oh, thank God," Martha sighs.

"What time is it?" I croak.

"Tuesday."

"Where am I?"

"In the hospital."

"Which hospital?"

"St. Mary's."

"Why?"

"This is where the ambulance took you."

"So why are you here?"

"I came with you in the ambulance."

"And you've been here for two days?"

"No, I went home yesterday, slept and did some errands. But I was back, bright and early this morning. You were in a coma!" Martha shout-whispers, like she's sharing neighborhood gossip. A coma. How embarrassing.

"Alcohol poisoning?"

"No."

"Then what?"

"Ed hit you in the head with a snow globe."

"Really?"

That's unexpected. So maybe this hangover is actually a concussion? I mean, it's been two days, so what else would it be?

"Were you guys at the church?"

"No."

"So wait, where did Ed hit me with a snow globe?"

"On your head," Martha says, making me wonder if she's just obtuse or if I'm not completely in control of my faculties. Is it you, or is it me?

"No, I mean where was I when Ed hit me with a snow globe."

"At the home."

"How did I get to the home?"

"You mean you don't remember any of it?"

And the truth is, I don't really remember anything after I said "Fuck the Church" to a whole mess of Sunday Catholics two days ago.

"No."

"Well, it was quite a scene."

"Sounds like it."

"So, from what the nurses tell me, you drove up to the home at around four o'clock on Sunday with a whole caravan of well-dressed maniacs and completely sacked the lobby lounge."

"Is that right?" Maybe Johnny was on to something about two bottles of Everclear being kind of a lot.

"Yeah, and apparently you or your people accosted the front desk nurse and locked her in the linen closet, then set up a full bar at the reception desk. You guys did the same thing to the floor nurse, Doris. And Doris is just a tiny little thing. Is any of this coming back to you?"

"No, but I can see how it might have gone down like that."

"So, your people weren't serving drinks to the residents, which is good. But the kids were scooping this kind of a fruit mash out of a cooler and giving it to the residents on paper plates, on your direction, so I heard."

"Ouch. That's not good. I suspect that fruit had absorbed a great deal of grain alcohol over the prior twenty-four hours. But the kids, you're talking about Elroy and Sally, right? They were still there?"

"Oh, sure. They were still at the home when I got there."

"And when was that?"

"Ed and I got there around five-thirty. Doris still had her cell phone when you guys locked her in the closet, so she called us. Ed was *not* happy."

"I imagine not."

"So, Ed and I walk in and you guys are blasting this rap song about jumping around on a big... what did we used to call them? Ghetto blaster? Yeah, a big ghetto blaster."

"House of Pain," nineteen-ninety-two one hit wonder, one of my go-to songs when parties unravel, typically when I've drunk myself beyond any possible embarrassment.

"Clear. So, you walk in with Ed, and..."

"And, well, the whole lobby was full of people jumping around. It was like a disco club in the seventies."

"Okay, so get to the part where Ed knocks me out with a snow globe."

"Oh, it took us a while to even find you. And when we did, you were up on the coffee table with Mrs. Liptenstein, singing a duet of *Something to Talk About* – you know, the Bonnie Raitt song?" My tastes in music are eclectic, but I don't recall that one being on my drunken orgy playlist. "And that Mrs. Liptenstein! Who would have known that she still has such a set of lungs? I wonder if she used to be a singer? Anyway, you were awful."

"Thanks. In my defense, I'd probably been blacked-out for at least three hours by that time."

"Yeah, well, you were still moving. That's for sure. Ed yells at you to get down from the coffee table before you kill Mrs. Liptenstein. And you weren't having any of it. So Ed starts walking towards you, and you reach over and grab a couple of snow globes from the mantel above the fireplace."

"Oh, no! Not Ed's snow globe collection on the fireplace mantel? He loves those things."

"Oh, yes. And I'm surprised that you even care."

"I'm not a total dick."

"Well, you were Sunday evening, because when Ed tried to grab you off the coffee table, you started lobbing those snow globes into the air, two at a time, forcing Ed to try and catch the snow globes. It was like an act at the circus."

"Did any of the snow globes make it?"

"Now, that's the strange thing, because the only one that actually broke was the one that blew up on your forehead when Ed threw it at you." Martha air-pets the bandage above my left eye. "All the rest were fine, even though they dropped like six feet. They all landed on the rug, which, I guess, is pretty springy."

"Except for the one that hit me in the head?"

"That's right! But what happened was, Mrs. Liptenstein saw you lobbing those snow globes, so she grabbed one herself and threw it at Ed. Overhand. Right at his face."

"Wow. So, is Ed in the hospital, too?"

"No. You wouldn't know it, but Ed has cat-like reflexes. He caught the snow globe one-handed, an inch from his face. And then, well, what he says is that he was trying to smash the snow globe against the fireplace to make a kind of statement and stop all the nonsense. I think he was just mad. But either way, I guess his aim isn't what it used to be because that snow globe, well, it just exploded on your forehead. Ed's still got the arm, though. He used to be a pitcher, in college."

"Did he?"

"Yes, second-team All-American."

"Good for him. Now Martha, maybe it's my banged-up skull, but I think I'm detecting some schoolgirl crush when you're describing how Ed acted on Sunday night. So, tell me."

"Frank, I think I actually had an orgasm when Ed caught that snow globe in front of his face. He was like a movie hero, just then. It so reminded me of when we were younger."

"Well, that's great, Martha! I mean, I'm not so happy about Ed fast-balling a snow globe at my head and knocking me out for two days, but I'm really happy for the two of you. So, are you guys back to, how should I say, doing it?"

"Oh, no. Not yet, at least. Ed's a wreck about criminal charges and civil suits and whatnot."

"Why? Is one of the inmates trying to get him in trouble for Sunday night?"

"No, he's worried that you'll press charges and sue him in civil court. I mean, he did put you in a coma for two days with that snow globe."

"Ha! Don't be silly. You know me, Martha. Am I the kind of person who would ever press charges or sue someone? People like that make me sick."

"That's what I told Ed, but he wouldn't believe me. Maybe, now that you're out of the coma, you can tell him yourself."

"Martha, I haven't even looked at Ed for over six months, much less talked to him. Do you really think I'd break that streak because of this fiasco?"

"I don't know, Frank. You've kind of got Ed over a barrel right now. He might be ready to break," Martha says.

I think about it. This whole performance art piece did kind of reach a crescendo on Sunday. I doubt anything in the next six months is going to top it.

"Okay. Get him to drive over here. I'll talk to him."

"He's in the waiting room."

"What? Seriously?"

"He was kind of worried that you were going to die. And that would be manslaughter, minimum. I told you, he's all worked up."

"Okay, well, send him in then."

Martha pats my arm, walks out of the room. About thirty-seconds later, Hardy comes in. Nervous smile on his fat face. I look him in the eye for the first time in six months.

"Feeling better, champ?" Hardy asks, nervously.

"I'm fine. Look, I'm not going to press charges or sue you or anything, so stop worrying about that."

He deflates, right in front of me. In a good way.

"Thanks," he says.

"And I'm sorry about the party. It started out as kind of a Church thing, but got out of hand."

"Thanks," he says again. "I'm sorry I put you into a coma with that snow globe."

"That's okay. I don't remember any of it."

"Look, Frank, I give up, alright? I'll refund you the unused balance for your stay. Hell, I'll refund you the whole twelve-months. But this thing has got to end. Like right now. You win, okay?"

"Thanks, Ed. It feels good to finally hear you admit that I was right the whole time. And, I don't want the refund. I mean, I did pay in advance. I just wanted you to offer me a refund. That's all. And if you'd offered me a refund six months ago, I would have said the same thing then."

Hardy closes his eyes and takes deep breaths.

"You are such a dick," he finally says.

"I know. I'll pack up my stuff when they let me out of here, okay."

"Alright."

"And Ed? That Martha is a pretty special lady, you know?"

"I know."

"Treat her right, okay?"

"I will. Thanks."

"Maybe watch one of those soap operas with her. It might be worth your while."

"Okay, champ," Hardy says and holds out his hand.

I shake it.

"Feel better, alright?"

I nod and he walks out of the room. But before the door closes, it opens again. Elroy and Sally walk in.

Elroy

"Look, it's the RMSOC candy-stripers!" Frank says, lying in the hospital bed, his head all bandaged up.

"We th… th… thought you were going to die," I say.

"I'm fine, Elroy. Just a bump on the head. Not even worth the stutter."

"You were in a coma for, like, forty-eight hours," Sally says. "Do you know how inconsiderate that is?"

"Sorry to worry you, Lambchop."

Sally rolls her eyes. I think she's actually mad at Frank now, not joking.

"The RMSOC is kaput," Sally says. "We took the rap for the whole alternative church thing. Mom says that Dr. Severs is on probation at our school."

"Good. That guy is a dick," Frank says. "Did you two get in any trouble?"

"Not really," Sally says. "I mean, a lot of the congregation sort of went crazy, so me and Elroy were treated more like victims than anything else."

"Any other repercussions that you know about? Prioritize anything that might involve me," Frank says.

"Not really. I mean, everyone at the church is pretty embarrassed about the whole thing," Sally says. "I think a couple older people and maybe a few kids went blind for six or seven hours because of the sangria, but no permanent damage."

"Man, I really should have listened to Johnny about that grain alcohol," Frank says.

"Other than that, everyone is kind of keeping to themselves, maybe trying to forget it ever happened. So, what are your thoughts?"

"My thoughts?"

"About the whole Church thing? What now?"

"Oh, yeah. Well, I mean, good times on Sunday, right? I think we did something pretty special. But now, to tell you the truth, I'm kind of over it, you know?" Frank says. He sighs and reaches up to rub his skull, then jerks his hand away like it's on fire. "Still a little tender up there."

And I can't believe that both of them are being so casual about this.

"Frank," I say, "th... th... there's no more RMSOC. So how are we go... go... going to get you out of the nursing home?"

And there's a pit in my stomach, like the size of a black hole.

"It's okay, man," Frank says gently. "I talked to Hardy. Seeing as how he almost killed me, he decided to fold on our dispute. So I'm moving out, anyway."

And that black hole pit in my stomach? Guess what crawls out of it? That careful part of me that I thought was stuck in a well somewhere.

"So, Mr. Hardy is go... go... going to pay back your money?" I ask.

"No," Frank says, "but he offered to. Sincerely. And that's all I ever really wanted. So I told him to keep his money."

"You are a bizarre person, Frank," Sally says.

"So wh... wh... what now," I say.

And I can't help it. These big, fat teardrops of mine are, like, splashing on the tile floor. And that careful part of me, crawling out of the black hole pit in my stomach, it looks just like the Walking Dead. Except it's smiling at me.

"Hey, Elroy," Frank says. "It's not like we're never going to see each other again. Come on, dude."

"Okay," I say.

But I don't believe him. Because that Walking Dead, black hole stomach pit part of me is pointing and laughing and saying I told you so. Saying, it's only been two weeks, do you think Frank isn't going to have a life when he moves out of the nursing home? Saying, how long is Sally going to stick around without Frank playing cruise director? How long before I'm all alone, with nothing, just like before?

"Dude, I'm gonna have, like, more flexibility than before. Buck up, huh?" Frank says.

"Okay," I say.

But I'm falling down that black hole pit.

The horror.

Sally

~ I wasn't sure if you'd still be here, once I decided to put off killing myself, like, indefinitely.

~ *I'm pretty sure I was the one telling you not to kill yourself.*

~ Still.

~ *Anyway, how are things going with your mom?*

~ She's kind of leaving me alone, I guess. I think what I said last Sunday, how everyone close to her kills themselves, it might have touched a nerve. Not that she's said anything about it.

~ *You know she's not really the reason that your father or I killed ourselves, right? I mean, that was only something that you were telling yourself to feel better about what you were planning to do. You get that?*

~ I think so. I don't know. I'm not really going to think about it, okay? I'm just trying to live right now. You know, no judgments, no worries.

~ *Very wise.*

~ I love you, Aunt Sadie. Please stick around, huh?

~ *I love you, too, Lambchop. And I'll always be here.*

Frank

So, it's been six weeks since I left the Hardy Managed Care Facility. And when I look back on that time, I honestly try to figure out what the hell I was thinking. But that's my life, I guess. One cause after another, and none of them with much legs after the first big push.

But I'm trying to change that, one small step at a time.

Elroy is still with his foster family, the Joneses. And it's not like I'm getting the kind of night terrors that I used to have in those weeks after I first met the kid, but it does bother me that the Joneses are still his foster parents. But that will work itself out, I'm sure, because things seem to work themselves out pretty naturally if you don't get all crazy about stuff. And like I said, I've been trying to curb this instinct to get all crazy about stuff, lately.

And, I mean, it's not like Elroy ever really sees the Joneses, anyway. I got myself a sweet three-bedroom condo in Rudolphsville, only three blocks from Sally's mom's place. And really, I just need a bedroom and an office, so the extra bedroom was gonna go to waste anyway. So, I let Elroy crash there every once in a while. You know, like, seven nights a week. Because, I mean, there's no way he was going to keep staying in a newspaper jail cell, sleeping on that skinny prison cot. So now he's got a nice room, big, with a sliding glass door that opens onto a little sixth-floor balcony. And he's got his own bathroom, with shampoo. And we share a washer-dryer, and he thinks the dryer is, like, the best thing ever.

So I think Elroy's pretty happy. But he'll be happier when we take care of the whole Joneses' foster kid thing. I'm waiting for Thanksgiving to talk to him about it. We're having dinner at Johnny's place. My mom and dad and kid sister are going to be there, too. I also invited Sally and her mom, because what are just the two of them going to do on a holiday like that, alone, anyway? But Sally says she'll probably come by herself because her mom will be busy serving holiday dinner at a leper colony or something. Which is great, because I'd really like Sally to be there when I talk to Elroy.

You know, it's remarkable how easy it is to adopt a twelve-year-old kid in the State of New Jersey.

The End

About the Author

Joe Barrett has spent the past twenty-five years as a chief executive of entrepreneurial organizations ranging from private, venture-funded companies to large publicly-listed multinational corporations. He has been a frequent speaker at National Retail Federation conferences and has sat on the boards of several for-profit and non-profit companies. His short fiction has been published in *Iconoclast, The Storyteller* and *The Palo Alto Review.* He lives with his wife and two children in New Jersey.

Thank you so much for reading one of our **Humor** novels.
If you enjoyed our book, please check out our recommended title for your next great read!

Parrot Talk by David B. Seaburn

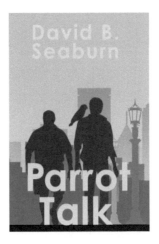

"...a story of abandonment, addiction, finding oneself—all mixed in with tear-jerking chapters next to laugh-out-loud chapters." *–Tiff & Rich*

View other Black Rose Writing titles at www.blackrosewriting.com/books

and use promo code **PRINT** to receive a **20% discount** when purchasing

Made in United States
Troutdale, OR
09/06/2023